BOOKS BY AL ROKER

THE MORNING SHOW MURDERS

The Morning Show Murders (with Dick Lochte)
The Midnight Show Murders (with Dick Lochte)
The Talk Show Murders (with Dick Lochte)
Murder on Demand (with Matt Costello)

NONFICTION

You Look So Much Better in Person
Ruthless Tide
Extreme Weather
Been There, Done That (with Deborah Roberts)
The Storm of the Century
Never Goin' Back
Big Shoes
Don't Make Me Stop This Car!

COOKBOOKS

Hassle-Free Holiday Cookbook
Big Bad Book of Barbecue

Murder ON DEMAND

NEW YORK TIMES BESTSELLING AUTHOR

AL ROKER

& MATT COSTELLO

BLACK
STONE
PUBLISHING

Printed in the United States of America

First edition: 2024
ISBN 979-8-200-92324-3
Fiction / Mystery & Detective / General

Version 1

Blackstone Publishing
31 Mistletoe Rd.
Ashland, OR 97520

www.BlackstonePublishing.com

PROLOGUE

1

A GOOD DAY TO FISH?

The man headed down a gravel walkway that led to the boats of the marina, all lined up on a series of docks, left to right, in a *mostly* neat, orderly row.

The serious fishing boats and trawlers were tied up on the far left—at the most expansive dock.

Then the pleasure boats, sailboats, and big inboards nearby.

But one last narrow dock—showing actual holes in some of the worn planks—sat all the way to the right, as if shunned, with its line of small boats, modest outboards, small daysailers, and largely forgotten dinghies.

But that dock with its affordable slips was serviceable enough for anyone who just wanted to keep his own unassuming boat tied up, ready for a little fishing . . .

Suited him just fine.

He carried his plastic tackle box, latched tight but, as always, a jumble of disorganized filament and hooks and bobbers inside.

But no problem there. All of that mess was familiar to him since he did this every single day.

Well, *nearly* every day.

When a really nasty storm threatened the Twin Forks of Long Island, with both the Atlantic and Gardiners Bay—even the normally placid Peconic Bay—suddenly threatening, he had to take note of that.

His sixteen-foot Bayliner boat had a little engine that *usually* could handle the normal wakes and chop with its decades-old thirty-horsepower Evinrude. But a serious storm? He knew better . . .

But even if it was really cold? With those so-icy ocean breezes that January and February could send skimming over the water? That never deterred him.

Now he stopped walking.

It occurred to him that he seemed to start this ritual earlier and earlier each day. Now—it was the cusp of dawn. The sun *just* inching above the horizon in the water, magically turning everything the light hit a deep golden yellow and orange.

Absolutely beautiful.

And most days he didn't really care if he caught any damn fish. No. Simply felt so good to be out there, in the sea, his line in the water, the air so fresh and salty at the same time. The sky putting on its ever-changing show.

For him, there was nothing better.

But first, there was another part of this daily ritual; he turned toward the "master's" shack, where he needed exactly two things before heading down to his boat, tied up at the very end of the last, and certainly the shabbiest, dock.

The man pulled open the office's screen door, held by a tight spring, giving resistance and then letting out a solid squeak more effective than any bell chiming over the doorway.

To see: Joe Cioffi, a stub of a cigar in his mouth, shuffling through a stack of paper. Bills, probably. An old-school thermos—probably as ancient as Joe—was open, a thin, steamy cloud still escaping.

Joe turned to him with a quick look up.

"Already? Tell you what, Jack, seems like you start your damn day earlier and earlier." Joe grinned at him as he continued. "Someday you'll be getting here before me, place still dark."

And the man smiled as he put his tackle box down, rested his rod against a well.

"Early bird—isn't that what they say?"

"Ha. Then you sure got *that* covered," Joe said.

And the man, older than Joe, didn't have to wait to be taken care of. He went to a squat refrigerator that sat in one corner. Grabbed a large paper container, as if for an oversized meal from a Chinese take-out, and—fridge lid up—began scooping out gloppy chunks of fish.

The bait. Most of it squid. But also a bit of fish parts that no one eats, at least in this country. The man knew he'd easily go through it all, as he usually did. Some fish were good at nibbling the damn bait right off the hook without getting snagged.

Occasionally though, if he ran low, he'd save some junk fish he just caught, like a nasty sea robin, to cut up. The fish—if biting—were not too choosy when the good stuff ran out.

And when done . . .

He walked close to Joe, who was still sifting through what looked like a pile of bills and receipts, and stood at a long table with a chart of the nearby waters, studying it.

To ask the same question he asked every single morning before heading out.

"So, where were they catching last night?"

Joe nodded at the question as if it were a weighty matter indeed. Then: "*Right.* Weird. Not where all the big boats' radar and sonar said they would, you know? Lot of disappointed night boats came home . . . *pretty lean.*"

That, the man knew, was the fate of all those who fish, whether for pleasure or for existence. It was luck, fate, and wherever the hell currents below took the schools of fish.

Important to remember . . . it was fishing, not necessarily catching . . .

"But turns out a few boats did head way out into Gardiners Bay. Deeper water there, you know? Practically the Atlantic. Got lucky, just nudging around out there. So some of 'em came back with a good haul of blues, striped bass, porgies. Just a few boats."

"Hm. That's pretty far out."

"Yeah. I *know*. Especially for a boat your size. But—if you're really in the mood to actually catch something today . . ."

And the man laughed at that, his right hand clapping Joe Cioffi's back. "I always *am*."

"Right, then, so I'd head right about . . . *here*—give it a try."

Cioffi sent a finger to a spot on the chart.

Not a spot the man normally went to. Certainly, well away from the normal fishing lanes. *But if that's where the fish were . . .*

"Okay. Will give it a shot."

"Might get an updated report later," Joe said. "Once the day boats head out? See if things have moved any. But worth a try to start out."

"Then that's what I will do. Oh—got to fill the spare gas tank. I'll note down how much."

Again, Joe laughed. "After all these years, if I didn't trust you by now, then whenever the *hell* would I?"

"Right," the man said, grinning.

He turned to pick up his tackle box, retrieve his rod. But there was one last thing from Cioffi . . .

"Oh, meant to tell you, Jack. The boats that came back? Said some chop kicking up. Something coming our way. Maybe more than you usually deal with? Just—word to the wise."

The man knew his small boat, plenty agile for normal seas, could be in trouble if a normal sea . . . *turned into something else*. The thirty-horsepower outboard, and in a boat that small? Could get dicey. And there had been moments . . . where he was glad to see the marina and land.

"Gotcha. Will keep my eyes open. Can get the weather updates on my phone."

"You get freakin' service out there? What a world . . . Just, er, be careful?"

A last smile. Joe took a swig from his coffee thermos. Then nodded as the man started out of the small shack. But he had one more thing to say. "You know, Jack, been thinking . . . You're a lot like that guy?"

"What guy?"

"In that movie? Spencer Tracy. Fishing in his small boat. *The Old Man and the Sea*. And damn knows . . . you're *old*."

The man laughed dutifully, adding, "That I am . . ."

He walked out of the shack, and—yes—felt a breeze, not steady, but with the occasional significant gusts.

He'd have to watch it out there . . .

$$\triangleright$$

Then, as he walked down the rickety dock—some planks actually popping up where rusty nails had fallen away—down the section of the marina with just small *nothing* boats, he saw someone a few docks away.

Will Sharp—a guy who always seemed to be here—gave a big wave.

And the man waved back.

Will was quite the local character, a worker here—*of sorts*. Probably not paid by Cioffi to do anything. But always around, eager to help out the big boats when they brought in their catch or troubleshoot a reluctant engine refusing to kick over for anyone struggling to get their big pleasure boat started after a long hiatus.

As he walked past, the man saw that a lot of the boats here looked abandoned. Covered tight with tarps that had begun to fray at the edges, pockmarked with holes, now no longer succeeding to keep rain, snow, *whatever* . . . out.

People liked their boats well enough for a while, he knew. But then, for most, real life intervened. The prized possession, the boat, forgotten.

Near the end of the pier, he came to his own boat. No name on its old hull, just the NYS ID in block letters on either side of the forward hull. NY 4985 GV.

His own canvas cover, he saw, was tight, secure.

So, he put down the tackle box and his rod and began unbuckling the tarp. First one side, then throwing it back, he stepped in, continuing all around the hull. He spotted a trickle of water on the bottom of the hull. Maybe some minuscule leak?

Nothing to be worried about.

He almost didn't notice that Will had scurried over, stood there watching.

"Mr. Jack, heading out?"

"Yup, Will. Gonna see if they're biting today."

This exchange, pretty much exactly the same every day.

But today—*maybe a bit different?*

Once the tarp was removed, folded roughly, and tucked under the rear plank seat, he looked up to see Will shield his eyes from the just-up sun.

But just a few degrees up from the horizon, a few dark clouds were hanging there, as if waiting, ready to cut off the sunlight before too long.

"Where you heading today, Mr. Jack?"

Mr. Jack. Will afforded everyone the familiarity of being on a first-name basis but also added the respect of "mister."

"Joe told me night boats had good luck, out past Gardiners Island?"

Will nodded, taking in the information as if it were something important.

"*Dunno*, Mr. J. Kicking up a bit already out there? You might run into something?"

The man knew that Will—probably someone who had haunted the marina as long as it had been here—had seen *lots* of weather out here.

Those days that start quiet and turn nasty . . . even dangerous.

The Atlantic could be full of surprises. Quick surprises.

"Could be. Gets too much, I'll head straight back in. Maybe have an early beer with you?"

Will smiled at that.

"You do that, Mr. J. But be careful."

Then Will looked on as the man retrieved his rod and tackle box, then took the big container of squid and fish chunks, wedging the bait in a space on the side of the boat so it wouldn't spill.

"Anything, you, er, need—anything I—"

"No, thanks, Will. Think I'm good."

The man smiled. Even this—a little chat with this fixture at the marina—a part of the daily routine.

And the man—by now, after all these years here—liked his routine. *It felt secure. Safe.*

He sat down on the wood plank seat at the boat's stern.

Key in, he gave the Evinrude's ignition a quick turn. Sometimes the battery would be low, even dead. Then it would require a strenuous pull-start, the same as the boats he grew up with back in Mill Basin in Brooklyn so long ago.

But now—after a hesitant *chug*—it turned over as he twisted the throttle a bit. A puff of smoke escaped, but still in neutral.

He quickly undid the bow and then the stern ropes that tied the boat to the dock.

"Catch you later, Will."

And Will just smiled, nodded as the man, sitting back beside the engine, turned the throttle more, the throaty sound deepening, and started steering his boat out to open water . . .

Away from the pier. Out of the marina, then more power, past the wake restrictions as he got away, steering nearly due east, he figured.

To deep water—and hopefully the hungry fish ahead.

He looked up to see that the sun had already vanished, gone into hiding behind the ever-thickening clouds.

Thinking: *Well, that was fast . . .*

2

A CHOPPY SEA

The more the man steered his boat, its bow cutting into the growing chop, the bigger those white-cap-covered waves ahead became.

Until, as he chugged along, hand tight on the throttle, his boat would ride one swell, then slap down and land with a belly-whopping *splat*.

Nothing he hadn't hit before. Get as many rough days out here as calm ones.

But all that chop, the white caps looking like icing atop the gray sea, continued to grow. One thing was for sure: when he finally found a spot, dropped anchor—assuming he actually could hit the bottom— the boat would be bobbing wildly as he tried to pull in any fish.

Maybe he should have stuck to one of the more sheltered spots in the bay itself?

Fewer fish. Maybe . . . no fish? But at least he'd be spared the rocking to and fro.

But, that thought aside, he carried on.

▷

Finally, looking around where he was, just past the tip of the North Fork, right between Gardiners Island and the much smaller Plum Island, he guessed he was close enough to the spot Joe had pointed out.

He looked just a little past Plum Island to an even smaller island. Supposedly private—but since when did that stop the curious?

Still—he imagined the Coast Guard kept an eye on it.

And there were stories about that island . . .

Yes, private, so no idle visitors ever went there. And for the past decades, maybe nobody at all went there, though once it did contain a mansion and—supposedly—secrets.

Some old Connecticut family who liked having the place all to themselves, even though no one ever saw it.

There were rumors of things hidden, even from hundreds of years ago. Blackbeard had indeed been in these very waters before being captured.

Anyone who tried to sneak onto it to look, to hunt, would, he imagined, be soon caught.

Of course, he well knew . . . *yes.* There were ways to do things like that—so many islands here—*and not get caught.*

For now, he grabbed his traditional fluke anchor, with big twin points to dig into the bottom, and lowered it over the side, hoping he'd still be at a depth where he had enough rope and it could indeed hit the bottom and dig in.

As the rope slipped through his fingers, now calloused and worn by doing this so many times, he watched the anchor sink fast between the fighting waves of the choppy sea.

Until—*there!* It went slack.

He hit bottom and went back to the motor to give it a few short bursts in reverse, helping the anchor's twin flukes dig in.

And with that, he took a breath. The air gusts felt so chilly here. Another sweater would have been good.

But it was time to fish.

One good thing about fishing out here, he knew, was that there was no need to cast the line far at all.

Just toss the line a few feet away from the steadily rocking boat. Let it drop, the weights pulling the hook down, and then slowly let the line play out until . . . guessing just when the hook and its chunk of bait would be some meters off that unseen bottom.

Lock the reel—and wait.

Then do what he guessed most people who fish *really* do.

Just sit there. Look at the show the sea and sky were putting on. Think about things, good things, bad things. The past. The future. Problems to be solved.

And problems that had been solved.

All while waiting for the bobber to dip. To feel that exciting tug on the line as something way down below went for the juicy and slimy piece of squid he had threaded carefully on the sizable hook.

Until . . . not too long . . . he felt *something* there. Always hard to tell whether it was hooked or just nibbling around the edges.

And he started to slowly, deliberately reel it in. Not so fast that it would slip away. Just enough to *drive* the hook deeper into the mouth of whatever fish had taken a chance dining on the chunk of bait.

$$\triangleright$$

Reeling it in, now only feet away from the surface, he saw something swimming, struggling.

The sea was making such choppy peaks and valleys it was hard to see. Never easy anyway, but nearly impossible now. But he kept reeling it in. Not a bad weight on the other end of the line.

What he had was no tiny porgy that he'd just unhook and throw back, free to get caught another day.

But in this case, the fish was wildly wriggling, violently twisting this way, and then . . . he saw what he got.

Right. A damn sea robin.

A spiny fish that was like a sea-going porcupine, with bony needles in its winglike fins and pointy parts sticking out all over that made getting the inedible animal off the hook so damn hard.

Everyone hated sea robins.

As he brought it into the boat, a series of even bigger waves appeared, surprising him, and rocked his boat so that it tipped nearly low enough to one side that water could rush over.

Bad enough that removing this thing from the hook was a pain, but to do it under these wobbly circumstances?

He debated simply cutting the filament and just fixing up another hook.

But he put a glove, well stained from the innards of many fishes, on his left hand and worked the sea robin's mouth roughly, left and right, its grimacing teeth showing it was not enjoying this at all.

As luck would have it, the hook was deep into the fish's jaw.

Until it finally slid free.

And then . . . well, this nuisance fish? He *didn't* throw it back into the sea.

It might not mean much, but at least he could make it so there was one fewer of them out here.

He tossed it hard toward the front, banging it against the hull.

He then turned to his box of squid. Grabbed a piece. Then, bent over the box of bait, the boat still rocking back and forth, he saw something out of the corner of his eyes.

He stopped—and looked up . . .

He saw a boat, a good-sized one too.

At first, he thought: *a fishing trawler.*

But then he noted its profile—*no*, not a fishing boat. Looked more like a high-speed pleasure boat, big enough with room for people to sleep.

Not the type of boat one would normally see out here, he thought.

For another second he kept looking, and then—strangest thing— *the boat turned.*

Now, though far in the distance, it was definitely pointed his way. The man kept watching as the boat seemed to be heading straight toward him.

Thinking: *What's this about? They out to do some light fishing? Want some tips?*

So what the hell was happening? With them speeding to the guy in the small boat, rod in hand, bobbing in what was fast becoming a much-too-choppy sea.

It felt strange.

He let his line and hook fall to the side of the boat and waited while what was now clearly a sleek and fast pleasure boat roared quickly toward him.

▷

Feet away, the boat came to an abrupt stop; whoever was piloting it cut into the left, making its own wave now that the boat was parallel to his own.

He gave those on board a smile, a nod—not having a clue what this was about.

Until.

Until . . .

He saw there were four . . . no, *five* men on board. None of them looked dressed for a casual day bouncing around the bay and the nearby ocean. No. *Something about them.* The pants . . . not jeans. Dress pants. City clothes. And zippered jackets, pulled tight. All of them were look-ing down at him.

Something about the clothes, how they looked, standing there— somehow *wrong.*

And for the first time, the man felt an ever-so-slight hint of alarm.

So, he said something.

"You fellas lost or something?"

And four of them turned to one guy as he took a step, grabbed the railing—as if for a closer look.

The thought again: *something very wrong here.*

Nobody said anything. As if they enjoyed watching him . . .

What was the word? *Sweat?*

And at that moment, the man saw the other four men move, reaching into the pockets of their jackets.

A move he had seen before. Long time ago . . .

And the man knew then that whatever the hell was going on here . . . *it was so very bad . . .*

ONE

WELCOME TO THE NORTH FORK

3

BILLY BLESSING, CHEF

Billy made sure not to touch the two-inch-thick bone-in rib eye sitting in the sizzling cast-iron pan, butter bubbling, happily spitting.

And the smell coming from that beautiful cut of meat as it seared? One of the best in the world.

And while that sizzled away, Billy went to where he kept—old school—his stone mortar and pestle.

He started grinding the pile of rainbow peppercorns into small chunks, then into finer pieces, ready to hit the steak just before he flipped it.

Usually, a dish like this? Classic French steak au poivre? You would do a filet mignon and dust the meat with the crushed pepper—both sides—*then* let it hit the pan.

But with this colorful array of peppercorns, some strong, all so flavorful, and this the king of steak, Billy liked them in the state when they weren't cooked to a char but sat atop the steak's blackened sear.

Outside the norm, but anyway—it seemed to work.

And for him, as always, that was the important thing.

He looked over at Miguel. Outside of some disinterested and distracted high school kids who helped with dishes back here in the kitchen, it was just the two of them.

Miguel, with his five kids at home in Greenport and—he told
ly—a dream one day of his own food truck. And much bigger
dreams for his kids.

Billy had to wonder: When did it become a thing that *everyone*
wanted a food truck?

But with closing time soon—and the kitchen in good shape—not
much to do after this last ticket was taken care of. That ticket, a regular
who always came late, once a week.

Same day, same time, same order. Nice old guy—cargo shorts, the
loudest of Hawaiian shirts, aged leather sandals, unruly beard, and
tufts of white hair shooting off his head at all sorts of angles—who sat
alone and read a book.

And best of all, then the place would be closed for a week. A bit of
a breather after an intense summer. Fall was knocking at the door, and
life on the North Fork was about to change, *big time*.

"Miguel—why don't you head home. I got this. Also, I want to
have a chat with Tom before we shut things down."

Miguel seemed unsure. They didn't make harder workers.

"Go on." Billy smiled. "You go start your small vacation, eh?"

That brought a smile and "Thanks, Chef. You too. Enjoy the
time off."

Billy smiled and nodded. Enjoying the week ahead? Not sure about
that at all.

These days, lately . . . he found free time a little difficult to manage.
He was used to handling *so* much.

But at least he liked the intensity of the kitchen here, especially
when it was busy, like it had been all season, full on steady with tick-
ets, the dining room bustling.

A week of nada? What was he going to do?

Hell, if he knew. He'd figure it out on the fly.

Miguel undid his apron, and Billy turned back to the pan. Been
about four minutes. Time now to sprinkle the rainbow pepper shards
on top.

Then he took tongs and flipped the steak, revealing the very nice dark char on the other side. He dusted that side as well. Before he made the cream sauce, it would get another quick flip, quickly gluing the pepper to that side as well.

"Good night, Chef," Miguel said, heading out the back door.

Door open, Billy felt a chill from outside . . . something new now after all summer when the door had remained wide open, when on those hot nights, it had done little to cut the heat of the kitchen.

He grabbed a fistful of his hand-cut fries and tossed them into the fry cooker.

Brandy and cream stood ready beside the cast-iron pan. This last ticket soon to head out.

Minutes later, he flipped the rib eye again and then added a splash of brandy. He tilted the pan toward the gas flame, and the pan briefly produced a deep-blue flame.

Then a matching splash of heavy cream, not too much. Swirling the two liquids together, with his other hand he scooped out a tablespoon of coarse Dijon mustard and sent it flying into the liquid, using the well-charred steak to mix it all together as it thickened.

And just like that, it was ready.

He turned to the fryer and pulled out the basket of perfectly browned fries. A moment's rest, drying from the hot oil bath, before emptying them onto a large platter, generously doused with sea salt.

Then tongs for the steak, placed next to them and topped with the now-thickened sauce.

And scene.

He hit the bell. The last server still outside, probably chomping at the bit to get home, appeared.

This dish was something ordered every Sunday night by this same guy who showed up minutes before the place would close.

The server, Crystal, who was taking a year off from college, took the platter.

As she started to sail away, Billy said, "Crys? You have a good break."

"You too, Billy. Don't get into any trouble."

He smiled at that.

een a long while since he had been in any trouble. Thank god. And he liked it . . . *just like that.*

▷

Billy gave the big gas stove a final wipe. She was a dinosaur, a massive black vintage Garland with ten burners and two big ovens, clearly built to get through a lot of frantic and messy dinners.

When you cook, Billy knew, you get attached to a lot of things.

The pots and pans, to be sure, each with their own ability and personality. The knives, *absolutely*. Needing as much attention as if they were alive, with regular honing, sharpening—using the right knife for just the right purpose. He'd almost rather lose a hand than these knives.

But in the eye of the storm, above all—the stove.

He stopped, took a look around; the kitchen was all set for its own brief siesta.

Now what? Billy wondered.

Owner Tom Foley came in from the dining room.

"Billy, got someone here—just came in—who'd like a word?"

Billy turned. As far as he knew, he hadn't run afoul of the local police. Any debts were pretty well cleared up by now.

(Okay—maybe not perfectly. But getting there . . .)

And now a visitor who would like a word?

"Yeah?" he said to Tom, letting his tone express his confusion at the impromptu appearance of someone "wanting a chat."

"Some woman. Um, not from around here, I can tell you. She's sitting at the bar."

Billy wiped his hands and—a last act—undid his apron.

"Says she knows me?"

"Um, didn't say that. Maybe, just er . . . go see what she wants? I'll finish getting the place ready to shut down."

The last lone customer was probably midway through his rib eye and frites, sitting way in the back at a table by the window that looked out onto the dark sea . . . no moon yet.

Tom would not be locking the doors soon.

"Okay. Be right there," he said to Tom.

Billy didn't have a clue what this was about. But this—well, after a lot of different experiences in a lot of different places in the world?

He had to admit . . .

Set off some kind of alarm . . .

And he never was a big fan of the unknown and unexpected.

Now, apron tossed onto a metal table at the kitchen's center, Billy headed out to the dining room and NoFo Eats's impressive wood bar, an always polished and gleaming red oak, where on a Friday night after five, the crowds would grow to be three-people deep.

But now—Billy was simply curious.

Mystery woman, sign in, please?

$$\triangleright$$

He saw her sitting there with a tumbler of ice, something brown surrounding the cubes.

Bourbon maybe? Jameson perhaps? One of the fine single malts Tom always kept in stock, despite the price?

As he walked to where she sat on a stool, she turned slowly, seeing him. A small smile. He noted a few things.

She was dressed like she had just finished her shift in a sleek corporate office on Park Avenue. A gray tailored skirt, the length perfect, and a matching jacket. White blouse. Auburn hair pulled back, but undone, clearly, it would be long.

Definitely not from around here.

Billy stood beside her. He debated grabbing himself a glass as well, something to mark that his shift was over—or maybe, in this case, to steel himself for what was coming.

But maybe, whatever this was, he could dispense with it quickly. Start whatever this break was going to be.

She looked at him, not taking a stool beside her, and then simply said, "Billy Blessing. As we live and breathe."

men, with—well, the word that was most apt and yet pretty rare these days—*spunk*, she said, "Why don't you grab yourself something to drink? Looks like you've been working hard."

Billy was about to demur. He never was one for taking direction from anyone, even when it came to a suggested nightcap. And from this stranger—beautiful, no doubt—who looked like she had just stepped from a transporter room located in a very expensive section of Manhattan to go slumming with the hoi polloi of the North Fork.

Seemed odd.

"I don't think . . ." he started.

Not really having a good reason, though, *not* to sit, not to have a drink. Other than, yes . . . *caution*. That and, oh yeah, fear.

"I have a proposition for you, Billy Blessing. But it may take me a few minutes to explain?"

Then, with a tone and shift of her eyes that indicated this woman—whoever the hell she was—was generally used to getting her own way, she said, "So why not take a seat at least. Hear me out? I think you will be interested. I think . . . it will be worth your while?"

I think this is definitely going to be trouble, Billy thought. And he also knew, from his various adventures in other towns, things done with other people, some legal, some less so . . . that there certainly could be skeletons left in various closets that could come back to haunt him.

In fact, being honest, for a few of them—from the Second City of Chicago to LA—possibly do a lot worse than just "haunt" him.

Was this woman maybe with the New York DA's office? No. Not dressed like this. Or maybe from a high-priced lawyer's office?

And the questions kept on coming into his head until Billy knew, well, he was hooked. Curious, at least this far . . .

"That a whiskey?" he said.

She nodded. "Well spotted. *Uncle Nearest 1856*? I hear it's your favorite."

"Nice. So you know a little about me. Okay. Think . . . I will join you."

Billy started to walk down to the far end of the bar, then around. Grabbed a classic crystal tumbler.

"Been on my feet for quite a few. And a few fingers of *that* might be just what the doctor ordered."

And then, the woman—pretty young, Billy guessed, but not sure exactly *how* young—said, as if showing how quick she could be, "Not my doctor."

And he had to grin at that.

Billy took the bottle of Uncle Nearest and splashed in a few fingers. Well, maybe all five fingers and a handful of rocks. Then he thought . . .

Curiosity.

Always did have a problem with that. We know it didn't work out so well for the cat.

4
SUSPICIOUS MINDS

Billy waited, intrigued by this stylish city woman sitting at the bar of what was the closest to an upscale restaurant in the North Fork, but still pretty rustic by NYC standards.

Tom had gone back to his cluttered office, probably to do the accounts for the night. Money in, salaries and bills to be paid, all the tedious paperwork that went with running a restaurant.

A world that Billy knew well. And—for at least that part—one he did not miss.

At least, he thought so.

The lone remaining patron still was way off in a far corner of the restaurant, tucking into what was left of his steak.

But then, the man stood. Money put down—always an ample tip—and he sailed off into the night without a word.

Then Billy was alone with the young lady. And, like the cat, ready to indulge that curiosity.

"Okay, Tom said you wanted a word. If it's about any of my still-outstanding debts, I have all those covered. No need for any legal—"

But she put up a hand and smiled. "Not here about *that*."

That smile, with her perfect teeth, faded quickly.

Billy nodded and moved on to his second guess. "And if you are here to do an interview, yet another story rehashing the rise and fall of one Billy Blessing—"

"Again—*wrong.*"

And at that, Billy was stumped.

"Then—you have me at a disadvantage," he said.

"Hmm?"

"Your name, for starters? Always a nice way to start a discussion of whatever the hell you came here to discuss?"

She nodded and stuck out a hand, showing her perfect French manicure, even in this dim light.

"Lisa Cowles."

The name meant nothing. Billy nodded and took the hand, feeling as if he were about to pay too much for a high-end luxury car.

Something he had, in fact, done—more than once. *Back in the day.*

Now, the ten-year-old Jeep Cherokee outside served his purposes—and the terrain here—just fine.

"Lisa. So—*Lisa*—you're not here representing any of the various debtors I still have hanging over my head. Not too many, mind you. Or here for that special hell that is known as an interview, hmm? Then—*what.*"

While he waited for an answer from this mystery woman who knew what bourbon he preferred, he took a swig. Always a treat after a long night. The strong, oaky smell of the liquor, the ice rattling, chilling the amber liquid. Some nights he'd go for a vodka on the rocks, Tito's always working just fine.

But other nights, especially when the true warmth of summer started to fade, chill in the air, the rich, warm taste of the Tennessee whiskey . . . perfect.

He let it sit for a moment on his tongue.

And then, in answer to his question, this Lisa Cowles reached down to a leather bag, too large to be dubbed a purse. Looking causal. But with a big "TF" at the clasp, revealing its lineage. A pricey Tom Ford design, and anything but casual.

She opened the buckle and took out what was clearly a newspaper clipping while Billy waited.

She passed the article to him, something clipped from the local paper here, the *North Fork Gazette*, a very small tabloid out of nearby Greenport, usually filled with news of town hall meetings, pumpkin festivals here and there, advertisements for the dwindling eating and drinking establishments that stayed open out here through the ever darker and colder months.

From a few weeks ago, he noted, seeing the date.

Something he hadn't read, but then it wasn't like you scanned this paper like the *New York Times* for what the hell was really going in the world. Or Wordle.

He skimmed the article quickly.

An article about a guy named Jack Landry. Fixture at Cioffi's Marina, it said. That place wasn't too far from here. Headed out to fish as he did every crack of dawn. Only this day, weather turned bad, things kicked up . . .

As they often did.

And he never came back. Presumed dead. Small boat never found either.

Basic information consumed, Billy handed the article back to the woman.

"Sad story. Got to watch the weather out here, what with the Atlantic right out the door, and it does change on a dime very quickly."

Just like Lisa Cowles's demeanor had changed. Face now set, serious.

"A few things, Billy. You don't mind if I call you that?"

"I have been called worse . . ."

"Right. That man. Jack Landry? He's . . . my father."

Billy nodded. Another sip. That fact was, well, interesting . . .

Then the obvious question: "But his name, and yours?"

"Right. Well, my father . . . See, long ago, he didn't stay with my mother. And she married a man named Cowles. Nice man. Successful.

Lawyer. Wealth manager. Very successful. Gave me a good life. The best education."

Billy nodded, still not seeing where this was going.

"I saw my birth father rarely. More of a stranger to me for most of the years. Though—before he moved out here—he opened up a bit to me. Maybe, sorry for everything that happened? Or didn't happen?"

"Regrets? As Ol' Blue Eyes sang, 'I've had a few'?"

"Yeah. Guess so. But here's the thing. I *don't* think my father, my real father, had a mishap out at sea."

Billy listened.

"He moved out here. Off the grid, you know—"

Billy laughed at that. "Oh, that I do. Can relate . . ."

"And I think something else happened to him that had nothing to do with the wind, the weather, the waves . . ."

"You do?" Billy asked. "Really?"

A nod. "And I want *you* . . . to find out what really happened to him . . ."

▷

Billy had gone behind the bar to retrieve the whole bottle of Uncle Nearest and a small bucket of ice. His plan for this meeting was suddenly changing.

And with Tom in the back and the last patron gone . . . they were truly alone.

"Okay, let's play this out, at least for a few minutes. What makes you think that your father, this Jack Landry, *didn't* have an accident at sea?"

At this, the woman looked away. And when she turned back, she fixed Billy with her dark eyes. Somewhere in the back of his mind, Billy heard Quint from *Jaws* describing similar eyes: "lifeless eyes, black eyes, like a doll's eye." He shook his head and took another swallow of bourbon.

"Okay, well, when he abandoned my mother and me, she always told me things, like what his real business was? That he worked with some very dangerous people and—especially when I was older—it was a good thing he was out of our lives."

"Okay."

Lots of stories like that in little old New York, Billy knew.

"He had been out here for what . . . almost ten years? Living a quiet life. I was able to find that out on my own. Just fishing, living in a small cottage somewhere. Got the address. And then—suddenly—vanishes."

She paused. Billy knew what the conjecture to come would be.

"Man like Jack Landry? My real father? Once powerful. Maybe dangerous. At least to others. Sorry—a man like that doesn't just *disappear*."

Billy had to smile at that. "Unless that is exactly what happened."

But something about Lisa Cowles's suspicions was resonating. He also knew one thing that he could feel in every word she said . . .

She knew more than she was saying.

But this whole business, none of his concern . . . what did it matter? Had a stiff drink with a young and beautiful woman, who had some kind of deep and dark suspicion.

Happens all the time, Billy guessed. But what did it have to do with him?

So, time to close the door here. The achiness from hours on his feet, the heat of the kitchen, the sheer frenzy of cooking both good and fast, suddenly, like the waves outside, hit him with a growing fatigue.

As it did every night . . .

"Look, sorry you believe that. Who knows? Guess anything's possible? But been a long night for me. Time I headed home."

He gave her a small smile. "Wishing you all the best, of course. Though I do suggest, next time? Try speaking to the local authorities? You know, the police? Seems an area that they would be much more interested in . . . than me."

He was about to slide off his stool, chalking it up to an interesting end to the evening, when Lisa reached down, grabbed her Tom Ford bag again, and this time took out something like a billfold. She didn't say anything but opened it to reveal a checkbook.

"Hmm. Don't see those much these days. Very old school," he said.

She paid him no attention and instead started to, apparently, fill out a check. And when done, she pulled it away from the check register with a crisp *snap*.

Passed it to him. He saw the amount. *Ten thousand dollars*. The payee, himself.

"I know you are still dealing with financial issues. Problems."

"Yeah, well, takes time, you know."

"And I also imagine you wouldn't mind"—she gave a look around the dining room of NoFo Eats—"having your own place again?"

And that was certainly true enough. He liked Tom a lot. And despite the pressure, the craziness, he enjoyed cooking again.

But not as much as he enjoyed it when he had his own place in Harlem, Blessing's Bistro. To run the joint, to be host, to oversee everything? The celebrity guests? The good reviews? That was all *so* much fun . . .

Until it burned down, and it turned out the insurance . . . just not good enough.

He took the check and looked at it as if it were from another planet. "And this is *for* . . . ?"

"Looking into Jack Landry's disappearance. See what you can learn. Find out what really happened. I've heard you are good at such things."

"Don't believe everything you hear."

"And I'm telling you, this 'accident at sea' could very well be no accident at all."

He tilted the check. "Yeah, well. Okay. I got a few days off here. But think I should, well, instead—go for a little R and R?"

He went to pass the check back. Not a bad amount.

"And you must be confusing me with someone else. Despite what you heard, I am no detective, Lisa Cowles. I am merely—"

"Oh, the things you did involving that Chicago outfit? And that murder out in LA? Seems like you somehow get pulled into things . . . ?"

She took a breath. The next words were a bit ominous, like she had really done her homework.

"And your *own* past, Billy? Well—plenty enough secrets there too. Or"—she smiled—"so I've heard."

Billy grinned at that. She had done her homework and hadn't

stopped at what kind of bourbon he liked. All that she was maybe referring to—the murders he somehow found himself in the middle of—was really such a long time ago. And it was more about his proximity in his other life as a morning show host than his sleuthing skills.

Still, it was true enough. He did, back then at least, appear to have a knack.

Somehow, he *did* get pulled into things. One way or the other. And some very bad people got caught. And he came out unharmed and unscathed, and that added to his celebrity.

But still, he shook his head . . .

"I dunno."

At that, she took the check from his fingers and ripped it in half. Then to the register again, more quick scrawling. Another tear, a pass . . .

"Hmm," he said. "Twenty grand? I feel like I'm on *Let's Make a Deal*."

"I have no idea what that is," she said, shrugging off Billy's reference to a long-ago TV game show. "This is just to see what you can learn. *That's all*. Look into things, as I said? And if you actually find out something that doesn't match this"—she picked up the newspaper clipping again—"this *bullshit* story, you get another check, except that one will have an additional zero at the end."

Billy now had to look at the new check. Then the promise of substantially more.

And he thought . . . *sure*. Could use the cash. And he was, in fact, planning on building a nest egg for a place someday, somewhere. Could take forever. A payout like this would definitely kick-start it.

And as luck would have it—

(Though a thought: Was it really luck on Lisa Cowles's part? She had done her homework. She probably had sussed out that the restaurant would be shuttered for a week.)

—he had a bunch of days free. And no real plans . . .

So, another sip of bourbon. Nodding, thinking. Until: "Okay. No guarantees, of course. I assume this check will clear?"

She laughed. "Oh, trust me—you have no worries about that."

"Tell me what you do know. About your dad, about this Jack Landry. And in the morning, well, I will, as they say, 'look into things.' *A bit.*"

"Good." And now, finally, again, she grinned. *"Let's Make a Deal* indeed . . ."

He smiled. This little negotiation had actually been fun.

"Okay. And I don't know a lot. But well—tell you what I do . . ."

And for a few more minutes, he listened, grabbing a pencil from behind the bar and a cocktail napkin to make notes.

Look at me being the professional sleuth. Eat your heart out, Sherlock, he thought.

And he knew one thing when she was done: she hadn't been kidding about not knowing much at all.

5

THE MORNING AFTER

Billy squinted from his bed, thick curtains keeping the rising sun over the sea mostly—and literally—at bay. But a sliver left uncovered let a blazing shaft land squarely on his face.

He rubbed his eyes. And after a moment, swinging to the side of the bed to get up, he tried to think if he had prepped the coffee the night before.

But stepping into the small kitchen of his very small cottage on the northern side of Route 25, with a sandy driveway and a few scraggly pines standing guard, he saw yesterday's coffee grounds, and the pot empty.

As he made coffee, he wondered about the night before: *Just what the hell have I agreed to do?*

He knew one thing, looking at the check sitting on the simple wooden table in the kitchen . . . first thing to do was hit the bank. Make sure there was indeed twenty grand behind Lisa Cowles's proposition.

With her promise to check in with him some days later, she had given him a stiff business card with just a name and a mobile number.

That was it.

The message is clear, Billy thought. *Call if he learns anything.*

He shoveled in a couple of tablespoons of ground coffee. No measuring here. Then, after the most cursory of rinses, he refilled the pot with tap water, which went sloppily into the well of a bare-bones, old-school Mr. Coffee.

Soon, he was ready to hit the ignition and start the thing brewing while he thought over what little the mysterious Lisa Cowles, daughter of a mysterious missing man, had told him.

▷

He peeled a banana and sipped the coffee, black with some brown sugar. *Breakfast.* In between bites of the banana, he got dressed. After all—amazingly enough—he was "on assignment," and the day well begun.

Lisa Cowles had said that she saw her father only a handful of times over the years. Always a dinner at a pricey Manhattan place. Sparks, The Palm Too, Keens. He liked his steak and oysters as well as—Billy guessed—those place's mighty-stiff drinks.

He tapped his computer to double-check where the Northold Police Department was. Just on Main Street, not far from the water. As a rule, Billy liked avoiding too much close contact with official authorities.

When you have had your history with such people, in his opinion—best to avoid.

But if he was going to do this thing—amazingly enough for money—he had, as a start, no choice. ·

He left his cottage with the front door open, the screen door slapping shut behind him. The October day was due to warm up, a little bit of leftover summer before the inevitable chill of winter kicked in.

He got to his Cherokee, started it up. Clutch down, and threw it into gear—glad that it was a stick shift. He liked the control, especially when so much of his life, as it turned out, *wasn't* in his control.

He pulled away, sending up a spray of sand as he rolled out to the main drag of Route 25.

▷

Billy went up the two steps to the front door of the police station, which, from the outside, resembled those tiny post offices that dotted the countryside. Like a very small house for very small people.

Only a sign near the roof indicated that, yes, this was "The Town of Northold Police Department."

Was it staffed, he wondered? Only one way to find out.

He turned the knob and pushed open the door, which—appropriately, considering things—gave out a noisy squeak from its weathered wood.

▷

Once inside, he saw someone at the desk. In a police uniform of sorts. A tan khaki uniform, worn by someone who—well, based on girth— would have a very hard time chasing anyone down an alleyway.

The guy's head was shaved as close as it could be. Glasses at the tip of his nose as he looked at a computer screen. The black tie attempting to be tight around his neck, but failing . . .

Billy waited a moment while the representative of Northold's finest looked up.

Then a simple "Yes?"

"Er, I wonder . . . could I have a word with the police chief?"

Simple enough request, Billy thought.

But it produced a look of confusion on the officer/gatekeeper at the desk.

"You have an appointment?"

Billy took a step inside. By now, most people he met would be going, *Aren't you that guy from TV? Years ago?*

But so far, the officer—now Billy could see his nameplate, one Officer Edgar Beck—had avoided saying that.

So Billy continued, "No appointment. Was just hoping to get a quick word?"

That sent Officer Beck spinning from his screen to a nearby book— apparently for appointments for the supposedly busy chief.

"Let's see, perhaps tomorrow, in the afternoon, could slot you in?"

And Billy thought, *Really?* Old Edgar here took his duties quite seriously.

"Look, I just need a quick talk with the chief if he is—"

At which point the inner door, to what had to be the smallest of offices, opened.

Billy saw a woman come out. Same uniform, but she stood barely five feet, he guessed. Black hair pulled back tight.

"Can I help you?"

Overriding Edgar's officiousness, which, he guessed, happened quite a lot.

Billy nodded. "Hoping you can. Had a few questions about a matter."

With Edgar now following this interaction, Billy chose to say no more.

"Oh, you have . . . a *matter*? O-kay. Right. Come in, then."

For a moment, Billy thought Edgar might protest this breach of protocol in the Northold Police headquarters.

But Billy nodded at him as he simply followed the diminutive chief into her indeed tiny office. She took a seat behind a modest desk and said, "You can shut the door . . ."

▷

The chief—Captain Lola Bristow, from her nameplate—did the usual when it came to recognizing him.

"*Billy Blessing*. Heard you were living around here, working at some place . . . ?"

"NoFo Eats."

"Ah, been a while."

"You wouldn't have seen me. I'm the chef."

"Really?" That produced a smile. "Well, I think I should be asking *you* questions, instead of the other way around. I mean, how did *that* happen? Wow. Fallen TV star lands here in the North Fork as a local chef?"

Billy didn't know whether to like this brash cop, who said exactly what she thought pretty easily, or to be pissed off at her directness.

Not sure yet if he liked that.

"Long story."

To which she replied, "Aren't they all?"

Billy was still waiting for an invitation to sit in the chair that faced the desk.

But since said offer did not come . . .

"Someone asked me to help them look into something. About their father. And what happened."

Chief Bristow took a ballpoint pen, gave it a click, grabbed a nearby yellow pad.

"That something you do? Besides cook, that is? *Look into things?*"

"Not on a regular basis but, well, hard to resist doing a favor. I'm that kind of guy."

Bristow's smile faded a bit; at least her curiosity was finally engaged.

"Okay, why not tell me what this is actually about . . . and why it brings you to my office here in sleepy Northold?"

And Billy—not really knowing a lot, or really anything—did just that.

▷

He watched the chief look away. Out a window that overlooked some kind of marshy area, tall, reedy plants waving in the wind. A few puffy clouds in the background. Not a bad view.

"Okay." She turned back to him. "Think I got it. So now, you tell me what you would like . . . from me?"

And Billy found himself curious as well. How did this woman, obviously quick, forceful, maybe a tad impatient, edgy—at least for laid-back Northold—end up being here, and being the chief?

He'd save that question for some other time.

For now . . .

"Well, for starters, if the man's daughter—"

"This Lisa Cowles?"

A nod. "Yeah, if she thinks it wasn't an accident—"

"For an as-yet-undefined reason?"

Another nod. And yes, this Chief Bristow was smart and quick.

"So far. I thought, well, this Jack Landry lived in the vicinity of Northold? Must be your jurisdiction, no?"

That produced a grin. "*Jurisdictions.* Mr. Blessing, you *really* must think you are still in Manhattan."

And Billy had to smile at that as well. Small department like this . . . the word was almost ridiculous.

"Um, yeah, wondering what you know about the so-called accident, his disappearance?"

Bristow nodded at that. Perhaps understanding. "Well. Do let me explain something to you. See, this Mr. Landry disappeared and probably died at sea . . . *see?*"

Billy smiled.

"And well—that's *not* in Northold, my 'jurisdiction' as you would have it. And though I am concerned about any resident residing in said 'jurisdiction,' and yes, pretty curious as to whatever happened to him . . . but responsibility for any investigation? Final determination? Based on location, that's squarely on the United States Coast Guard, who, of course, kept me informed."

"And that information?"

"Well, in this case, *nothing.* Guess that's why they call it a disappearance?"

Billy nodded at that. "I imagine then—that you don't mind if, for my friend—I do some looking around? See people. Ask questions? That sort of thing?"

"*Look* all you want. Though considering what likely happened—and I do not see you as the seafaring type, hm—doubt you will learn much?"

Billy laughed. "You got that right, about me and bodies of water. Still, when in Rome—"

"Or on the North Fork . . ."

"Right. One other question then. Though guess I could find out on my own . . ."

"Ask away. I find this all very entertaining."

"The marina he used? I imagine that *is* in your jurisdiction?"

"That it is. Cioffi's. Down Sunken Hollow Road."

"Know the area. Where I cook is pretty near there."

"Speaking of which, I must come by and sample your work. Not often we get cooks out here with such a pedigree."

Billy turned to leave. "If you do, I will be sure to do my best."

And just when he thought this was over, the chief came to the door.

"One thing, Billy Blessing. A request, I guess? If you learn anything that you think I should know, please give me a call?"

Billy nodded.

"Good. Hang on a sec—"

And the woman went to her desk, wrote something down on a Post-it, and freed it from its pad.

"My cell. If you do discover something, best—in a small sleepy town like this—yeah, best to keep it nice and quiet."

Billy took the Post-it. "You got it."

And then, Billy turned and sailed out of the small office, past the guardian Edgar at his desk.

Thinking . . . *the chief.* One interesting character. For a lot of reasons.

Which prompted the thought, perhaps not entirely without some vague hint of curiosity, maybe suspicion, *How interesting . . .*

6

CIOFFI'S MARINA

Billy made his way down the gravel path. Over sandy hummocks, to the rows of docks with boats of all sizes, commercial and otherwise. To the office of the marina. Not more than a very weathered slat-board shack.

Sun was well up, sky perfectly clear.

Almost the exact opposite of what the weather had turned into when Jack Landry took his small boat out of here.

He went to knock at the office door, but it was open a crack, so Billy just gave it a gentle push and entered.

To see who he assumed was Joe Cioffi, sitting at a beaten-up table marked by cigarette burn marks. Smell of smoke from an inexpensive cigar in the air. A clear glass with brown liquid nearby that, Billy guessed, *wasn't* tea.

Always five o'clock somewhere, Billy thought. Even for a sleepy marina at the end of Long Island.

But before Billy could say a word, Cioffi barked, "Got no boats."

"Um, well, I—"

"*No* boats. All rented. So, see you later. Kinda busy, *capisce?*"

Only then did Cioffi turn and look at Blessing. For a moment, the look on the man's face showed that *maybe* he also knew who Billy was. Or maybe just dimly registered that the man in his office was someone he'd seen before. *Doesn't anybody recognize me anymore?*

Or more likely, someone not dressed in any nautical "let's hit the sea, mateys" fashion and just looking like a really unlikely visitor to the marina.

"Thanks. No boats. *Got it.* But not here to rent a boat."

At this, Cioffi finally pivoted, giving him his full attention.

"Okay. Then, what the hell *are* you here for?"

Billy smiled. "Just had some questions about someone who kept his boat here."

Billy clocked Cioffi's face. Eyes narrowed even more. Did he know or suspect what was coming next?

"An old guy named Jack Landry?"

Cioffi nodded, grabbed a stub of a cigar sitting in a sooty ashtray. Then he picked up a box of wooden matches, got one out, and gave the cigar a quick light, a few deep puffs to get it going.

Then—well, guess he was ready for the rest of this so far not very convivial conversation.

$$\triangleright$$

"So, pal, you like a *detective* or something? Come here, asking questions? You don't look like no Columbo."

"Not that I don't appreciate the throwback reference, but no, I'm not a detective. But I played one on TV." When the only response Billy got was a blank stare from Cioffi, he said, "Just, dunno—friend of the family?"

Cioffi shook his head. "Old Jack Landry has family? Sure didn't seem like that."

"What do you mean?"

Cioffi gave his lit stub a few more puffs. "If an old guy has kids, grandkids, any of that crap? They *talk* about them. Know what I mean? Seems like he lived alone, *was* alone."

Cioffi leaned forward.

"And I'll tell you one more thing, Mr. Friend-of-the-Family . . . All I knew of him was he kept his small boat here. Liked to fish. Lot of old guys out here like to do that. Keeps them busy, y'know?"

Billy nodded as if some ancient mariner mystery were being explained.

"But—if you don't mind, and it might put someone's mind at ease—that morning, when he went out. Weather was bad?"

Cioffi shook his head again. "Not really. Not at the start. Not a bad dawn, you know? But then right after he left, I guess, *yup*—clouds rolled in quick, something nasty heading this way, *and fast.*"

"And Landry knew that?"

At that question, Cioffi paused. "Sure. I guess. Guy takes a boat? Out there? You gotta check the damn weather reports."

"But you didn't warn him or anything?"

That produced a laugh.

"Who am I? Freakin' Al Roker on *The Today Show*? Got what—over a hundred boats here, from the big day fishing boats, the commercial trawlers, the big pleasure boats, and then little crappy sixteen- or eighteen-footers . . . like Landry's. People *s'posed* to do their *own* homework, see? Make their *own* goddamn decision. Go—or no go."

Billy nodded. Though he had to wonder . . . Cioffi seemed agitated to be talking about this. His puffs came faster and were now interspersed with sips from his glass.

Billy had been around enough blocks to sense . . . this guy here? *He's really nervous about something.*

"And that morning, you know where he went?"

Quickly, a shake of the head. "Nope."

Billy waited to see if a pause—always an effective tool in any interview on television—triggered something.

Then—*abracadabra.*

Cioffi continued, "I mean, probably he had his favorite spot to fish. Places he got lucky. All these guys in their shitty little boats do."

"Yeah. So, you have absolutely no idea where he went . . . in the bay, or maybe farther out?"

"That *is* . . . what I *just* said, no?"

The smoke hitting the air in this tight little office was getting difficult to breathe, so . . .

"Okay then. Thanks for talking."

He was about to add: *Been a big help.*

But Billy was sure the sarcasm would be lost on the oddly agitated marina owner.

Instead, he turned and opened the door to leave. The air outside felt so good, the sun hitting his face as he shut the door behind him. Though he still didn't know anything about Landry and the day he disappeared.

But steps away, he looked down to one of the piers.

Off to the right, where there were rows of smaller boats, one was just now putt-putting away. Probably a lot like Landry's boat. And a man was standing there on the pier, looking like he was coiling some ropes.

A worker here?

Well, sometimes information could come from an unlikely source.

So, Billy started down the path to the piers, heading to where the man waited.

Billy thinking: *Maybe time I got a little lucky here?*

Joe Cioffi waited. Sitting at the table, his stub smoldering. Waiting . . . until he guessed that the person who came to ask questions was gone.

Then he grabbed his phone. It had been dropped more than a few times, so the screen had become a spiderweb mesh of cracks. But worked well enough—that is, when it found service out here.

He opened the desk drawer, filled with scraps of paper, receipts, notes written and forgotten.

But also, a white business card with only one thing on it.

A phone number. He hit the keypad on his phone with the numbers. But made a mistake. Did a backspace to correct it.

Nerves, he thought.

The number entered, he started the call.

Ringing once, twice, then—middle of the ring—an answer. He

did not know who was on the other end of the call. That was not important.

He was just doing what he had been told. Because it had been made clear that was a very important thing to do. *Do what he was told—exactly.*

The voice on the other end said simply, "Yeah?"

"He came here. Asked questions. Some guy. Don't know him."

The voice on the other end didn't seem surprised at this, as if this visit was to be expected. The voice gave a quick description, to which Cioffi said, "Yes. That's him."

Then: "He comes back . . . see what you can find out. What he's up to? What he knows? What he *doesn't* know."

Cioffi was about to say, well, all that was not something he could do, *should do.*

But before he could figure out how to say that, the voice said, "You got that?"

So, all Cioffi could say was, "Yes. Sure." Then for added reassurance: "Got it."

And then the line went dead. And Cioffi sat there a moment holding his phone, so overdue for a replacement, he guessed, the battery barely working these days, and thought, *Who the hell was I just talking to?*

7

A DIFFERENT STORY

Billy walked down the long pier. Most of the boats here were covered in weathered tarps, bobbing in the water. His target: a tall, lanky guy, a baseball cap with the NY Yankees logo on his head, the blue of the cap well faded.

As he approached, he heard the guy muttering to himself.

"Hey, friend," Billy said.

The man spun around.

"Yes? Er—?"

The man seemed confused by Billy standing there. His bushy, unmanaged gray beard caught the sunlight. Wild eyes squinting in the light. A stained T-shirt that said "CBGB" with the worn letters "OMFUG" below.

Billy never knew what those letters under the CBGB logo meant.

That Lower East Side place that gave birth to Blondie and the Ramones . . . *long gone.*

"You work here?" Billy asked.

The man put down the coil of rope he had in his hands.

"Um, why, I help the boaters out. You know, some of this, some of that."

Billy nodded, smiled at that. "You work for Joe Cioffi?"

The man rubbed his beard, and Billy could see the lanky guy projecting caginess.

"Who are you?" the man said.

Whenever Billy heard that question, he thought of a book he had as a kid. Maybe the first book he had actually loved since it had such great pictures in it.

That line, spoken by a caterpillar smoking a hookah. Strange now to think of that . . . in a kids' book.

Who are you?

Kind of a key question.

"Oh, sorry. Name's Billy. *Billy Blessing.*"

Again, nothing. Well, Billy did think, with his living out here, his years of being "known," a celebrity, almost famous—well, here, with this crowd—didn't count for much. But, come on.

But giving him the name seemed enough for the man, who now stuck out his dark and bony hand, with fingers that looked troubled by arthritis, like they might not work together all that well.

"Will Sharp."

Then Billy found the need to bring the conversation back to his original question. But first, Billy shot a look back to where the marina's office sat. No one was standing outside, seeing where he went.

That was good.

"Well, Will Sharp . . . this pier here, these boats? Like I said, you work here?"

Will smiled. "I help people out. With their boats, you know, getting them ready. Help the old fellas get out. You know . . . but they just tip me whatever they want." His grin broadened. "Not like a *real* job. Had those! Didn't like them."

Billy smiled at that, now liking this character who haunted the marina. Probably a useful nonemployee to have around.

Billy decided that maybe an early tip was called for. Took out his wallet and dug out a twenty-dollar bill. Passed it to Will.

He took the bill, pleased, and said, "You got a boat here? You need help?"

And to alleviate the man's confusion: "No. Boating's not my thing. But looking into things, all about a friend. Who did have a boat. Guess somewhere right along here? This pier here with all the small boats?"

Will nodded, then said, "Friend?"

"Yeah. He went out a few weeks back and didn't come back."

That made a light bulb go off in Will's face. "Oh, you mean *Mr. Jack*." Will shook his head. "Terrible thing, that. Nice man, you know? Your friend? Nice guy."

Billy didn't confirm or deny, just nodded.

"You working that day?" Bill corrected his terminology. "I mean, helping out here? Did you see him?"

"That I did. Have to admit, was even a little worried."

"Worried. What about?"

"Why, the weather! This time of year, early morning can start out *real* nice and sunny. But if you know the signs . . . gonna change so fast."

Billy, having no knowledge of such things, said, "Signs?"

A nod, then Will pointed to the east. "The dark clouds gathering way out there and, depending on winds, moving fast. Imagine the weather reports must have said to expect rain, maybe some storms? But that would be for inland. But out there . . . ?"

Will now gestured to the bay, quiet, calm, and beautiful.

"The farther you get out, the *faster* things change. Different story out at sea, that's what I always tell people. When you're out on the open water, it's always *a different story*."

"I bet. So, Jack Landry—*Mr. Jack*—he knew he was heading out into it?"

A nod. "Guess he thought he could get out there, do some fishing—tell you, that man *loved* to fish every day. Some days he was even out before I got down here. Nice man, as I said."

"Sure," Billy said, relieved he hadn't, so far, been asked how he knew him. "And that day, he just didn't come back?"

"Right. I mean"—Will pivoted and pointed to an empty space in the pier—"that's his slip right there. Tell you, Billy Blessing, it must have kicked up something bad out there. And fast."

"Why do you say that?"

"Well, you see . . . Mr. Jack, like I told you, went out every day. Seen good weather, bad, and everything in between. Things pick up, storm kicking in, and he'd know!"

"Know?"

"To get his damn boat *right* back here, quick as he could."

Billy waited. Thinking: this accidental disappearance at sea seemed less and less likely.

Then, the big question: *If not that, if not an accident . . . then what?*

He was tempted to ask Will for a bit of speculation: *Why* did he think that Jack Landry didn't do just that? Get his ass back to the bay, to the marina?

But he doubted that level of insight was in Will Sharp's comfort zone. Besides, he had another question. One which he thought would be a dead end.

"Guess you have *no* idea where he went that morning? Big bay out there, open ocean not far beyond. Bunch of islands out there if he got into real trouble?"

Will's eyes focused on him as if the question wasn't unexpected. And he had an answer.

"Well, *I do.* See, he went out past Gardiners Island. Out where . . . well, the bay isn't the bay anymore. You're really in the Atlantic Ocean. Different animal, being out there. Especially a small boat."

Billy had to register: *This was interesting. This hanger-on at the docks down here knew where Jack Landry went.*

"He told you that?"

"I always asked where he was going. All the people heading out on their boats. Just curious, you know? Thought that—going out that far? Those clouds in the sky? Not sure how I felt about that."

Billy paused. He wished he had a notebook of some kind. Isn't that what he should have, asking questions, getting answers? Columbo would.

He could make notes once he was back at his place. And next time, make sure he kept a notebook with him . . .

But Will's confusion over this . . . Could it be important?

"Will, why do you think he went way out there?"

"Well, I *know* why."

Billy waited. About to nudge with an *And . . .*

But not needed.

"See—he probably did what he did every morning. Got his bait. And asked Mr. Cioffi where they were getting reports from the night boats. You know, good fishing spots? Usually all around these waters just fine. But guess—not that day."

Well, thought Billy, now holding a bit of information that completely contrasted with what Cioffi said.

Or, in fact, pointed to the fact Cioffi had just lied to him.

The sun felt warm; the heat was surprising with fall already here. October—a funny kind of month.

And just to make things absolutely clear: "You're saying Joe Cioffi probably told him that's where to go?"

"Yes. Sure. That's what Mr. Jack even said." Then Will turned, looked at the empty slip. "Just before I helped him untie. Get all his gear in the boat. Watched him motor away. Morning still beautiful. But, well, all about to change."

And Billy looked at the empty slip as well.

Suddenly thinking, wondering: *What's going on here?*

And for the first time, not knowing what was in play at all: *What am I getting into?*

8

A LITTLE BREAK-IN

Billy found Jack Landry's cottage . . . no problem.

It was stuck at the end of a once-paved road, now well into disrepair. Great chunks of asphalt were missing, crumbled, leaving only sandy holes to bite at his Jeep's tires.

But the Cherokee handled them pretty well—just as long as he went slow.

First thing he noticed as he came to the small place: it was about as isolated a joint as he had seen out here. Farther along the coast of the inlet, he could see really serious houses, waterfront mansions—complete with their private docks, boathouses, and expansive windows looking out to, he guessed, the east and the rising sun.

So—why are there no other places right here?

Good question, he thought. Could be no decent foundation to build on—not a spot for anyone's dream waterfront home. Maybe a flood issue? *That does happen out here.*

Or maybe owned by some eccentric who liked the isolation amid the sandy hummocks—and for some reason did not want to sell. *Just let this little cottage be here.*

He pulled close to the place, killed the ignition, and got out.

No police tape here, he saw.

Which—based on what Chief Bristow had told him—made sense.

No evidence of a crime, so this place—not a crime scene. Just awaiting the next of kin to come check out the weathered cottage. Get what
they could.

Like Landry's daughter, who, according to her, he rarely ever saw.

And Billy also doubted he'd find anything of interest, at least about
the man who supposedly vanished at sea.

He walked up the two splintery steps to the front door . . .

The door was locked. But he saw that it was the type of flimsy lock and
doorknob arrangement that could be easily jimmied open. Billy hadn't
done that, well, in a long time. But it was an old trick he'd learned when
he did his own stay behind bars.

Actually, considering his stay in prison for fraud, he often thought of
it as a very useful education. The school of hard knocks . . . *squared*. Let's
just say he graduated magna cum laude with a degree in useful shadiness.

He guessed there must be another door around back.

But to get to that, he had to step off the small porch, down to the
sand, and tromp around back, past a white propane tank showing its
age with exposed rusty spots.

He had to admit—as he got to the back—the view here, looking
over the dunes more like rolling waves and the tall waving stands of
phragmites . . . beautiful.

Not a bad place to escape from the world.

Billy wondered: Did Landry own it? Rent it? All things he needed
to look at.

More notes for the notebook he did not have.

He walked to the back door. The entryway was raised about a foot, as
if a step should have been there but never got put in. The windowpanes
of the door were smeared. One of those things that just never got cleaned.

But he could just see inside a small kitchen area. A mug sat on a
table. Maybe the morning coffee from when Landry headed out for his
early morning of fishing.

He tried the doorknob. Also locked. But in this case, wobbly, as if not terribly interested in keeping the door shut or locked, it seemed to be missing a needed screw.

He kept playing with it, rattling it . . . then a bit more forcefully.

Until it simply popped open.

Billy thought: *Well, that was easy.*

And he walked into the missing man's home . . .

The refrigerator was stocked with, well, what he imagined any old guy living on his own kept. Some milk, nearly gone, probably turned into a white sludge by now. A container of OJ. Egg carton with two eggs. The usual condiments. Something in tinfoil that Billy didn't unwrap. Slice of pizza? Half a burger?

The freezer with an assortment of items ready for the microwave and a decidedly downscale and solitary dinner.

Then out of the kitchen, just steps away, over the creaky wood floor, he walked into the bathroom. A tight shower stall. To the right, the lone bedroom, also small. Bed unmade. Sure. Why make it?

A table with a book. A nearby closet.

But Billy sailed on to the living room.

There was a TV. Flat-screen, of course, but the smallest you could actually buy. Despite the isolation, he must get cable here. An easy chair: modest, no recliner. Footstool. A small table to the side with two wooden chairs.

He'd need to go check out the bedroom. But Billy had the sudden feeling that this place—so far—said absolutely nothing about the man. About as generic and empty as it could be.

Then considering his chat with Will at the marina, he thought, *Why not indulge suspicions?*

Maybe . . . *too generic?*

But then he saw the one thing that looked different from anything else in this bland cottage.

A small bookshelf with three nearly full rows of books.

And maybe with the idea that it might have something to say about the man, he walked over to it, bent down, and scanned the spines of the books.

▷

The top row—fiction, Harlan Coben. Good mystery writer, Billy knew, having read one of his books a long plane ride ago.

A few older books, even a pair of Ian Fleming's hardbacks with original dustcovers.

You Only Live Twice and *Thunderball.*

Billy had read those too—would have been decades ago.

Below that, a shift to biographies and histories: *The Life of Ulysses S. Grant* alongside volumes on the Civil War. Stephen Ambrose on World War II. Then a few books that, well, didn't fit the mold.

One simply titled, *The Mob in Manhattan.* Next to it, another book on crime, *The Havana Connection.* Last, one with an intriguing title: *The Oath.* With the subtitle *How the Global Crime Syndicate Built Its Empire.*

Empire. Billy knew that organized crime was pretty powerful. But *empire?*

He slid that one out.

A clearly well-read volume, pages dog-eared. Yeah. Sure. Never a bookmark around when you need one.

He was about to put it back when he saw that the back of the bookcase—a cheap piece of what looked like thin plywood—was loose. Like it might pop off. Or rather, it already had come off and had been haphazardly hammered back into place.

And Billy, trying to be as observant as possible, saw through an opening in the back a sliver of what *should* have been the wall behind the bookcase.

But it wasn't the wall, which in this room was painted a faded lime green.

As if anyone would like *that* color.

No. Something metallic, a dull gray.

But there was only one way he'd get to see what it was.

Probably nothing, guessing that this room backed up to some kind of crawl space with the small boiler, a water heater.

Only one way . . .

$$\triangleright$$

Books are heavy. Billy knew that, which was one reason why he chose to patronize libraries versus bookstores. Boxes of books could weigh one down, especially if you had a reason to move around quite a bit.

So, this bookshelf—when he started to nudge it away from the wall to cantilever it out so he could satisfy his curiosity about what was behind it—took a lot of grunting and full-body shoves.

But it moved. And as it moved, whatever was behind it became visible.

Billy saw—flush against the wall—a *safe*.

He took out his phone and turned on its flashlight. To see: a combination lock—old school—the name of the safe and its combo lock visible as well: *Yale*.

And he knew, as far as investigating what it held, what secret about the missing Jack Landry, it would require skills that Billy did not have.

It was so tempting. He even reached out, gave the dial a twirl.

But he also knew . . . a safe like that, hidden? Might contain some mighty interesting things.

He used his phone to take a picture of the safe and its lock.

And while Billy didn't know how to crack it, there were people who did.

But for now, he put his phone back into his pocket and pushed the bookcase back into position. The nondescript cottage was now back to being just that.

Its secrets were safe for now.

A place that looked like it held no secrets or revelations. And yet, behind the shelves of books, it clearly did.

He stood up to head out for now. Thinking of what was next in his little investigation—and the prize at the end of it all keeping him motivated. A nice amount of cash and the possibility of his own place, his own restaurant . . . *once again.*

▷

He went out the front door. Immediately he spotted a car in the distance. It was so empty out here that seeing that car, just sitting there, facing the cottage at a distance . . . made him stop.

No houses near the car, just more dunes and grass. The road it sat on . . . barely that.

He kept his eyes on the car. *A black sedan, facing this way.* An Audi S8 maybe? Hard to tell. But an impressive vehicle, even at a distance.

He had the immediate thought: whoever was in that car may have even followed him.

So, what now?

Get back in his Cherokee, turn back to the pitted road, drive toward it?

Somehow that didn't seem like such a good idea.

But another idea did: he was all alone out here. Again, not a good idea, either.

And when he thought of what Will had said at the marina—that, sure, he knew where Landry went that day, that Landry had most *certainly* talked about it with Cioffi—Billy had to wonder: *What have I wandered into here?*

Certainly not the way he had expected his week off to go.

He took the two rickety steps down to the sandy path, his eyes still on that sedan.

Billy slid out his phone as circumspectly as he could—after all, you don't want to alert someone following you, spying on you, to know that now you are worried, that maybe you are thinking of gingerly hitting 911 on the keypad.

Which would—no doubt—summon Chief Bristow to see . . . well, what? There was a car parked in the distance? That it seemed to be watching him?

And then her likely question: *You just broke into Landry's cottage here? Really?*

Still—it felt better holding the phone in his hand.

As he reached the driver's side door, one hand to the door latch, the headlights on the ominous sedan *came on*. Then he could see a bit of movement.

The car moving.

For a moment he thought, *Whoever this is . . . is driving straight here.*

But no. The car did a sharp, broken U-turn, back and forth until it had turned completely around, then pulled away fast, kicking up a spray of sand from its back tires.

Billy wondered: *Who the hell was that?*

Why were they looking at me?

And why am I standing out here exposed?

He popped open his car door, slid in. Shut it. Hit the lock button.

Then he had the important thought: *I could use some help with this . . .*

He pulled away from the cottage, turning around, avoiding the tall grass that closed tight around the narrow road and property.

Driving away from Jack Landry's cottage, he thought, *What's with that safe in the wall?*

To know any more, he'd have to be back soon . . . hopefully without his sinister escort.

9

KNOCK, KNOCK

By the time Billy got to his place, it was fully dark. No moon, and the few neighboring cottages and bungalows, all nicely spaced out, were dark as well.

He knew—once the summer season was over—a lot of people started showing up on weekends only.

And by the time the real chill of winter hit—with the choppy Long Island Sound on one side, a blustery Peconic Bay on the other, both fed by winds from the Atlantic—cottages here would stay dark for weeks, patiently awaiting that first break of spring.

He didn't mind that.

Though now and then, he thought, *Some companionship might be nice.* All work, no play . . . maybe not the best recipe?

But for now, this was *okay.* He parked right at his front door. No pathway, just a sandy stretch, followed by some wobbly wooden steps up.

A very modest rental, to be sure.

But as he took those steps fast, he found that the front door was open.

Now he knew—some nights, some days?—well, he didn't bother locking the door.

Not like he had anything much of value inside.

No, all of that was in a storage unit over in Red Hook, just sitting there until perhaps he resumed some version of his previous life.

Not likely soon.

And yet, Billy thought, *this is where, when you're watching a movie, you yell at the screen, "Get the hell out of there."*

But he didn't. Instead, he gave the door a push.

Thinking: *Well, that's interesting . . . not even closed.* The door jamb mechanism was not engaged.

But then, thinking . . .

Well, anything's possible. Maybe the door didn't latch this morning when I left.

So, he entered.

▷

He hit the switch that operated a table lamp near the lone easy chair. A thick book was on the table where he'd left it, a bio of John Lewis, courtesy of the small Northold library. *Walking with the Wind.*

He did love history . . .

Cool inside, heat off all day. And now, with night, that early October chill quickly falling.

On into the kitchen. He hit the overhead light.

He'd check his fridge soon for dinner possibilities—always something in the freezer, whether some leftovers from the restaurant, or random cuts of beef, or maybe flounder, cod, sea scallops.

Bag of frozen vegetables to make it all nice and nutritious.

Though if people saw that, he imagined they would have a hard time believing that he once had been something resembling a real chef. With his own restaurant! Cooking intricate dishes on national television. Everything prepped, of course, so even on the blurriest of mornings, after a late night, he could toss this little bowl of something into whatever mix, then that . . . and *voila,* a tangy shrimp-and-corn salad would suddenly materialize.

He was about to reach up for a glass.

And here was what brought a little something special to this more than humble abode. A set of quality crystal glasses. Seemed to him that a good Scotch, a quality vodka, swirling with a cube or two, always tasted better in a beautiful glass.

Well, that deserved something, as the Brits would say, *proper*.

But then he noticed something that was *not* proper.

One of the drawers under the row of cabinets was slightly open.

Now he thought, *Why am I noticing that?*

And he realized it was born of a life spent in kitchens, where there were procedures, routines. End of shift, end of day, you always left everything buttoned down. The place ready for its next duty. Countertops totally cleaned, sink empty, everything put away.

Drawers and cabinets shut tight.

But now—not this one.

Again, he thought, *Interesting . . .*

But he was not yet alarmed. However, something was not quite right.

Going for that better-safe-than-sorry approach, he did not take down the cut-crystal glass.

Not yet.

Instead, as if—oh, yeah—remembering something, he turned and walked down the narrow hallway that connected the compact kitchen to the bedroom.

▷

The hallway—no light, a few dark steps, at least until he reached his bedroom.

Then, light switch thrown, he walked in slowly, not sure what he was expecting.

To the side table by the bed. An assortment of over-the-counter bromides on it. Acetaminophen. Ibuprofen. Melatonin. Cooking caused pain. And boy, did he ever need his sleep at the end of the day.

The bed was not really made. At least he and Jack Landry had that in common. Covers pulled back, pillows still dented from last night's bout of sleep.

He looked around, not seeing anything out of place.

Yes. At first—*nothing out of order here at all.*

And whatever hint of suspicion he had vanished.

Until he looked *down* at the bottom drawer of his dresser.

It was open wide, as if, yeah . . . someone had been pawing through it, looking for something.

And suddenly he was on full alert again.

But the place was empty. No sounds. He hadn't interrupted anyone in the middle of what the cops back in the city would call "tossing" his place.

Searching for something.

Maybe the drawer was possibly left like that? No. Maybe he was just feeling a little edgy, he guessed. Doing this investigation, looking into someone disappearing at sea—not the type of thing he had done in a long time.

So, sure. Guess a bit of nerves makes sense.

One more thing to check.

He turned to the closet at the other end of the room, next to the lone window that still had the blinds pulled tight.

The way he usually kept them when the morning sun sat right out there, bright and early.

He walked to the closet . . .

Opened it.

Just a closet, stuffed with all the seasonal gear he needed for a year. No light inside.

But as he turned the knob, pulled it open, something came out of it, heading right toward him. With no time for him to react, a fist in a gloved hand landed squarely in the center of his face, hitting his forehead hard, pounding the bridge of his nose.

Billy felt intense pain as he was kicked backward, then tripped up by the bed.

He began to think. That punch out of the closet might not be all that was on the menu. And if that were the case, he was clearly at a disadvantage, now flat on his back, head throbbing.

But instead of another attack by whoever had been hiding in his closet, the person, wearing a woolen face mask, hurried to the door and out of the bedroom.

Billy scrambled off the bed, and—old instincts don't die—he started running too.

He never did like sucker punches. Then again, who does? Not even suckers.

But by the time he reached the living room, the door outside had already been slammed shut hard, the attacker—whoever the hell they were—already out of the house.

Billy hadn't seen any car out there. *Did the person come here on foot? To break into my place?*

Then a partial answer to that question: the sound of a motor. It took a minute for Billy to recognize the deep rumble of a substantial motorcycle.

As he opened his front door, he saw the bike shooting away from the back of the house, where it had been tucked away, off the road, where no one would notice it.

As it sped away, Billy saw that the light to show the license plate number was out.

How convenient.

And in seconds, the motorcycle—who knew what kind, not something Billy was savvy about—was gone, the throaty motor vanishing in the night.

So Billy knew how his assailant had got out here, but now he faced new questions: *Why was he out here and what was he looking for?*

Those questions receded as the pain, now centered on the sensitive bridge of his nose, pushed front and center.

He reached a hand up in the darkness to feel—yup—a bit of moisture. He was bleeding, so he headed back inside, not sure what to do next except to get something to stop the damn nosebleed . . .

▷

Billy sat, his phone near, with a second glass of Monkey Shoulder, a very nice Scotch blend, as he pressed at his nose to check that the little balls of cotton he had wadded there were doing their job.

The bleeding, though, had not stopped.

With just the light of the table lamp near his chair, he sat down, facing the flat screen as he thought over things.

Namely, *Who the hell was that?* Somebody broke into his place, then attacked him. (And that, he realized, could have gone worse.)

Then the big questions: *What were they looking for? I actually have something that someone wants that badly?*

He considered whether it could have simply been a random attack.

But any degree of logic kicked *that* argument out of the arena.

A random break-in of one of the dozens of anonymous shabby cottages down a narrow country road? Those almost-shacks were well away from the water and the beaches, which might be the only reason someone would live on this stretch.

Not a place to break into and rob.

No. He came up with only one possible explanation. It had something to do with what he had been asked to do.

Paid to do, actually, he reminded himself.

Namely: find out what really happened to one Jack Landry.

Whatever it was that led to Landry disappearing, he now knew that—*hello*—people who play rough were involved.

Another press to his nostrils, to the cotton balls. Hoping he could take them out soon.

Gotta look weird, he thought.

Then more thoughts . . . If the attacker, the search of his place, had to do with Landry, and yes, some not very nice people were involved . . . then exactly how dangerous was this?

Sure, he'd like to get that chunk of money to maybe, *possibly* start to rebuild things.

But there was, of course, another question, one which he hadn't answered at all.

He had been physically attacked. Assaulted in his own place.

Generally, a matter for the police. But at this point, not knowing what he didn't know, was involving them a good idea or a bad idea?

He took a sip of the Monkey Shoulder, a bit of melt from the ice releasing that heady aroma of what was a rather good blend of Scotch.

And with that question unanswered, his phone began vibrating, the sound amplified by the wooden table. So much for having the ringtone off.

He picked it up.

No number appeared, just the words *unknown caller.*

No one I know, he thought. *Spam, most likely. But all things considered . . .*

He hit the green button and said, "Hello."

10

NEW YORK CALLING

By the time he heard the voice on the other end, now on speaker, he recognized who was calling him.

Northold police chief Lola Bristow.

Isn't that funny, he thought, *just debating a call to the local authorities myself . . . and now here they are.*

"Billy Blessing . . ." she said.

"Chief. To what do I owe the pleasure?"

"Something has popped up. And considering things, thought you would like to know. Take a look at it with me?"

Billy was surprised at that—a professional officer of the law asking for his help? But maybe, with her limited resources and questions surrounding Landry, well—all hands welcome.

"*Popped* up?"

"Yeah. Got the call about an hour ago. From a marina down in New Suffolk. There's a couple of small private beaches there. The marina is just a few slips where summer people tie up their boats. And someone coming back from a day of fishing saw it."

Billy didn't have a clue what "it" could be. At the moment, there were a number of interesting possibilities. But he was patient.

"Really. What did they find? 'Popped up,' as you say?"

"A boat. Well, apparently a wreck of a boat. Was dark, the guy said, but clearly been smashed here and there, bunch of holes. But he used the light of his camera. He got the number."

"Number? Not sure I . . ."

"All boats are registered. Just like cars. This one, well—I ran it through the database. It's Jack Landry's boat."

"No kidding?"

Then Billy thought: a wrecked boat, smashed in here and there, couple of holes in the hull . . . and maybe a clue as to what happened to the old guy, to Lisa Cowles's father. Maybe it would put suspicions to bed.

He imagined that after a boat gets in trouble out there, it starts drifting, then hitting the rocks out of the marked channels.

And there you go.

But then, Billy recognized he didn't know a hell of a lot about boats or the sea or wrecks. So the thought: *Is that what happened?*

He asked, "Suspicious?"

"Ha. It's nighttime, Billy. Told the guy to pull it well onto the beach. That I'd go take a look in the morning, See *what's what.*"

And Billy felt that, from the chief's tone, maybe with the small boat in that state, there could be a lot of ways it could have gotten that way . . .

"So, as I told you—not my jurisdiction. Coast Guard's already alerted. They'll come take a look . . . sooner or later. But was thinking of going there first thing, early. Curious, you know? See for myself? Thought . . . maybe *you're* curious too?"

Billy definitely believed the expression about curiosity and cats of all kinds, but in this case, if he was really doing this thing—trying to find out what happened to Landry—then:

"Of course. Not that I will be able to tell anything."

Bristow laughed. "That's okay. Figure, doesn't hurt. Another pair of eyes on it."

"Good," Billy said. "Shall I meet you . . . where?"

"I'll text you the spot. Near that fried clam joint."

He had not yet wandered down that road to New Suffolk or its beach. So . . .

"Haven't tried it."

"They do good clams."

"Great to know."

In a second, a text message with an address popped up with an offer to open up a map app on his phone.

"About nine. See you there?"

"You got it. And, Chief—thanks."

"Right," she said. And the call ended.

Wasn't that interesting? Billy thought. Suddenly this investigation actually had *something* to investigate.

He was about to get up and check the fridge and freezer for something quick to cook up when he got another call.

Busy night on the old mobile phone.

This time, the name was displayed. Except it was one he hadn't seen in a very long time. One of his contacts who had—when things changed at the network—moved on.

And yet, here she was . . .

Gretchen Di Voss. Once, she was the head of the network before her world fell apart about the same time as his own.

But maybe—who knows—still in charge of the once mighty Di Voss Industries?

He hit the green button and answered . . .

"Gretchen," Billy said.

"Billy . . . Blessing."

He shook his head. "Now that we got the formalities over, names and all, what planet did *you* just beam back from?"

She laughed. Di Voss was always a good target for his sense of humor. A big fan and supporter of everything Billy touched until everything, all that success—somehow, someway—began to slip away.

For her too . . .

He was curious, not having heard from her in years. And certainly—not keeping up in any way with media and business back in the canyons of Manhattan—he didn't have a clue. Her name and her world—like his, he assumed—had simply vanished.

People hit something, a bad turn, and then they are quickly erased. *Like they never were there at all.*

"You got my number?" he said. "It's new. Or newish. Not a lot of people have it."

"I know," she said without detailing how she had his new mobile number, adopted when he had to flee the mounting debts and relentless calls. He had some low-rent lawyer back in the city who was handling all that.

The aftermath of his restaurant burning down . . .

Accidents do happen, the detectives had said.

And the morning show, *Wake Up, America!,* being canceled, catching Billy exactly at a time when he was financially overextended. Too many days of flying business class back and forth across this great country . . . it does add up.

Then finally, when his cable show got yanked—last minute, unceremoniously—suddenly he realized *no one* was calling with offers.

Or even condolences.

Certainly not Gretchen. Smart, savvy, and who knows—*maybe* there was a heart in there? But he would have bet against that.

"Okay. So, you found me. Well done. Now *why?*"

Di Voss did not face the question head-on. Instead: "You still at that little restaurant out there? Cooking?"

"Not so little. And yeah, cooking. It's kinda what I do, remember?"

"Among other things . . ."

Right, he reminded himself. *Gretchen knew all of his—well, let's just call them "extracurriculars."* From the dark days of Billy's stint in jail to somehow getting in the middle of other people's murders.

With Billy not at all sure how all *that* happened.

"Billy—I got something that I think you're going to like."

But before Billy would bite at that, he had a question. Or more likely, a dozen of them.

"First, if you don't mind, Gretchen. You know where I am, what I have been doing. What about you? After—let's just call it the *collapse*?"

She paused.

"Took a break." The words that didn't ring true at all. Not when you knew Gretchen Di Voss. "Did some travel. Lot of thinking. That's sort of thing? While—Billy—the world changed."

"Doesn't it always?"

"I mean, the world you had? TV, cable. All that jazz? Gone. And *transformed*."

"Really?"

Billy still had enough curiosity about the real reason for the call that he remained patient.

"It's all 'on demand' now. Guess even you know that. Out there in wherever the hell *you* are."

"Northold. North Fork, Long Island. You should visit. You'd like it."

"Sure. *Right*. The cable networks transforming into these streaming behemoths . . ."

"Hm. Behemoth. That's a nice word. Means large, aggressive—"

"Right. And guess what, Billy?"

"I'm still here."

"There is a new streaming network that Worldwide is starting. Going to cover lifestyle in all its dimensions. Leisure, travel, and, well . . . cooking too. *Big time*."

"Aren't there, um, streamers that do that already?"

"Sure. But there's always an appetite for more," she said, perhaps not realizing how apropos the word just used was. "Way big. Lot of the cooking stars you knew, who you were friends with—Pascal, Jimmy Lund, Katie Coole?"

"Would not exactly say 'friends.'"

"They're all signed up. So—this new venture is going classic. And see, *you* have a name and history that are really worth something."

"Lucky me."

He could see that his responses were starting to wear on Di Voss as she tried to build her little fire of enthusiasm.

"Billy. They want to put you *front and center*, in charge of their whole range of cooking shows. Competitions."

"Oh, not them. Those cooking competitions?"

"But not just that. Hang on. Also, deep dives into the classic chefs, classic dishes. And the kind of food you created at Blessing's Bistro. Your background matched to a hundred years of classic cooking from around the world. Listen, Billy, they want you to do that, but on a giant scale."

Billy stopped for a moment. The call felt almost like a prank.

So, he paused. Took that last sip of Money Shoulder . . .

▷

"Okay, Gretchen. You're saying this, um, company . . . part of Worldwide?"

"Yeah. New streaming service. Has a couple of *very* behind-the-scenes, big-wallet investors."

"And they want a whole array of shows involving food, cooking?"

"But with travel and culture, all *that* mixed in."

"Ah, great. So finally, I would start earning air miles again."

Finally, Di Voss laughed. Maybe she was thinking that she was getting through to him.

And maybe she was . . .

"And they want *you*—like I said. Front and damn center. You'd be lead creative."

"Lead? So other people would be playing in this sandbox then?"

"Well, yes. Sure, some of those chefs I mentioned. Most of them you know—"

And I don't particularly like, he thought.

"Nothing locked in stone yet. But they are all set."

"They are?"

He waited.

"Listen, can you skip the restaurant gig you have out there for a day or so?"

"Well. So happens I'm off all this week. Why?"

"Got a meeting set up the day after tomorrow. The old Monolith Studios building in SoHo. You meet them, they meet you. And if a deal happens, we're off and running. And fast."

"*We?*"

Another hesitation. Something held back. And Billy had to wonder what else she wasn't telling him . . .

"They brought me on as a creative consultant, and when the on-demand shows start getting put together, I'll be an exec producer. You know . . . just like the old days?"

Billy did know this: before that world went away, Gretchen had not only headed up Di Voss Industries with dear old Dad out of the picture, but she had basically told the network what they would be doing.

Real power. For as long as it lasted.

Oh, how the mighty have fallen.

"Day after tomorrow?"

"Yup. And if it all sounds good to you, your life *changes*. They even have a catchphrase."

"Yeah? And what is said catchphrase?"

"*Blessing's Back!*"

Billy laughed. "Hadn't noticed I'd gone anywhere, except out to the North Fork of Long Island."

Another pause from Gretchen. Then, as if no decision or debate were required at all: "I booked you a room at the Soho Grand for tomorrow night."

"Oh, *that* dump," he said, laughing. The place was anything *but* a dump and was perhaps the key spawning ground for media types, no matter what the hell the media was.

"I don't know," he said.

Because he didn't. Things were kind of settled here. And he was even up to old tricks, dealing with a mysterious disappearance.

Sure, money was a little tight. And having his own place again would be great. He certainly missed that.

And then he thought of one very good reason to go. A case of two birds, one stone.

"Okay. Text me the details. The meeting. Hotel reservation. And I'll be there."

"Yay. You are the best, Billy Blessing."

"Sure. But at *what?*"

Another laugh. "One thing—this is a business meeting so—"

"Got it. So, no farmer overalls and plaid shirt. Think I have a few things in my closet that will still fit."

"Good! Till then—"

"Right. Bye, Gretchen." Then, not sure he really meant it: "And thanks."

And the call went dead.

▷

Billy sat there, thinking he really should eat something.

But he also thought of this sudden big meeting, about making a splashy return, and hopefully boatloads of cash, in the brave new world of "on demand."

Didn't sound too bad.

But there was still the matter of Jack Landry. And now, well, tomorrow after meeting Bristow at the missing man's boat, he would hit the racecourse that is Long Island Expressway.

Always fun, that road. Fast until it all comes to a sudden dead stop when a tractor-trailer goes flying on its back. Seems like every day it's the same tractor-trailer. They just tow it to a different spot and crash it.

Check in to the mighty Soho Grand.

But then, he had an idea. While there, he could meet someone from the past. Someone who could be helpful.

Maybe even in the hotel's grand lobby, where the party light was always on. Might as well enjoy it while there . . .

He picked up his phone.

Scrolled his contacts, some more than a decade old. Some probably even gone, or at least maybe with new numbers, new lives somewhere.

He found the one he was looking for.

Detective Deacon Solomon.

Actually, he remembered, Solomon had retired almost about the time Billy's career imploded . . . and he had been Detective First Grade in the Major Cases Unit. If there was something big and bad happening in the Big Apple, Solomon had been on it.

Billy could hardly imagine a man like that, who had spent so many years fishing bodies out of the river, exploring messy crime scenes where, well, when you got home, you probably would just ditch the shoes you had been wearing straight into the trash.

Blood always makes one resistant strain.

So now, was Deacon still in Brooklyn with his wife? Doing what?

But he also knew, someone of his rank? *You never lost your contacts in the department.*

In fact, you might officially retire, ample pension in place, but for someone like Detective Solomon, Billy guessed, you never really leave.

He pressed the name on his phone to call.

Ringing. Would Solomon know it was Billy, see the name? *Who knew.* Either way, he might kill the call or let it go to voicemail.

Some people—a lot of people these days—don't like talking on phones.

But instead, a voice answered—more gravelly than he remembered. The first burst of words had a slight tell-tale slur around the edges.

"Yeah, who the hell is—"

And all Billy had to say, with a laugh, was, "Deacon. It's Billy Blessing . . ."

11

THE BOAT ON THE BEACH

Billy thought he'd missed the first turn that was supposed to take him toward the coast and—from the map—a small bay dubbed Cutchogue Harbor, which the town of New Suffolk curved around.

But then, ahead, he saw a police car parked tight to a wooden-slat beach fence atop a dune near the pathway to the shore.

But also, another car. A cream-colored Ford Bronco.

Interesting, he thought, having expected to simply meet the police chief. But it looked like she wasn't alone.

He slowed as he got near, pulled over to a space where two warning signs stood atop poles tilted at slight angles. One said: "Private Beach! Residents Only."

Cheery, he thought. The other: "No Parking Anytime."

So he parked.

Billy was not so new to the area that he wouldn't know—for the locals, the longtime residents?—they took these little rules and regulations *quite* seriously.

He hopped out. The morning air was chilly; the water, though still and flat, was apparently cold enough to give the slight breeze a cool bite.

He started walking, his shoes (a pair of trail shoes he'd got when he realized his suede broughams by way of Nordstrom didn't fare so well in the sand) nonetheless giving way with each step.

He got to the opening at the fence, looked down.

And along the stretch of beach, he saw Bristow, who—looking up, spotting him—gave him a wave.

With another person . . . crouched down to what looked like a small motorboat. Sixteen, maybe eighteen feet long, pulled well up onto the beach.

No one else in sight. And Billy started his walk to them.

As he got closer, he could see that the boat looked in real bad shape. A wreck really. The other person had moved around to the other side of the boat.

"Morning," said Bristow.

"Good morning, Chief. Thanks, um, for the alert."

At that, the man examining the boat looked up. Young, dark hair. Serious black glasses. And a shirt with a badge, which meant Billy could finally read who this person was.

Lt. J. Talbot. USCG – CGIS.

Coast Guard, Billy guessed. As to what the other letters meant . . . no clue. Billy nodded at him.

The man's eyes narrowed as he looked up.

Bristow made the introduction: "Billy, this is Lieutenant Jerry Talbot. He's with the Coast Guard station out here."

The man crouched by the boat added, "I'm with the Coast Guard Investigative Service. Out of Riverhead?"

Billy gave another nod. Curious, but not enough to ask a question.

Though, he did find it interesting—this Jerry Talbot here being Coast Guard, a sea-based force, but he came in the Bronco and not a boat. Or what did they call them? A *launch*?

Racing over the water. Wasn't that how they did it?

He remembered what Bristow had said: if it happened at sea, then it was the Coast Guard's jurisdiction.

Though it seemed clear what was happening here. Might have *started* at sea, but the boat was most definitely on land now.

Bristow added, "Told him you'd been asked by a family member to kinda look into Jack Landry's disappearance. Friend of the family."

Billy nodded at that version of the story. Not exactly true, but would certainly cause fewer questions from the young Coast Guard investigator.

Finally, the man stood up.

He looked at Billy, rubbed his chin, hesitating. Taking a moment, as if unsure what to do, then stuck out his hand.

"Mr. Blessing . . ."

"Lieutenant."

Then the Coast Guard officer turned to the chief.

"Okay. Seen my share of bad wrecks, chewed up by rocks, shoals— and that's precisely what we have here."

"Meaning?" Bristow prompted.

"Well, you see all those odd dents, the hull pushed in here?"

He pointed to a spot near the front.

The bow, that's what it is, Billy thought. Doing his best to stay in a nautical state of mind.

"Yeah—and look back there, the stern? Mighty big hole, just below what would have been the water line."

Bristow looked over at Billy as if urging him to get into this. Perhaps . . . *ask a question?*

"So, Jerry. What does *that* mean? What do you think happened?" Bristow asked.

"Well. My guess—hit by a real bad sea? Any number of spots out there where you slip away, out of the channel markings . . . and all of a sudden, you're in trouble, hidden rocks all over the damn place. And whatever small engine the guy had . . ."

Billy noted there was no outboard motor in the back. A casualty of whatever accident had happened to the boat.

"Well, once water starts to churn up—lot of chop, swells, boats gets swamped in seconds—and you might as well have no motor *at all*."

Billy nodded. He also saw Bristow slowly walking around the small boat.

Then the lieutenant turned to her. "So, guess . . . it's good we found this?

I mean, that I was called in? Kinda makes a clear case for what happened. Boat this small, bad sea—and that old guy didn't have a chance."

"One thing," Bristow said, still walking slowly, still looking down. She said the words slowly. *Casually*, Billy thought.

And having been around a lot of police, from here to Chicago to LA, he knew . . . that kind of question? Asked exactly that way? Bit of a technique.

One thing?

Sure. *As if.*

"This boat. Lot of metal. Big gashes in it, so sure—it took water. So, how did it end up here? Why didn't it sink?"

Good question, Billy thought. Seemed like an obvious one too, and he was interested in the answer.

"Oh. Common mistake. People see a metal boat hull and assume, once it is scuttled, then down to the bottom it goes. Not so. Lot of metal but enough wood inside, pockets of air here and there, the thing could end up suspended a few feet down. Then, water kicks it up again, and she starts moving . . . with the tide, right to the shore."

"All the way here?"

"Yup. Seen it before."

Now Billy had a question. Why not, as long as the lieutenant was still up for answering them.

"Lieutenant, what about Mr. Landry? Boat starts to sink, getting battered, going down. Shouldn't—?"

Already the lieutenant was nodding. "You mean the body? Right? Where is *that*?"

Billy nodded.

"Well, *lot* of things can happen. Perhaps bobbing in the same water with those swells, getting battered by the same jagged rocks. In a sea that bad, he wouldn't last long, even with a life vest on. And who knows whether he even had time to put it on?"

But Bristow now seemed interested in the question. Or rather the answer.

"Okay then. So—what happened? The body. Where is it?"

"Well, you know, it could, possibly, wash up just like this did. But won't be much left of it. I've seen that before. The fish, well, they would get to work on it, and then keep right at it."

Billy had the thought: *Landry became the wrong end of a surf and turf special.*

"So, eventually it would sink, but maybe just not much of a body to recognize anymore. Or a nasty current catches it? Takes it out of the bay here, out to the Atlantic, and well, then . . ."

He watched Bristow nod at that. Billy realized that, although the chief led a very small department in a town sandwiched by two great bodies of water, she also might not be much of a beach and sea person.

Had *she* ever seen a body like that?

Probably not yet, he thought.

Then the lieutenant made a show of looking at his watch. "Um, I got to get back. Desk jammed with paperwork. Will file a report on this, though."

Said as if all done; case closed.

He took a step away—and then stopped. Something seemed to occur to the young lieutenant before he left the scene.

"Oh, the boat's registration number. Texted that in. This boat is registered out here, no problem, to a 'Jack Landry.' Address as you told us. But there *was* something wrong . . ."

"Wrong?" Bristow said.

"Yeah. Kinda odd. It should also—however it was purchased—be registered with the State DMV. All boats with a motor need to be. No matter how small the motor. But this boat's number *didn't* pop up."

He grinned. Then added: "Like a little ghost ship. Oh, and just in case . . . can you put some of that yellow tape around this until I get some people to pick the boat up?"

Billy assumed he meant the yellow crime-scene tape. Though the lieutenant had just made a convincing argument . . . well, when it came to Landry and this smashed boat?

No crime at all.

Then Talbot started walking back to the path and their "illegally" parked cars.

A young mother and father had come down that way, a small kid with them, racing around the sand, hooting and hollering at the gulls, which were seeing what was for breakfast.

Billy thought, *The family isn't seeing the* story *over here.* Old man dies at sea in bad weather.

And not much story at that.

But he was wrong on that score . . .

▷

Lola Bristow turned to him. Her face serious, catching the morning sun now that it was a few fists above the horizon, giving the air here, finally, some warmth.

"Well, I guess I'll head back. Guess this—".

He saw the chief watching Talbot back up, do a fast three-point turn, then pull away.

And Billy felt . . . *something is up here.*

"Anything else, Chief? Looks like a nasty accident at sea. Boat got wrecked. Open and shut, as they say."

But Bristow quickly shook her head and said, "Come here."

She walked over to one side of the boat, Billy thinking, *Right side, starboard. That what it's called?* So much he didn't know about *any* of that.

But he guessed, if he stayed out here long enough, well . . . *when in Rome . . .*

Bristow crouched down and, with a glance to Billy, signaled that he should do the same.

As he came beside her, she said, "See *this?*"

At that, she put a finger into—not a dent, not a big gash in the hull—but a much smaller hole.

She nodded to the rear—*aft!*—and said, "Saw another couple back there."

Billy looked at the hole, and, well, he had been around enough to know there was one thing that could make a neat little hole just like that.

"Bullet hole?"

"*Bingo*, as they say. I probably can figure out what caliber the bullet was. I haven't looked at the interior of the boat. Maybe more holes there that didn't puncture the hull. Maybe even a shell."

She stood up.

"Guess the young Coast Guard officer hasn't had much practice identifying such things," Billy said.

"Yeah. Important thing he missed here."

"But not by you. A little out of your typical duties, here in the quiet jurisdiction of Northold?"

"Here?" She laughed. "Got that right. But back in the city, on the force. Well, I got to see bullet holes *everywhere*. Even in people."

And Billy realized what she just said, what it meant. Those bullet holes . . . the boat had an encounter not just with rocks, not just a choppy sea, but someone firing a gun, *right at it*.

But also, now he had a more pressing question.

"Force? You were NYPD?"

"Yeah. Was it showing?"

"Not at all. Though I did think you were just a North Fork—and female—version of Andy of Mayberry."

She laughed. "Kinda what I swapped the city streets for."

"And how did that happen?"

But Bristow let the question slide.

"Things happen, yeah? So, look, what *this* means, for now, is that Jack Landry, well . . . who knows? Maybe someone drilled holes into him as well?"

"I get that."

"It also means, well, your little investigating on behalf of the long-lost daughter—"

"Technically, she wasn't the one who was lost . . ."

"—could be dangerous."

This prompted Billy to look down at the boat, more like a crumpled and massive chunk of tin foil. Only—not well-hidden—the signs that something else had happened.

"Got it. *Dangerous.* Good safety tip."

"So—" She smiled a bit. "How about . . . um, you want to know how I migrated from NYPD to here? Meet for dinner, tell you the whole story? And also, you see, with this, um, boat now. Though the Coast Guard may not know it yet, now this boat, this evidence . . . yes, squarely *in* my jurisdiction."

Dinner. That was interesting, thought Billy. Was Chief Lola Bristow asking him out?

But he had to decline.

"Sorry. In a few hours, I will attempt to drive back to the city. A few things have come up . . ."

"Things?"

"Yeah." He didn't elaborate. "Back tomorrow sometime, dunno, before dark. How about then?"

"Sure, just got to make sure my daughter is covered. Almost old enough to babysit herself. *Almost.*"

So many intriguing facts about Bristow coming out.

"Great. Will text you tomorrow. After I take care of things."

"Good. And of course, as discussed before, you find out *anything* . . . like I did just now? You tell me."

"You got it, Chief."

She turned back to the boat. "Got to get some crime-scene ribbon around this thing . . ."

"Need any help?"

"Nah. I'm good. You go tend to your things in the big city. Oh, and drive safe. LIE these days? Like out of Mad Max."

"I know. And I'm out of practice."

As Bristow walked beside him, heading back to her Northold squad car, Billy went to his Cherokee.

"Tell you what. That's what living out here will do."

"Hm?" he said.

She pressed a button, and the trunk of the car popped open. "You get out of practice . . . *with a lot of things* . . ."

Billy nodded, smiled, then got into his car. He'd go soon. But first . . . well, bullet holes, gunshots—caliber yet to be determined? Maybe he should do some searching with his computer.

About Jack Landry. His daughter, Lisa Cowles. And maybe—on a completely different matter—try to see what Gretchen Di Voss had been up to lately.

To see what useful stories the internet could reveal.

Might as well know what I am heading into, Billy thought.

And he pulled away, flapping his sun visor down as the morning sun poured in . . .

TWO
SECRETS AND LIES

12

A DETECTIVE CALLS

The waiter in the lobby bar area of the Soho Grand Hotel came over and—Billy thought—with just a smidge of pique asked, "Have you decided *yet* what you would like to drink, sir?"

Billy had already explained that he was waiting for someone and had decided to hold off and wait.

A place like this, a waiter like that? So New York. It had been a while, he thought. And this "grand bar and salon," as they called it? He knew, from his days working in Manhattan, it was a place to see and be seen, especially if you were at all involved in the gargantuan media world.

After some time out on the North Fork, amid the farmers, the fishing boats, and those who had fled the city—and then had simply decided to stay—it was . . . well, *kinda fun.*

Detective Deacon Solomon was late.

Not that Billy was surprised. Trekking in from the far reaches of Bay Ridge, Brooklyn, could be a journey, even on the best of traffic days.

Billy seriously doubted the detective ever took the subway. Not when he had a car on which he could still display his NYPD Detective car sticker and—unlike most who drove into the dense city—could park wherever the hell he wanted to.

Still, getting in and out of Manhattan—some things never change. *Not that easy.*

The waiter still standing there, Billy decided to give him what he wanted. *An order . . .*

"Yeah. Um, how about—well, what bourbons and whiskeys do you have?"

Again, the waiter seemed to feel getting a drink order out of Billy was turning out much harder than he had signed on for.

"We have *lots*. Gentleman Jack, Maker's Mark, Uncle Nearest."

Billy put up a hand.

"*That* will do. Uncle, with a few rocks. That's ice, by the way."

The waiter didn't crack a smile. Instead, he said, "Right away . . ." and hurried in the direction of the bar at the other end of this sprawling sea of easy chairs, love seats, and low tables, ready for cocktails and bowls of complimentary nuts and pricey hors d'oeuvres.

Billy went back to people-watching, and being out of practice at that, he saw a couple had suddenly appeared by his chair.

A man and woman of similar shape and age—mid-fifties, maybe? Married long enough, he guessed, that they had come to physically resemble each other.

"Excuse me, um, but my husband and I couldn't help but notice, wondering . . . ?"

She looked at her husband for reassurance.

"You're *Billy Blessing*?"

Billy smiled. Finally! He didn't get recognized *that* much anymore, though often anyone new to NoFo Eats catching sight of him would do the old "Hey, aren't you . . ." or even worse, "Didn't you used to be?" bit.

The regulars—god bless them—let him be. They just came for the food he cooked.

And now, years away from his daily appearance on national television, sure, why not? It felt good to be spotted.

So, he answered: "Why, yes. Yes, I am." He produced a smile to match the pleasant admission to his identity.

The woman turned again to her husband. "*See*, I told you, Henry. It *is* him." Then she looked back at Billy.

"We enjoyed watching you *so* much, so funny, always with new ideas for things to cook, to try—"

Billy nodded at that.

Having been recognized, he thought it best to let things peter out on their own. He also wondered if he should have picked a more secluded place to talk with Solomon. But with his staying here for the night, this lobby bar was convenient, and with enough noisy chatter around the room, their conversation could be discreet.

The woman wasn't quite done. "Will you be coming back? To the new *Wake Up, America!*, I mean?"

Her face—*how sweet*—seemed genuinely concerned at raising the question, as if she were bringing up the loss of some distant relative of his she had just heard about.

He produced his pat answer to that question. "Don't think so. I'm enjoying my life out on the North Fork. For now, at least."

After all, Billy did not know what would be happening at tomorrow's meeting. New opportunities in the exploding world of streaming? If so, maybe his days out there were numbered. *Time would tell.*

Then, finally in the role of a now-welcome interloper, the waiter returned and put down a Soho Grand coaster, then his drink, a very generous pour.

Billy nodded to the drink, smiling at the couple. "I er . . ."

He was afraid they might ask for an autograph or—*god*—even a selfie. When all he really wanted now was to have a sip and think of just what he was going to say to Detective Solomon.

What to leave in. What to leave out.

The husband—perhaps with a smidge more awareness—took his wife's hand.

"C'mon, Susan. Let the man enjoy his drink."

Indeed, thought Billy.

And to close the moment, Billy added, "And thanks, by the way."

The woman, smiling at that, let her husband guide her away. And as he did take that first sip, the bourbon strong, the ice chilling it, he thought, *People still remember me.*

And there isn't a single thing wrong with that.

With the drink nearly halfway done and the bar lounge nearly full and buzzy, Billy looked down at one end, where a staircase from a street-level registration desk led, and saw Detective Solomon.

Looking entirely like a retired detective should. A rumpled sport coat, a collared shirt, no tie. If such things were allowed, he could easily picture Deacon with a cigarette in his mouth. Those days—smoking anywhere?—pretty much gone.

Solomon spotted Billy and walked over. A chair facing Billy, nice and close, was occupied by his messenger bag that he now removed.

He stood up.

"Detective—"

"*Billy Blessing . . .*" Then Solomon looked around the room, taking on the mostly glitzy crowd. Billy's fan group of two had sailed on. Only media types were left, all quite practiced in acting as if they were somebody—or perhaps a somebody to be.

"Join me in a drink?"

Solomon laughed at that as he sat down. "Sure. Didn't come all the damn way from Brooklyn for a *quick hello.*"

The waiter, seeing the new guest, had reappeared.

No waiting for Solomon: "Um, whiskey. Large."

But the waiter seemed a little stumped at that.

"Whiskey? *Any* whiskey?"

Again, Deacon laughed as he looked at Billy: "This is where you wanted to meet? Sheesh." Then to the waiter. "Give me any good whiskey. *You* pick."

And the waiter, challenge presented, turned away. Then Solomon looked back at Billy.

"So, here you are back in the big city. How the hell have you been doing? And *what* the hell have you been doing?"

Billy, after another sip, gave the detective a quick update.

▷

"I don't get it," Deacon said. "Really. The life you had? TV, cable, your own hot restaurant in New York—"

"Yeah, until that pace got *too hot*, I guess."

"Yeah, heard about that. That fire? Damn suspicious, hmm, Billy? But then, you know, the different things you got into? You *did* have enemies."

Billy didn't like talking about his restaurant burning down. How the insurance turned out to be a mess, the place a near write-off. And how the FDNY—while also suspicious, to be sure—couldn't find any definite evidence pointing to the idea that someone had done it, that it was arson.

"I know. A lot of things happened."

Solomon nodded. His own whiskey, whatever it was, was nearly gone. Billy was going slow—after all, he did have a big meeting the next day.

"But still, Billy. What I don't get is how you go from all you had to just . . . what, cooking out in farmland? I mean, don't get me wrong, I like it out there as much as the next guy. Nice fishing. Wineries. *Sure*. Wouldn't even mind getting me a little boat. Do some fishing. But *you*?"

And Billy had to admit that those questions, all good. But he also knew that, as long as he could cook, for now, he was okay.

But he turned the tables on the detective.

"And you? Happy being off the force? Not flashing your shield around? Keeping the city safe from crime . . . ?"

Deacon finished his whiskey, then raised his glass to signal the distant waiter: *Another, ASAP.*

Then . . .

"Tell you one thing—the city was safer when I was working the mean streets. But I keep busy. Always things that need fixing. An old house."

And Billy could tell: retired homicide detective Solomon was bored.

Hence his eagerness to show up here without knowing anything about what he was to learn and what he'd be asked to do to help an old friend.

"So, tell me. You asked me here. Something up? A problem? Anyway, I am, as they say, *all ears.*"

So, Billy told him . . . just what was "up."

13

TAKING NAMES

Solomon scratched his head. He had brought along a small spiral notebook, curved, the spirals bent from having sat in his pocket for too long. But at least—Billy thought—the gesture of the notebook showed Billy that he was being taken seriously. For now, Billy kept his in his pocket.

"So, let me see if I got this straight. You're working one night, and this woman walks in, yes? Knows you, but more importantly, somehow knows things you have done in the past, right? And wants you to figure out who did what to whoever, and why? That is, if something was done at all. That it?"

"That's about it."

Solomon shook his head. "And did she say *how* she knew these things? I mean, about the supposedly bad people who might have come for her father?"

"I didn't ask."

"Might have been a good question. *Just sayin'.* Okay then, and she tells you about her father, this"—he looked down at the notebook—"Jack Landry guy. Kinda old fella—"

"Not *that* old."

"Who went missing after heading out to go fishing one morning real early."

"Yup."

"And you spoke to some people . . . the police chief, the guy who runs the marina, some worker there . . . oh and even the freakin' Coast Guard."

Solomon grinned at that and looked up.

"And you have learned pretty much *nada*?"

"Well, wouldn't exactly say that. Almost nada."

Billy looked around. He wondered if his conversation with Solomon looked any different from the dozens of tête-à-têtes that filled the lounge, now without a seat to spare.

"I did learn that it was a nasty day. Weather turned bad."

"Yeah, I hear it can do that."

"And the Coast Guard has it all written off as an accident at sea."

Solomon nodded. "Any sign of the guy's boat?"

Billy mentioned the battered boat but—for the moment—held back the small but key detail about the bullet holes.

"And a body?"

"There has been no body found. Still, guess an accident could make sense. Least to the Coast Guard."

"Yeah, but this daughter—Lisa Cowles?"

A nod. "She says her father had 'enemies.'"

"For reasons she did not specify?"

"Not yet, at least. Everyone has enemies, hmm?"

"You got that right."

"I had the week off. She wrote a check. With an even bigger one to come."

"Ah—so the money is your motive?"

"I *do* think of getting my own place again."

He refrained from mentioning tomorrow, the big meeting and its possibilities.

"Well, then—think I got the picture, Billy. What there is of it. So, why did you feel the need to give me a call?"

Billy nodded. As he was about to find out . . . when a detective leaves the NYPD, *do they ever really leave?*

▷

Billy leaned forward. "I'd like to know who the hell this Jack Landry really *is*. Or was. And why someone might have wanted him to disappear."

He saw Solomon writing down the name. "And this Lisa Cowles?"

"The daughter."

"Yeah. Told you she was a lawyer?"

"Yup. In some big Manhattan firm, I imagine. Might be good to check that out."

Solomon wrote that name down too and looked up. "You could have just asked her."

"I could. I have a phone number. But call it instinct. Sometimes not asking is a better way to get at the truth."

And the detective laughed at that. "Ha. *Not* in my line of work. But then, you have mixed it up with some—shall we say—shady characters?"

Billy grinned as he realized he was enjoying this. Those times when he got involved in some "nasty" things—New York, Chicago, LA—well, part of him somehow always enjoyed that.

Despite the danger . . .

"For either of these two people, you got anything else?"

"Well, Cowles paid me by a check—"

"And it cleared?"

"Did indeed. But no address or info on the check. Just a company name of some kind. Her own business?"

"And that was . . . ?"

"LC Holdings."

"Hmm. That could be anything. Okay, and—"

"Oh, and the boat was registered with the town, but when the police chief—"

"This Lola Bristow?"

"Yeah. When *she* checked, no New York State record was found, which—I guess—all boats are supposed to have?"

"Beats me. But I can look into it. Gotta tell you, Billy . . . when this is over, think you may owe me a nice steak dinner? Sparks perhaps?"

"Deal."

Then Billy hesitated. There was an additional fact he hadn't shared yet. He debated for a moment: good idea, or a bad one?

Then . . .

"One more thing, that boat, well, showed a lot of dents and gashes."

"Yeah, backing up the Coast Guard theory of an unfortunate accident in a stormy sea."

"Exactly. But when the lieutenant left, the chief showed me something else."

"Really?"

A nod. "On one side . . . what looked like bullet holes? No. Sorry. Not 'looked.' *Were* bullet holes."

At that, Solomon froze. Lowered his pen. "You're *kidding* me? Now you're telling me this? The boat looked like it had been shot up?"

"Apparently."

"And I'm guessing this local-yokel cop of yours can tell a bullet hole from—"

"Hey. She's former NYPD. So yeah, that hole versus a gash made by a rock? I guess so. So can I . . ."

Solomon paused a moment and looked at his watch. Taking his time. Organizing his thoughts.

Which Billy guessed was a detective thing to do.

Then: "Look, Billy, you are your own man. *I get that.* And it's not up to me to tell you what to do, what to watch out for. But do you really want to get involved in whatever mess this is? Bullet holes in some old guy's fishing boat. Doesn't sound good to me . . ."

"Me either. Makes me think that this daughter knows things she hasn't shared."

Now Solomon leaned across the table, keeping his voice very low. But also very urgent.

"Got that right, Billy. But think you better consider how wise it is to dive into this, hmm? Bullets can make holes in other things besides fishing boats."

"I know. I'll be careful."

Solomon leaned back.

"I get that you once, as we say, had another life . . ."

Here Billy knew the detective was referring to Billy's stint in prison. Something he had worked very hard to keep out of any of his résumés and bios.

"Like that insurance commercial: *'You know a thing or two, because you've seen a thing or two?'* Sure. So you're not just some blow-dried TV guy. With your cooking. Your restaurant, back in the day. An entrepreneur. *I get that.* But if I were you, dunno . . . maybe best you just *drop* this whole thing?"

And for a moment, Billy considered Solomon's warning. He had a point there. His quiet and steady life out on the North Fork . . . not too bad.

Predictable. Sure. And certainly sleepy in the offseason.

But not that profitable. With the money from Lisa Cowles, he could change that.

More than that, though, he felt—well, he was *already* involved.

And just like cooking, from the meal prep to the cleanup, he liked seeing things through.

He told Solomon, "I'll take that under consideration."

And with that, the detective stood up and let out a small laugh. "I doubt you will. Meanwhile, I will use what little info you gave me here to see *what I can see.*"

"Why, thank you, Detective."

Then another pause.

"Billy, since what is happening out there with this Jack Landry guy may involve some bigger players, I've thought of someone you maybe should talk to."

"Go on."

"He lives in some rathole in Greenport. Near you? Kind of low-level mob guy who did a bit of this, a bit of that. Helped us out from time to time and—lucky for him—never got caught by the big boys. They leave him alone."

Billy took out a pen. "And his number . . . ?"

"Ha. This guy? No number, Mr. Bill. But I get reliable reports that he spends the bulk of the day haunting the Wayward Tavern in Greenport. A real old-school gin mill where he can just let the days go by and disappear. But here's the thing . . ."

Solomon looked around. The expansive lobby was standing room only.

Then, all of a sudden, music. Down at the far end, by the staircase to reception, Billy saw a DJ on a raised platform, nodding, headphones on . . .

"Oh, brother," Solomon said. "You have *got* to be kidding me. They're now gonna turn this damn hotel lobby into a disco?"

"Guess, technically it is not a lobby. An extension of the bar maybe? So, this guy—?"

"Yeah. Named Danny Pippo. Some name, hmm? And he owes me. Kept him out of a lot of stuff without anyone knowing. You go find him, tell him all about your lovely little investigation out there, and see what he says. Is there any information on the street that what you're doing is maybe a little dangerous? Or more than a little. You know, so—what do they call it?—your due—"

"Due diligence?"

"Yeah, that's it. Maybe learning some very good reasons you should just drop this."

"Anything's possible."

At that, the detective looked around at the crowd, now all of them talking at a louder volume to overcome the music.

After the sleepiness of the North Fork, Billy sort of liked it.

But not Deacon Solomon . . .

"I will call you soon as I have something—or nothing."

Billy stood and put out his hand. "And then I will look forward to that steak dinner."

Deacon said, "You do know the, um, infamous history about that place? Sparks? The gangster who was gunned down right outside?"

Billy broke into a grin and said, "Yeah, when someone yelled duck, too bad the mob guy thought they were suggesting his entrée."

Deacon grinned and turned to leave. "And they do a pretty good rib eye as well . . ."

"Thanks, Deacon," Billy said, standing as the detective navigated his way through the sea of people, waving a hand over his head to signal *so long.*

And with no plans for the night before his big meeting, Billy sat down—ready to order another bourbon.

14

THE ART OF THE DEAL

Billy walked beside Gretchen Di Voss, the morning chilly, people bus-tling to get to their meetings, their office cubicles, or any of the host of boutiques and trendy shops that filled SoHo.

Billy had a latte, Gretchen a mocha; both sipping as they walked and talked.

This was the only time he'd get a quick briefing before heading to a meeting room over toward the west, near Keith McNally's classic bistro, Balthazar.

"Okay, Billy. First, so good to see you."

She shot him a look as she said that.

They had history. And Di Voss still had that winning smile that always made her strong executive style of ruling her domain go down that much easier.

Now, since her father passed, she was the sole head of Di Voss In-dustries . . . with Billy not sure how extensive a realm that currently was.

He still knew Gretchen could be sweet, charming—and within a heartbeat, slice and fillet you and put the knife back in its sheath better than any chef *anywhere*.

"Great to see you as well."

Niceties out of the way . . .

They walked down Grand Street, filled with people, all hurrying.

Billy was glad to see that. The city back to normal, with all the crazy business that meant. He took a sip of his latte, the coffee so hot coming out of the small opening on the plastic lid.

"So, what more can you tell me about this meeting?"

Gretchen turned to him as she walked, eyes flashing. Bit of a smile. "Big opportunity, Billy. *Really big.* They recognize your name, its value, and want to exploit it all over the place . . ."

"Exploit?"

"Yeah. I mean, you are a 'brand.'"

"From 'exploit' to a 'brand'? What's next? My own line of frozen food?"

She paused a moment. "Not sure you understand. This could be a gateway to so much of what—*I hope*—you still want."

"Like?"

"Being on air with a new streaming network? And running shows. Leading to a new restaurant. Hell, even chain. Imagine . . . Blessing's Bistros everywhere . . . LA, Vegas . . ."

"Got it. *A brand.*"

"Yes, but see, you'd be—in this new world of on demand—in charge. I dunno, call it producer, creator? With money to match. You can escape whatever the hell you are doing out there at the butt end of Long Island."

"North Fork. It may be the butt end of Long Island, but there are a lot of assholes here. And I cook. I like cooking."

She laughed. "Sure. Right. Anyway, that's what's in play here."

But Billy knew that Gretchen would not be involved unless she would be a sizable part of it as well. So . . .

"And your role in all this?"

She nodded as if expecting the question. "The usual. An exec. But you, me—we *have* had a good working relationship in the past, right? I can run interference for you."

"Oh—there will be the need for interference?"

"It's not *all* that different from the world of broadcast TV. Still have shows. Still have ratings—of a sort. Cash is still king, whether it is subscribers or advertisers. But hey—none of that ever gave you a problem before. Has it?"

"No, it hasn't . . ."

As Billy walked, he noticed some people doing a double take as they saw him. But New Yorkers being New Yorkers, they let him proceed without confirming that sudden awareness.

Hey—he's somebody.

Or used to be. He had to admit, Billy missed the attention.

He turned to Gretchen, Broadway dead ahead, the office building close.

"Okay. Got it. And hey—want to say thank you. You know, for this. Even if it doesn't work out."

"Oh, it *will* work out, Billy. Don't you worry about that."

They hit the corner. Waited for the signal to cross where, though the cars would stop, a delivery person on an electric bike could still steam-roll you in the out-of-control bike lanes.

Nothing against bikers, Billy thought. But he wasn't sure the people who lobbied for those lanes knew they would become express lanes for food deliveries all over the city, with traffic rules be damned.

They got the signal to cross, and a brisk countdown began to when that option to cross safely would have passed.

"Going to be interesting. To hear what they say."

Gretchen had regained her smile again. "Why, yes it will . . ."

$$\triangleright$$

The meeting room was on the top floor of the building. High enough that Billy—sitting at one end, a place where they had thoughtfully put his name card—could see a chunk of the crisp blue sky.

Gretchen to his side.

A scattering of young people were at the table, many with laptops open, all looking serious, focused on the "momentous" event about to happen.

Billy hadn't brought anything. Besides a notebook, now he had to add a laptop to his list.

Just a meeting, he thought.

At the other end of the table, a guy was smiling and nodding as he said a few quiet words to his troops at the table.

But also, to that exec's right—and actually sitting a foot or two *away* from the table—was another man.

This guy, examining his phone, looking too well dressed for casual SoHo. Crisp, well-tailored suit. Power tie with blue stripes.

Billy didn't get to check the guy's shoes, but he imagined they'd be impressive as well, pointy and polished to a glow. All of it saying—clearly—*money* . . .

And speaking of financial resources, the man's watch—a Rolex Submariner—was catching the sunlight, gleaming on his wrist.

That man simply sat there with his eyes on the screen and occasionally, rather disconcertedly, looked straight at Billy as if it were *his* job to start the meeting.

But finally, the exec at the far end (he had briefly introduced himself, but the name and title had quickly escaped Billy's brain) said, "Okay, we're all *set*. So, first, welcome, Billy Blessing! Welcome indeed! We are all *so* glad you could come in for this meeting. Again, I'm Jim Collins from Worldwide."

He grinned at the others at the table. "You can meet the rest of the team later—but we all think you are going to *love* what we have to say."

The man in the sleek gray suit—if that's what it was—continued his sitting and looking. *No name offered there . . .*

"So—I've been tasked with heading up this brand-new division of Worldwide. A *stand-alone* division, I should add. And the gentleman to my right is one of our key backers, Mr. Tony Hill of Hilltop Entertainment. Maybe—the key backer?"

That name, that company meant absolutely nothing to Billy.

As it seemed it was expected for Billy to say something . . . he did: "Hi."

"*Great.* I assume Gretchen here has briefed you on our plans, the rough outline of it all?"

"Somewhat," Billy said. Then, since it seemed best to show some interest, "Enough to have me intrigued about what you propose . . . What you are up to? When it comes to me, that is?"

At that, Collins nodded to a young assistant to his right, who went to what Billy guessed was a digital whiteboard.

Only this one . . . so many generations removed from anything Billy had ever seen in the studio.

With a touch, it flashed the animated letters of a logo . . .

Blessing's Back!

The assistant remained there.

"Okay, we'll go through the whole deal. Our vision, if you will. First take and all. But there you see it: *Blessing's Back*. And wow—is it ever gonna be big . . ."

And then the pitch—because that's what this was—began . . .

For a crisp ten minutes, with nice graphics and pretty pictures and a pie chart or two thrown in for good measure—also slickly animated, of course—Billy quickly got the general idea . . .

First up, a streamed cooking show. Billy all over the country, cooking with local chefs, finding amazing dishes in all fifty states.

Then, of course, a competition show. Still very much—Billy heard—in the very early planning stages, but the general idea was finding amateur cooks who came from unlikely and unusual backgrounds to compete for a cash prize and some kind of title.

How original . . .

Billy had to wonder: *Would that include people who did time in jail?*

Then, a year or two on, the launching of a franchise, a chain of restaurants with the Blessing's Bistro name.

Again, as Billy heard, the details were still fuzzy, but it started with Vegas, where it seemed all great chefs, like elephants trudging to the biggest money water hole, ended up. But then rolling out to the big cities . . . Chicago, LA, and to be sure—New York.

And then they were done, the presentation fast and crisp, finishing with a great image of Billy from some years ago, holding a platter of visually appetizing food, a nicely frenched rack of lamb.

Billy knew that, although often, when on *Wake Up, America!*, people got to taste what was prepared, it would have already chilled a little from sitting, those fresh flavors evaporating.

Though—in the magic land of television—everyone would be oohing and aahing anyway.

Finally, the man at the end of the table, Jim Collins, grin broadening, leaned forward: "So, Billy—what do you think?"

Billy nodded. Having lost it all—and now to be presented with this? Somehow it didn't seem real at all.

Or possible.

But he said, "Pretty ambitious."

"You bet. You have a name, Billy. A reputation . . . and this plan we just showed you will maximize your brand."

Billy looked at Gretchen as if she might have something to add. And she caught that glance.

"Oh, and steering the whole thing with my team here, Gretchen Di Voss, of course. Someone you have worked with for such a long time."

Billy could have added that those years, well, had their ups and downs, not to mention flickers of other more personal distractions, which he and Gretchen had wisely never revisited.

Old romances were best forgotten when it came to this world.

"Um, yeah. Gretchen. Well, guess that guarantees you will have someone really savvy running things. Assuming this actually happens."

He realized his last words tossed a wet blanket on things.

But then Billy noticed something, well . . . odd.

The other man, in his perfectly tailored sharkskin suit. This Mr. Tony Hill? Leaned over and whispered something to Collins. Not heard by anyone at the table.

And Billy thought: *What is this? Grade school?*

Though the man's face, not so quick with the easy smiles, looked a little too hardened for any schoolkid.

But Collins, at the head of the desk, nodded. "*Right.* So, just to be clear, Gretchen would join our team. In a leadership role, of course. And she'd be working with everyone across all the initiatives."

"Good to know."

Because she would, he knew, have his back.

Now Billy waited for whatever would bring the meeting to a close. Which, if the past was a prologue, would be some discussion of a "deal."

But first.

"Um, Billy, Mr. Hill here reminded me that there is some urgency— on his part—with all these plans . . . ?"

"Urgency?"

"Yes. Er, the plans are already moving, steps being taken, various important negotiations already underway? So, you know, it would be"— again that toothy smile—"all set for you."

"Right," Billy said, not at all sure what point was coming. But he didn't have to wait long.

"*So*—as soon as we have a deal memo outlined, we'd want you back here, in the city, hands on it all. *Pronto!* You know, first make sure every detail passes muster with you, and Gretchen too, of course."

In other words—Billy could figure—he'd have to leave NoFo Eats rather peremptorily and leave the North Fork.

And probably even walk away from whatever the hell he had been doing during this week of downtime.

Digging into an old guy gone missing at sea . . .

And now maybe not missing. Maybe murdered.

But this wasn't Billy's first rodeo. "Yeah. Makes sense. I mean, things move fast these days. Just call this the Blessing Express."

Murmurs of polite laughter bounced around the table.

Gretchen spoke up with words of reassurance: "But I guess when Billy looks at the offer, the outlines of a deal, and we all come to an agreement, should be fast? Then, well, think that should be no problem."

She looked over at Billy, who nodded with a small smile. But he was feeling rather noncommittal at this point.

Even the sharkskin-suit man—this Tony Hill—smiled at that. Something behind that smile . . .

Smiles all around . . . while Billy kept thinking: *Who* is *this guy, sitting like he's king, with this dog-and-pony pitch for his benefit?*

"So, if you give us the name of your agent, we can—"

Billy nodded and put up a hand.

"Um, I don't have an agent. Have not had one since, well, things changed?"

A big 'O' on the lips of Collins. *After all, who in the biz* doesn't *have an agent?*

Suddenly, someone had pulled the emergency brake on the Blessing Express!

Gretchen filled in the gap.

"That's okay, Jim. I've done enough deals and projects and contracts with Billy. I can look at any offers with him. Time comes, I have a good entertainment lawyer to check the fine print."

The 'O' disappeared, train back on track once again.

And at that, the relieved exec stood up.

"I am *so* glad to hear all this. I will have my legal team get on the memo ASAP. Should be superfast"—a glance at sharkskin man—"to get this all going. Then, guess, once you sign off, Billy, you and Gretchen should be ready to roll."

Gretchen had stood up, matching smile for smile.

Billy did as well. Thinking, wondering: *Shouldn't I be more excited about all this?*

"Sounds good," he offered innocuously.

And—he *guessed*—it did. But a little voice in his head did whisper . . . *Was it?* His quiet but not unpleasant life was about to vanish in an instant.

"I best get back to, well, you know. North Fork."

The expression of everyone around the table looked as if he might as well have said he was returning to Mars.

Billy shook hands with everyone, though. He didn't care whether it was the lowliest assistant or someone who was a mere rung or two below the executive.

Back in the day, he didn't care about position, titles, or even power. People are people, and that was all that mattered.

When he was done, Gretchen was beside him as they said their goodbyes and walked out of the office.

Past a young guy at the receptionist's desk, whose owl eyes tracked them to the elevators.

Billy thought, as Gretchen hit the button, *Been a while since I walked corridors of power like this.*

Then a real interesting question: Did he really miss it?

15

AND BEFORE HEADING BACK

Billy noticed that Gretchen didn't say a word in the elevator, not with other people there. Or even when they hit the gleaming lobby with its two security officers and Lucite barriers, which opened only when a pass or badge was scanned.

Not until they hit Grand Street did she stop, take a breath, and turn to him.

"Well—mighty quiet, Billy. What do you think?"

Billy looked around at the busy SoHo scene. Did he miss this, now that it might all be coming back, the crowds, the rushing around so fast?

He smiled. "Guess . . . *Blessing's Back*?"

And Gretchen laughed. "Sure. Why the hell not? Not like you're an unknown."

"And you will be, what, my boss-slash-manager?"

"Doubt I will *really* be a boss. Think there will be lots of mini-me's heading up various divisions. And that guy who said nothing at the table? New to me. But obviously with *muy* cash and pulling strings on this."

"Talk about quiet . . ."

"As to an agent, well, you've been around long enough you can read a contract. Know a good deal—or bad one—when you see it. And we can use my lawyer when the time comes . . ."

A moment to recall. Then: "Larry Schaefer?"

"That would be the one. He'll find any hidden traps in the deal memo, then the contact. Wouldn't worry."

"I'm not. Worried, that is."

"So, you excited? You *in?*"

Again, Billy took a moment, looking around as people weaved their way around the two of them. They could grab another coffee, sit down. But he wanted to get back to Greenport.

Funny how that pulled at him . . .

To track this Danny Pippo.

Where he sat in a dive of a bar . . . and might know things.

After all, I did *take that check*, he thought. Did *promise to do something . . .*

Even if it was to put the daughter's mind at ease.

So . . . just a quick few, final words now as they walked . . .

▷

"Well, sure," Billy said. "I never wanted to pull the plug on my life. I liked doing TV. *Loved* the damn restaurant. So—all these ambitious plans? Guess I'm in?"

"Good. Knew you would be. Maybe start thinking about how you will, er, tie things up out on the North Fork, get ready to migrate back to the big city? And fast. That's been made quite clear."

Billy looked away. "Yeah . . . that will take some doing. Kinda in the middle of some things?"

And that drew a glance from Gretchen.

"*Uh-oh.* From past experience, I have a suspicion what *that* may mean."

He smiled. "I imagine you do. But, you know—not to worry—it's all probably nothing."

Gretchen shook her head. "You do have a knack, don't you? Getting involved in stuff . . . dangerous stuff where—well, in my opinion—you clearly don't belong."

"What can I say? I am a man of many talents."

"Okay, just be careful. The future beckons, Billy. Lot riding on this. For you, and for me."

"Yeah, got it, boss." A grin. Then: "One thing, can you try to find out who that other guy, that Tony Hill, is? What's *his* story?"

"The whisperer who I suspect is the man with the money?"

"Yeah. Like to know who I'm jumping into bed with."

"Don't we all. Will do my best."

"Okay. Got to hit the lovely LIE."

"Better you than me. You know there are other ways to get out to the end of Long Island."

"Yeah, but it's the fastest."

Gretchen took a breath. "Sure, that is if an eighteen-wheeler doesn't flip over along your journey."

"I always try to avoid them . . ."

Then Gretchen leaned close and gave him a kiss, taking Billy by surprise. Thinking of their history, though . . . maybe not unsuspected.

"Be careful. Okay?"

And Billy turned back in the direction of the Soho Grand and the car park.

"I'm *always* careful . . ."

And as he turned and started back, he thought: *Was that true?*

There had been some close calls. In fact, his life was a series of them.

Luck does run out, he had heard.

But his? Maybe not just yet . . .

And sure enough, around exit 42 at Jericho—and thinking he was almost home free—the LIE, a four-lane behemoth with a dedicated HOV lane, forbidden to him as a single driver, was reduced to one horribly slow, crawling lane of traffic.

As Gretchen had predicted, the cause—revealed in an alert from Waze—was a massive truck that had flipped over, causing a series of cars to crash into it. That same damn eighteen-wheeler!

Great . . .

It had been a while since he had fought his way through traffic. And this trip, which *should* be two and half, maybe three hours, would now turn into a much longer one. But he thought: *Not like I have an appointment.*

Detective Solomon had said his "contact," one Danny Pippo, spent his waking day at the bar, aptly named the Wayward Tavern.

In midcrawl, the accident site still well ahead, his phone pinged with a message.

He picked it up.

From Police Chief Lola Bristow. A text:

> Still up for a drink and bite when you get
> back? Have a bit of news to share.

One-handed, Billy typed back:

> Sure.

Then hit the send arrow with his thumb.

Quickly followed by another message:

> 7 p.m. Touch of Rome restaurant.

For this, he hit a thumbs-up emoji, sent it—and then wondered . . . *What had Bristow learned?*

And then another interesting thought: she was—apparently—helping him in this. But was there some other interest also in the air?

Not that Billy would mind that.

Been a while, he thought.

But for now, he inched his car forward along with the giant creeping row of cars, vans, and trucks . . . all struggling to get past the accident.

▷

The accident was a nasty one; the truck lay sideways like a giant beast that had taken a fatal shot. And around it: four cars, all horribly dented, windshield glass all over. The front end of one was crumpled like a piece of discarded paper.

But it seemed that the drivers—standing by their now wrecks, looking as if they'd just landed on a totally terrible alien planet—were rattled but alive.

Squad cars were all over the place, EMT, and farther along: a flatbed ready to remove the wrecks.

Everyone passing was rubbernecking, adding a lot to the jam—but how could one *not* look?

Then he rolled past it, and like a magic wand, the four lanes opened, and the pent-up line of cars roared away.

Some going—in his opinion—way too fast, letting their built-up frustration put them in line for the next multicar accident.

Billy sped away too . . . albeit more steadily. And he thought: *So many, um,* curious *things ahead.*

This Danny Pippo character in Greenport. And later, drinks. Dinner with the chief.

And the thought: *What an interesting week this is turning out to be.*

But he also knew that interesting wasn't always a good thing . . .

16
MEETING DANNY PIPPO

Billy found the Wayward Tavern on a narrow street set well back from the bustling center of Greenport, with its shiny new restaurants and matching boutique hotels and shops.

What was probably once a sleepy fishing town now clearly was . . . *a destination.*

But this street—with an auto shop on one corner and a bodega anchoring the other—was something from a different world.

And across from the crummy-looking auto shop, with a stack of tires and cars jumbled outside, was the Wayward Tavern.

And while aptly named, only the word *Tavern* could still be read in the pale color of the actual neon sign in the window; the *Wayward* part only displayed "Way."

This tavern clearly had not taken any part in the town's gentrification and booming times.

But this would not be the first time Billy walked into a dive bar, so he grabbed the door handle—and entered.

▷

The first thing was the smell; there was something about dry beer spills on both the wood floor and bar that just hung in the air.

And Billy had to admit, for him at least—not the worst smell. Been in enough bars that there was something almost comforting in the strong aroma.

However, the atmosphere was drifting strongly from aroma to stench. Nothing a fifty-gallon drum of Pine-Sol and a power washer couldn't take care of.

Sitting at the bar were three customers, all hunched over their drinks and radiating the feeling that they had been there a long time . . . and today's shift for them was far from over.

The bartender, with an appropriate expansive belly, took note of Billy's entrance.

No smile cracked; this was not a place for the causal drop-in or the curious.

Still, Billy came close to the bar, only a few feet away from one of the barstool habitués.

The bartender did not issue a request for an order—no "*Whaddya have, pal?*"—as if sensing this visit was not about grabbing a quick beer before racing home to the missus.

So Billy cut to the chase.

"Hiya. I'm, er, looking for someone who hangs around here? A Danny Pippo?"

The bartender didn't flinch at that. Took a few moments as if debating how to react. Did he serve as Danny Pippo's informal gatekeeper?

And then: "He's in back. At a table. His usual place."

Billy wondered if the bartender was expecting a drink order, but instead he said, "Thanks," and walked down the long bar area, the smell deepening along with the gloom.

The occasional incandescent light above was barely able to keep this place lit enough to prevent patrons from stumbling over a table or chair, or even—as must certainly happen—an errant, inebriated customer from hitting the floor face down.

But as he got to the back, he saw an actual jukebox there. A classic Select-O-Matic. Something from a long time ago, which, maybe, still worked?

And then he spotted some kind of machine that Billy guessed was for people to bet on something or other. A light bulb hung over a side hallway, illuminating the word *Gents*.

That, considering the venue, was kinda ironic.

And at a table to the left, tucked away, someone was sitting, facing front as if he had been expecting Billy—or someone.

(And that reminded Billy of something, though for the moment, he couldn't place it. Some western film, maybe? How Doc Holliday sat at a back table, facing front, ready for whoever walked in, gun raised—as he drank himself to an early death?)

Billy walked over to him.

$$\triangleright$$

Pippo cradled a shot glass in his hands.

"Danny Pippo?" Billy said matter-of-factly.

To which Pippo said, "Who wants to know?"

This is going to be a scintillating conversation.

Billy looked back at the bar area. The three barflies were back to their own preoccupations, once again hunched over the bar, not watching whatever was transpiring in the back of the joint.

But the bartender *was* watching closely. At this distance, he probably could not hear. Still . . .

Billy leaned down.

"I'd like to talk to you. Ask you a few questions?"

Pippo nodded. Then, with a grin showing that dental work was well overdue—though, Billy guessed, not likely in Pippo's future—he responded with, "I'm busy."

Billy smiled. When he got involved in things in LA, Chicago—bad things being done by bad people—Billy found he had an unusual quality.

It didn't faze him.

So this, while not the most promising of beginnings to asking the guy questions, didn't deter Billy.

Not at all.

He leaned down even closer.

"I was *told*," Billy said, keeping his voice low, "by Detective Deacon Solomon that you would be able to, just *maybe*, help me?"

"Don't think so."

This was, so far, proving more difficult than Billy had expected. But he continued: "The detective, we go back, you know? And *he* said, well, that *I* should say to *you* that he fully expects you will assist me in absolutely any way you can . . ."

"He did?"

A small flicker of more attention from Pippo.

"That he did."

"Like I said, I really, er—"

But Billy put a hand on the man's shoulder. He wore a collared shirt of some kind, short-sleeved, collar worn and frayed, shirt erratically stained, of course. One that probably hadn't seen the inside of a washer in a very long time . . .

And it too had a certain . . . aroma . . .

"He said to, well, guess the word would be to 'warn' you? That if you didn't help me, he would have no choice but to tighten certain strings? Make things a little difficult for you?"

Billy smiled.

"Not that I know what he meant by that *at all*. I'm just passing it along . . ."

Billy let his smile fade.

"And hoping you decide to talk to me for just a few minutes. Hey—I can even give you some cash. Cash is king, right? Especially in a joint like this."

Pippo hesitated then . . .

"Alright. Okay." He licked his lips. "But not here. Meet you by the carousel—"

"The carousel?"

Pippo nodded. "It's by the waterfront. Out in the open."

Pippo looked down to the bar, to the bartender at his post watching the scene. Probably curious as hell.

"In a few minutes. You go. I'll follow."

Pippo drained his shot glass.

But Billy felt compelled to add: "You won't play any games with me, hmm, Danny? Sending me off to this carousel? Now would you?"

To which Pippo said, "I don't play games."

Billy nodded, started to turn.

"See you there, Danny."

And then Billy continued to walk down the bar to the door, barely letting in any light from outside. Late at night, he imagined that door had to be a real challenge for a good number of the patrons.

He pushed the door open, the bartender's eyes tracking him, then out to the fresh air.

And did that air—not far from the nearby bay—feel and taste *so good* . . .

▷

The carousel was spinning, half-full with kids on the painted ponies, with moms and dads holding those too young for a solo ride firmly in place on stationary ponies.

The clang of calliope music rang out. And close by, the harbor with charter boats, docks, a scattering of waterfront restaurants.

But this park also seemed to be home to other denizens, he noted.

Guys hanging out, looking around. Billy saw one pair engaged in a tight tête-à-tête, obviously some kind of deal going down.

These days, with legalization going full tilt, the rules about such things probably had changed. The cops probably had a lack of interest in such scenes. Who could blame them for not cracking down?

Still, the dichotomy of that, a drug deal and the sweet fun of the carousel . . . *just weird.*

But he realized why Pippo had picked this spot. Lot of open space. They could talk and no one would hear. And with so many other people milling about here and there, no one would take note.

But so far, no Pippo.

Billy looked at his watch. He did have another appointment . . . dinner with the police chief.

Which he had to admit, he was looking forward to.

Then, from across the street, near a bookstore, he saw Pippo, head swiveling left and right to avoid the cars coming his way—the move aptly demonstrated by Ratso Rizzo so many years ago . . .

Billy took a breath, wondering, *Where will this encounter go?*

Pippo immediately started looking around the open area, as if checking who might be here, who might be seeing.

"Okay, right. I'm here. *Whatchawant?*"

At that, Billy told Pippo about Jack Landry, leaving out details like his suspicious daughter and the bullet holes in the guy's wreck of a fishing boat.

Pippo nodded.

"So, what the hell do you want me to tell *ya?* People go out there, in the damn ocean, *shit happens.*" A smile. "That's why I stay right here—*on land.*"

Billy had to wonder: a guy like Pippo, who had obviously crossed paths with Deacon Solomon back in the city, how did he end up here?

Hiding out?

If so, from whom, from what?

"Yeah, I know. So I have been told. But see, I have reason to believe . . . just isn't that simple, Danny."

Pippo was looking right at him.

"That something else might have happened to this guy Landry?"

Another sloppy grin from Pippo. Another display of the gaps in his teeth.

"Whadda *you?* Some kind of cop? A detective?"

"None of the above. Just one of those people who—now and then—tries to help people . . . who need help."

Pippo licked his lips. He seemed mighty unsure about all this.

"Okay. So, why me?"

Now even Billy took a look around. And in that moment . . . he saw something.

A parked car down on one end. With someone in it. Giving the driver a clear view of the two of them. Just someone parking? But then—why not get the hell *out* of the car?

Instead, just sitting there.

Probably nothing, Billy told himself. *Probably . . .*

"My friend, the detective? He said, if some things were going on out here, things that could lead to someone disappearing? Maybe it was no accident at sea, but something else? And suggested that you might be a wellspring of knowledge on that subject."

"A *well*—what?"

Billy reminded himself that he best watch his vocabulary.

Another look to the black car, the driver. *Still there.*

"Um. That you might know if any, guess, *moves* were being made? Payback for something or other? Somebody wanting someone *gone* for some reason? You know. That sort of thing?"

Now Pippo nodded, getting it.

"Okay." Pippo looked around as well but did not take in the car that Billy could swear was spying on them.

"Tell ya what I heard. 'Cept you didn't—"

"Hear it from you? You got it."

And Pippo talked . . .

"You know, I got friends. And these friends of mine—"

Billy could well imagine who Pippo's friends consisted of. Would make for one very interesting book club . . .

"And they have been talking, you know, like guys do?"

Billy nodded.

"That, well, some players from the city have been around here. Asking questions, looking into this, looking into that?"

"*This, that?*"

"You know, stuff maybe involving *someone* they might be interested in? Who the hell knows why? But they did say they were asking about this old fellow that disappeared out near Gardiners Island—"

"Jack Landry?"

"Look, I don't know *any* names. Got it? But they were asking what people knew of him. What people thought."

"Thought? About . . . ?"

"His just, um, disappearing in his boat? Yeah, questions like that."

Billy sensed this guy, whose words so far were proving mighty interesting, was holding something back.

"Get the feeling—you heard something else." Not a question, Billy knew—and hopefully a nudge to Pippo.

To his right, the carousel had stopped.

The kids with their moms and dads got off. And then a few more got on. Slow day here for the carousel. But Billy guessed this place, in season, with summer tourists everywhere—there would be a very long line for a ride on the painted ponies.

Pippo's eyes darted around a bit, as sure a tell as Billy ever saw. Yeah. *Pippo has, at least, one more nugget he isn't sharing.*

"C'mon, Danny. I'll tell nice Detective Solomon just how helpful you were."

Bit of a gulp, that squeeze having the necessary effect.

"Right. They also asked about whoever it was . . . that was 'looking into' that old guy. You know? Asking questions about him. Nobody knew much. But guessing . . ."

Billy waited.

"That guy they were asking about? It was *you.*"

A smile at that, and Billy—though glad to learn of it—also realized that wasn't the best news he could get. It was one thing to be asking questions discreetly for a worried daughter about dear old dad.

Another to know that certain people were now asking about . . . *you.*

"Thanks for that, Danny. The more you know, eh? Well, you just make sure you don't tell anyone about this little chat. Think you can do that?"

Again, the guy's lizard tongue snaked out to dab at his lips. Probably time to retreat to the Wayward Tavern and resume his daily regimen.

"You got it, boss."

Billy guessed that Pippo now thought, mission accomplished, information delivered, and he was off this particular hook.

But . . .

"Oh. One more thing, Danny." Just like Columbo used to do before lowering the boom on the killer. "Before I let you go. Like you to see if any of these friends of yours can get some names. Just kinda curious exactly who might be interested in me? And maybe why?"

For a second, he thought Pippo would try to squirm out of that task but—well, whatever Solomon held over Pippo's head must be something pretty powerful.

So, instead—a nod. "Damn. Okay. Will do."

At this point, Billy would have texted his mobile number to Pippo. But he already knew that this man standing before him—rather remarkably—had no such device.

Still, the dive bar had a phone.

Billy took out his small notebook. Full of notes and ideas on everything from recipes he wanted to try, to new books he might want to check out at the local bookstore, Split Fork Books.

Not a lot to do out here during the winter. *Usually* . . .

He wrote down his mobile number. Ripped the page out and handed it to Danny. "Don't lose that, Danny, okay? And you learn something, find yourself a phone . . . *and call.*"

"Okay. Sure. Got it."

Then Pippo crunched up the piece of paper—not a great sign it would survive what remained of the rest of the evening.

"And can I, um, go now?"

Billy smiled. "Sure. Have a pleasant evening . . ."

Pippo turned and made his wobbly way across the grass, still spongy and green, back to the streets of Greenport.

Billy took a moment . . . enjoying the view, getting dark now, a splash of purple in the sky behind him in the west.

People were walking around, enjoying the cool but comfortable evening this would be, strolling beside the waterfront.

He looked to where he had seen that parked car. With someone inside looking right this way. But it had moved on.

Probably nothing, Billy thought. Just getting edgy. *That's all.*

Then Billy looked at his watch. Time for him to get moving.

Dinner with the police chief awaited.

17

A TOUCH OF ROME

Halfway back to Northold, Billy's phone, on the seat beside him, vibrated with an incoming call. He hit the button next to the steering wheel, and Detective Deacon Solomon's voice filled the car from its speakers.

The wonders of Bluetooth.

As Billy moved to lower the volume, he said, "Deacon? That was fast."

"Yeah, thing about retirement. It gives you a *lot* of time with not much to do with it."

"So I've heard. You learn anything?"

"Could say. First, this Jack Landry? Well, found no record of any such person, least one that fits your description, where he lived, any profile . . . all that. *Zippo.*"

"And your guess?"

"That's easy. That this Jack Landry is a pseudonym."

"Oh. Interesting."

"And as I am sure you can guess, Billy, people who use pseudonyms usually have things to hide. Or maybe people they are hiding from?"

And Billy thought that was even more interesting. A bit of evidence that, if something bad had happened to Landry, involving bullets out at sea, then there may be a very good reason.

And Billy also realized . . . if *that* was true, then he might indeed be way over his head.

"And this Lisa Cowles?" Solomon continued.

"Yeah?"

The detective laughed. "Guess what? Did a *big* search there. Someone, you say, from a large Manhattan law firm? Age about what, mid-thirties? And maybe this is not surprising . . . *no* 'Lisa Cowles' who is a Jack Landry's daughter. Actually, no one who fits your description of her."

Billy slowed, coming to one of the North Fork's farm stands. People were already out, buying pumpkins, getting ready for Halloween. Those last bursts of sunny days before the locals settled in for a quiet and frigid winter.

He said, "That makes sense. If Landry isn't Landry, then his daughter was—"

"*Lying* is what we call it."

"Yeah. But why? Why the interest in what happened to this guy, her supposed father. Guess the mystery man could *still* be her father?"

"Anything's possible."

Billy thought for a moment. This was all something worth sharing with Lola Bristow, over whatever bowl of pasta he ordered.

But again, another question: "Deacon, *okay*—if both names are bogus, is there any way to try to find out who they might *really* be?"

"Been thinking about just that question. Maybe. First, the check Cowles gave you? Surprised, actually, considering how things are shaking out, that it wasn't cash."

"Yeah, me too. But no . . . a check. Cleared."

"But not a personal check?"

"Um, no. Some company name. She signed at the bottom. A scrawl. Didn't really bother to examine it. I mean, call me gullible. Thought she really was the daughter."

"Never know. She may still be. This thing you have gotten yourself involved in—"

"Whoa. *Hang on.* I didn't *get* myself involved in it."

"Right. Well, you took the damn check, right? So, guess what? You're *involved*. And so far, with way more questions than answers. I'm also guessing this may be the beginning of more surprises to come. And by surprises, I mean . . ."

Billy jumped in before Solomon could elaborate.

"Gotcha. So, anything more you can do on your end?"

Billy hoped that the boredom of retirement might spur Deacon to want to keep playing with this *stuff.*

He didn't call it a "case." Not yet.

Though bullet holes in the boat? Sure, looked like it . . .

"Maybe. First if you can find me a picture of the canceled check. And is there any way you can get a picture of this Landry? You said that the boat registration was a dead end. He have a car? Damn hard to use a pseudonym with that, the DMV being what it is these days."

"Can send the image of the check. And look into the car question."

"Oh, yeah, Billy—did he rent the place he lived in? Guessing so. Might be some info there. But doubt it. Imagine such things are pretty loose out there. You spoke to Pippo today?"

"Yup . . ." Billy updated Solomon on Pippo's reluctantly given report, including uncomfortable questions being asked about Billy himself . . .

"As to what might be happening, questions being asked, who and why—he doesn't know. But—after some pressure—said he'd ask around."

"Okay. He better be careful. Those type of questions? Usually don't go down well."

Billy heard a woman's voice in the background.

"Oh, that's Ellen. Dinner's ready. Her night to cook. Makes one great pot roast. You should come over sometime."

"I'll plan on it . . ."

Though Billy couldn't imagine a universe where that would really happen.

"Oh, and, Billy? Maybe I don't need to say this . . ."

"Yeah?"

"You be careful, hmm? I don't know, and *you* don't know . . . what we're dealing with. So—"

"Be, um, careful?"

"*Exactly.*"

"Will do, Deacon. And hey—will send you the stuff I get together. And thanks."

"Sure."

The call ended, Billy entering the small business section of Northold's Main Street, spotting the small Italian restaurant to his left, with its small private parking lot in the back.

Billy pulled in. Ready for his meeting with the local police chief.

▷

Lola Bristow was already at the table, white wine in front of her. Out of uniform. Giving him a smile as he entered.

"Sorry, bit late. Had to slow down at every farm stand I passed."

"Oh, yeah. When the pumpkins come in, seems it gets more like summer around here again. The swarm of tourists return— briefly."

A young woman, college-age, came over, chewing gum.

Nice touch, thought Billy.

"Something to drink?" she said.

Nice tableside manner.

"Yeah . . . think a vodka martini *up*, with a twist?"

For a second, he thought the girl might not know what "up" meant. But she nodded as she dutifully wrote down the order and wandered over to the bar area.

The small restaurant, tables adorned with the appropriate red-checked tablecloths, was nearly full.

"Got a question," he said, looking at Bristow.

"Shoot."

"You don't mind, what with being the police chief and all? Eating here, people knowing who you are?"

She laughed. "Not like I'm going to pull them over for speeding, now is it?"

"Guess not. I was also thinking, I mean, going from a tough beat with the NYPD to *this*?"

"Yeah, took some adjustment. But I like it. The people . . . well, they may have not taken to me right away. For a few reasons."

Billy could have guessed that.

"But now, I do the job. Help people out. Just like"—another laugh—"that Andy of Mayberry."

"Except," Billy said, keeping his voice low, "don't think anyone got murdered in Mayberry."

"Murder? Oh, that where you think this is heading?"

The waitress came back with the martini. A substantial one, Billy saw. He could do the backstroke in that glass. The bartender knew how to keep his customers happy . . .

The waitress waited, pad at the ready, for a food order.

Bristow said, nodding to the menu, "I've looked already—you just got here."

But that wasn't a problem for Billy, not in a place like this. "I'm ready to order. Chicken parm? Comes with pasta?"

The waitress nodded. "Spaghetti and a small side salad."

How nice . . .

"Great."

Bristow said, "Penne alla vodka."

Another nod, then the waitress walked away.

Then Lola Bristow returned to the topic at hand: "Murder? Because of the bullet holes?"

Billy nodded, then shared what he had learned—that this Jack Landry wasn't Jack Landry. And that some serious people from the city had been asking about him.

And now, yes—all of it was looking more like it might very well be a case of murder.

With the sudden and very important question right there in front of them . . .

Why?

▷

Billy cut into a piece of the chicken parmigiana.

The sauce wasn't too bad, a tangy homemade marinara, not

something from a can or a jar. The cheese was nicely browned on the top. Pasta—not homemade, but one can't have everything.

And with Bristow's penne gone, and now that he had ordered a glass of the house red, he decided he needed to put all his confidence in the chief.

"Look, there's something I didn't mention. Wasn't too sure what to do about it."

"Really. A secret?" Said in a way that indicated she *wasn't* surprised at all.

"When I, um, broke into Landry's place. Looked around. Found a safe."

"Really? Do tell, just before I slap the cuffs on you."

First, Billy was more than a little intrigued at the playfulness in her voice; then he began to wonder if Lola Bristow already knew about the hidden safe. Had she already—despite none of this really being in her jurisdiction—gone into the place herself and looked around?

"Right, well—was hidden behind a bookcase. Some interesting titles on that bookshelf, by the way."

"I bet."

"And—there was this small safe embedded in the wall."

She nodded as the waitress put down another glass of wine.

And then Lola, not responding yet, added, "The desserts here aren't too bad. The cheesecake not quite what you'll get at Junior's in Brooklyn—but tasty. Passable tiramisu. Maybe an espresso? Unless you have to hurry away?"

She smiled at him, and again Billy felt a bit confused. *What actually was going on here?*

Though he had to admit—he was enjoying himself.

"Yeah, so this safe. Hidden safe? I'm guessing it might just have a lot of things in it. Things this Landry guy wanted hidden, secret?"

"Safes are good for that," Bristow said.

"But well—you see, no way in. Not without the combination."

At that, she laughed.

"Um, excuse me. But a little bird told me about your past. Before *Wake Up, America!*, the cable show, the restaurant, all that?"

And Billy knew one thing the chief had certainly done: namely, looked into Billy's past.

Discovering what he'd hoped would remain buried forever.

His time in prison, back in Chicago. A short stay under another name—William Blanchard—before he reinvented himself. Reinvented his life.

But for now, all he said was a simple "Yeah?"

"And I imagine with that past—interesting one too—you know that there has been no safe invented that *can't* be cracked?"

Billy knew that to be true. But so far . . . he hadn't had the opportunity to pick up *that* particular ability.

"Well, sure. Simple combination. I know. It *can* be cracked. But not in my skill set."

"'Skill set'? That what you call it?" she said, laughing. "There are also a ton of videos—how-tos—on something called the internet? Surprised everyone isn't cracking safes all over the place . . ."

Billy didn't doubt that. But he had little confidence a YouTube video on opening a safe would do the trick.

So then—he had an odd question to ask, especially of someone who was the local police authority . . .

"You maybe know someone who might help me out in that regard?"

She looked away.

Then, North Fork being the North Fork, most of the diners had hit this place early. Now Billy saw only another couple or two left in the dining room. And he knew that, in the back of the house, people were eager for the evening to be over. Clean everything up, head home . . . get some sleep before starting the whole thing all over again tomorrow.

Lola returned her gaze to him. Putting on a faux southern accent, she said, "Why, Mr. Blessing. I do declare, I cannot *believe* you just asked a law enforcement authority to help you break into someone's safe."

And Billy had to laugh at that as well.

"Just like to know what's inside the safe? Could tell me . . . tell us something since—"

"Since—so far, you don't have much? Save for the evidence of the bullet holes."

He nodded. "Save for the bullet holes."

And then she leaned close, lowering her voice even more.

"Tell you what, Mr. Billy Blessing. Let's order ourselves a nice dessert. Take our time. And when all done—"

A look around.

"I can drive you to Landry's. You can show me the safe and—believe it or not—I can probably open it."

For a moment, Billy couldn't believe what he was hearing. But he knew this Chief Lola Bristow of the Northold Police was . . . *something else.*

"Sounds great to me."

"Good then . . ." And he saw Bristow look around for the waitress. Dessert and espresso to come.

Billy thinking: *This evening just took a very interesting turn . . .*

18

THE DANGER OF ASKING QUESTIONS

Danny Pippo knew better than to start asking a lot of questions. About a missing guy, and a boat being found, and people from the city being seen around here.

Certain kind of people . . .

Yeah. He knew a *lot* better than to do that. But when squeezed, he had no choice.

And now, late in Greenport, the sidewalks about to be rolled up, he was in a hurry to get back to his one-room apartment above the hardware store, having just spoken to some low-level drug dealer he knew.

Asking questions that made the dealer *clearly* uncomfortable . . . even saying, *"What the hell you doin', man? Asking about things like that?"*

And the guy had nothing much to say. Like most of those that Danny tried to lean on.

Though a few, maybe feeling somehow safe—the city and its mob guys so far away—told him . . . *yeah, seemed like some things were happening out here.* People from the city in their dead-giveaway cars prowling around.

Looking for something. Or maybe—looking for someone.

As to the specific question . . . an old guy who disappeared way out there near Gardiners Island? He had less luck with that.

Except more than a few of the lowlifes—guys who did illegal things now and then if the pay was good enough—said . . . *"Sure, disappeared? That what it is, a disappearance? Well, there are all kinds of disappearances, now aren't there?"*

Leaving Danny with the idea that they maybe really knew more than they were saying.

There were a couple more guys he could hit up tomorrow, not that he was looking forward to it.

But he also knew it wouldn't take much to have Solomon—back in the city, retired or not—make a call, and suddenly Danny's parole agreement would disappear, and he'd be back in jail.

He didn't like jail. Did not want to go back. So, if it took doing this, then that was exactly what he would do.

Now, walking down a dark street, heading to his crummy room, he felt a steady breeze from the nearby bay. Though blocks away, the breeze was strong enough, the damp night air actually cool enough, that he was chilled.

He didn't like winter out here. Hell—he didn't like winter *anywhere*. And this late-night chill just reminded him of what was coming down the road. Out here, you got some nasty winter weather.

He picked up his pace . . .

He came to a corner with a streetlight; Danny wasn't sure why they put a light here. No cars as far as he could see in either direction.

He crossed on red.

His room, with its so-so heat, was not far now. But he had a gas stove. Sure. Could crank that. Warm the damn place up. Still some Four Roses left to help warm up his insides.

Then to crash—and forget this whole evening that began with that guy walking into the Wayward Tavern.

He moved past the lone streetlight on the corner, shadows deepening. Equally crummy houses on either side, paint peeling as if they were blistered. A deli that mainly sold junk food. Not like a real New

York deli, he thought, not with any kind of meat you actually wanted. And those nice hard rolls. And salads, all fresh.

Lot to be missed about the streets of New York.

Nearly there when he heard something . . .

Steps. Behind him. For a moment, he thought of stopping and looking behind him. But he just kept up his pace.

Until—well, those steps were now closer. Like someone had hurried to catch up with him. And now Danny turned and gave the figure behind him—because there definitely was someone behind him—a look.

Tall guy. In one of those puffer jackets. Like it was already winter. And a skullcap. The lone streetlight was behind the guy, so his face . . . a shadow.

But now he was close enough to say, "Yo, Danny. You got a minute?"

And at that, Pippo had to think. *Well, what to do? This guy could be anybody, looking for anything.*

Thinking he could turn and run as fast as he could to the side door, open it fast, then to the rickety stairs up to his room.

Could do that.

But this guy . . . maybe he was fast? Maybe what he wanted to talk about was nothing?

Though, after what Danny had just spent time doing, he had that creepy feeling that—having done something bad, something he really shouldn't have—well, *really* bad things could happen.

And usually, in situations like this? Running didn't help.

So—he stopped.

And simply said, "What? *Whaddya* want?"

And then the man who had moved fast to get close to him, now slowly closed the remaining distance between them . . .

"Some of my friends in town . . . they heard what you were doing tonight, Danny."

Danny thought, *Oh, shit.* But he responded by shaking his head, saying, "What are you talking about?"

"That you were, y'know, asking about, well . . . *people* who might have come here, asking about somebody looking into something? About some old guy, disappearing. Something like *that*? Someone who came to *you*, wanting to know what you know. Or if there might be other people curious about this old guy."

The man smiled, and now his teeth caught the scant light.

Danny had to make a quick decision. And as soon as he said it, he knew it was perhaps the wrong one.

"I don't know what you are talking about. I was just hanging out at the—"

The man raised a hand.

Then Danny noticed. He was wearing gloves.

Sure—it was chilly out. Right, and a breeze. But gloves?

Why gloves?

The man took a step forward. This street, so late here, so dark and deserted. Pippo licked his lips.

"Look, I said—"

But the man shook his head.

"You really *aren't* hearing me, are you? Who did you speak to? What did you find out for him? And what did you tell that guy who came and visited you in that stinkin' dive you call home?"

Pippo started to open his mouth.

But the man continued quickly: "I'll tell you what *I* think, what my instincts tell me. You have gone around asking a lot of questions you really *shouldn't* be asking, hmm? Not healthy. And also guessing, maybe you haven't told this guy anything at all yet."

Danny had started nodding even before the man in front of him finished.

"Isn't that right?"

Danny nodded even more, eager to agree, eager to end this. To get back to his junky room, off the street. Away from here.

But . . . it happened so fast.

A movement of the man's right hand, and something slipped out of pocket. A *click*, and it opened. And there, moving toward Danny Pippo, was something shiny.

And as it came close, faster that anyone could ever move to get away from it, the blade hit home. Right into his midsection. Then, a quick twist of the blade.

And Danny knew—in a last flash—he'd never see that room of his ever again . . .

19
DEAD OF NIGHT

"This old door," Billy said as he mostly forced the back door to Landry's isolated cottage open, "just opens with good push."

It seemed incredible that the local police authority—in this case, Northold police chief Lola Bristow—was actually with him, breaking into Landry's place, and soon to "crack" into a safe that, Billy hoped, might hold some very important secrets.

And once they were in, Lola said, just as Billy was reaching for a nearby light switch in the small kitchen, "Best *not* do that. Know we're pretty out of the way here. Still . . . you never know, hmm?"

And Billy realized her instincts from whatever she got into as a cop back in New York were clearly intact—even here in the usually quiet North Fork.

"Yeah. Good idea." So now with no light, the night moonless, he navigated to the front living room, slowly.

Though, if they were to crack the safe, he imagined *somehow* light would indeed be needed.

And with Lola behind him, he made his way into the room—remembering the rough layout—and over to the bookshelf.

"It's behind here."

"Okay," she said.

Billy began to pull at the shelf until he was sure that the wall safe would be visible. Visible, that is, if they had any light!

At which point, Bristow leaned down—close to him, Billy noticed. This, well, was definitely in the category of things never done. And he had to admit, more than a bit exciting.

Lola kept her voice low.

"Okay, Let's have a look at it . . ."

And then, her phone in her outstretched hand, she put the light on; there was the safe, combination fully illuminated, secrets waiting to be revealed . . .

"First impression?" Billy said.

"Well, not the most difficult of combination locks to crack. But no piece of cake."

"You still think—?"

"I can open it? Only one way to find out. Mind holding this?"

She handed him her phone.

"And a bit of room?"

Billy realized he was in the way, so he moved to the side, then angled her phone so the light came from above the safe. Squarely targeted on the combination.

And as he did, Bristow put out a hand and gave the lock a slow twirl.

"Are you trying to—" Billy started.

But that brought a look from Bristow. "Um, *if* I am able to crack this safe—no guarantees at this point—it, well, requires *quiet.*"

And to show he got that, Billy made a locking gesture over his lips and tossed away an imaginary key. She smiled, then returned her attention to the safe. She leaned close, one ear right near the numbered knob of the combination lock. He would have liked to ask another question as she did so. Like . . . *what exactly was she listening for?*

But once warned, he kept silent—and just watched.

Lola seemed to be moving the combination one way, then the other, slowly now, as if each small movement was so important, potentially revealing something. After a bit of that, she turned to him, and— no smile this time—said, "This might be harder than I thought. I mean, I have not done it a lot. And I'm a little out of practice."

Billy nodded as she turned back to the safe, and her slow, methodical twirling of the dial.

He heard her take a deep breath and hold it, as if even steady breathing might interfere with her focus, her listening.

Then, she turned the dial to the right. And stopped.

A small nod to herself. Then, after expelling a breath, another turn, now to the left, farther around this time. But the chief still moved the dial steadily, slowly.

Until again—a stop. She took a deep breath. Now—a longer pause.

Since—well, like most combo locks—Billy guessed the third number, the "open sesame" moment, was about to happen.

Or not.

Finally, as if more waiting would do nothing, Lola started turning the dial right. If anything, more slowly this time, her cheek planted flush on the metal door of the safe.

Until—she stopped again.

Moved her face away. A look to Billy.

"Here goes nothing," she said, reaching down for the handle, just inches away from the lock. She gave it a steady, firm yank downward.

And now . . . an amazing moment as Billy saw the handle *move* with a submissive click, as if giving up on the fight, *the door swung open . . .*

▷

Chief Lola Bristow stood up and stepped back, like maybe something very bad was within the safe.

Billy had to ask: "Something wrong?"

At that, Bristow laughed. "Could say that. Look, Billy, I like you.

And maybe, I guess, you could do a lot more about finding out what happened to old Jack Landry than the young Coast Guard lieutenant. Or me. But you see, if *I* reach in, pull out those documents . . . well, that is a whole other thing."

"How so?"

"As long as I *don't* see them, I have something they call 'plausible deniability.'"

"I believe I have heard that phrase before."

"Bet you have. Well, opening the safe, and not reaching in? I still don't know anything about anything. But if there is something inside that tells me things. Important things."

"I get it. You'd have to share with the Coast Guard?"

"Yes, and they'd be all over this. That is, if there is something in there of importance. Your little fishing expedition here—"

"Interesting choice of words."

"—would come to a quick end. I'd even have to make sure that was perfectly clear to you. And let's not even get into the legality of tampering with evidence."

"Think I really get it."

"Yeah. You're smart. I am sure you do. So, this is where, well . . . think I will go look outside the house? The night sky. Clear night over the bay. Bit of fresh air?"

"Beautiful night indeed . . ."

And Billy knew that she meant he could reach in and grab what was inside, the police chief none the wiser.

With plausible deniability as in . . . *I didn't see or know anything about any of that. Swear to god.*

And as Lola turned and walked to the front door of the cottage, Billy turned his attention back to the open safe.

Could be nothing in there. Or could be something.

Either way, he was about to find out.

▷

Billy reached in and immediately felt a stack of items.

From the feel, he could detect some envelopes, then folders, all held in one big pile with a thick rubber band.

He pulled the stack out and then leaned closer for another swipe inside with his right hand.

Empty.

So he closed the safe—still marveling at how Lola had just opened it. Maybe a skill he should work to acquire? Though he had to wonder— opening safes—was that something he would be doing more of?

As opposed to hosting a cooking competition show!

The safe latched shut, and he gave the tumbler a twirl, not sure whether that was something important to do.

Then he stood up, put the stack of folders and envelopes on top of the bookcase, and pushed the case back into its place, hiding the safe.

If someone came investigating, someone who actually knew what they were doing, they'd find a safe. And they'd find it empty.

And at that, Billy turned. It was late. Had been a long day. He started for the door out to where Lola Bristow waited, looking at the stars.

▷

He noticed she didn't say a word about the stack of items held by rubber bands tucked under his arm.

"Beautiful night," she said.

But he knew—she had to see that he had indeed found something.

"Yes. So, er—"

"Thanks for meeting me for dinner, Billy. Not maybe your level of cuisine—"

"It was fine."

She nodded. "Been thinking about something else. An idea."

"Depending on the specifics, those are generally good."

Billy took a look out to the sandy road, to the distant trees where less isolated homes could be seen, lights coming from windows.

No one could be watching them, he thought. That was a good thing. Best no one knew about this illegal collaboration.

"And so—your idea?"

"Landry's boat. The bullet holes?"

"Which Lieutenant Talbot missed . . ."

"Uh-huh. Well, I was thinking if Landry *was* killed out there—"

There we go, Billy thought. Murder on the table and being discussed . . .

"Then where better to dump the corpse?"

"You have any experience of that? I mean, back in the city?"

"That I do. Not a lot. Had a body pop up in the Gowanus one time. Not much left of it. Still, the lab was able to get an ID."

"I've seen *CSI.*"

She shot him a withering look before replying, "Yeah. And another time, not my beat, a mob hit, from who knows when? And the victim, in a body bag, somehow finally popped to the surface. Drifted over to the South Street Seaport."

"That must have ruined some people's dinner arrangements."

The Seaport, he knew, had become a trendy place, with flashy new restaurants, clubs, a hotel or two—its ancient role in the story of New York and the selling of fish honored on plaques, but largely forgotten.

"So—you were thinking?"

"Yeah. Landry gets shot out there. Who knows why."

"He's on first."

"What?"

"*Who?* Ah. Before your time. Mine too actually. Old Abbott and Costello routine. 'Who,' the baseball player on first. Your dad would get it."

"Um, you lost me. But they would, pretty obviously, dump the body there."

"Which means . . . no one would ever find it. Case kinda closed?"

To which Bristow responded, "Not exactly . . . Let's get in my car. Bit of a chill, hmm? And I will tell you why."

▷

The chief's engine turned on, lights still off, some heat on. Yeah, October was a beautiful month, still with warm days. But the nights now carried a chilly warning about the winter to come.

"So—and trust me, I don't really know a lot about this kind of thing—but they dump the body. Making sure that it *won't* pop up to the surface."

"Which would be unfortunate. For the murderers, at least."

She looked at him. "You know, you are very funny?"

"That's one reason why America loved me. Least until they didn't. Or at least until the network execs *didn't*."

A laugh from her. Then: "So—the body dumped, weighted, the boat left as a wreck since it added to the story of an accident at sea on a bad day."

"Makes perfect sense."

She paused a moment. "So that means—the body would still be there."

"*There?*"

"At the bottom of the bay?"

"Um—and I am guessing, not being a seafaring person at all, that it could remain there, undiscovered, for a very long time, or whatever is left of it after Flounder, Sebastian, and all his 'Under the Sea' pals get done nibbling?"

"Yeah. Maybe. That is—if it ever was found."

And for a moment, Billy waited to hear . . . what exactly the Northold police chief was suggesting.

In Billy's mind, the word *plausible* was likely to pop up again . . .

▷

"Okay, so this is just an idea. Again, we are off the record here."

"Yeah, think I got that by now."

Billy had to wonder: what motivated the former NYPD cop, turned chief of a small North Fork town, to want to help?

Could be a lot of things, he imagined. Maybe she didn't like the idea of something going unsolved? Maybe she wanted to break the humdrum of her daily life here—probably pretty quiet as far as homicides went.

And maybe, well—thinking about all things possible—maybe she just liked him.

That would be interesting . . .

"So, if Landry *was* killed out there, he could still be there. A pretty standard way to dispose of a victim."

"So I've heard."

"Which means, if it's found—the body, that is—you have a whole other thing you are looking into. And then, well, a resident of my town? Suspected murder? Guess I could get genuinely involved."

"Wouldn't that be nice? Imagine you don't get many murders out here."

"Now and then. Things happen everywhere."

"Don't they though? So, your idea?"

She turned to him.

"There's this guy been living here like forever, well before I arrived. Runs Humphries Search and Recovery."

"I like a business name that tells you what it does."

"It's a commercial dive shop. This area, always having its share of wrecks, salvage, whatnot. Also, the place does the more common stuff like helping marinas put in new docks."

"You need divers for that?"

Lola laughed. "Beats me! I'm from Brooklyn! But guess anything done underwater, he does."

"But not taking tourists out to see the underwater sights?"

"Not sure we have those. Seen the gray water out here? This isn't the Caymans."

"I noticed."

"But sure—there are a couple of those dive places too, in Riverhead, and up near Orient Point."

Billy nodded, perhaps beginning to see where she was headed with this.

"You go to him. Describe the situation."

"Mentioning the bullet holes or—?"

"Can't hurt. I mean Ted—"

"Humphries?"

She shook her head. "No. That guy, the original owner? Long gone. Ted Willits worked for him, learned the ropes. And amazingly enough, was left the operation in a will."

"How nice. So let me guess. I tell this Ted Willits where Landry went out. The general area. And he would have some way to search it?"

"Believe so."

Billy nodded. "And then, he could go down. Find the body?"

"Then it is a case of habeas corpus," Bristow added.

"Though, in this case, there may be more habeas than corpus."

"No matter. That makes it a murder case. Enough that I can step on all the Coast Guard toes I want to."

"Get the feeling you wouldn't mind doing that."

"But one thing: you keep me in the loop all along. Okay? About anything at all that happens with this. Still think you might be in over your head."

"Wouldn't be the first time."

She smiled. "Yeah. I know Billy *Blanchard . . .*"

She knew . . .

His real name. His record. Pretty savvy on her part to find that out. And yet—

Still willing to help him.

Remarkable. And he thought, *I really like this expat city cop.*

Interesting, because he hadn't liked anyone in a while.

"Okay. Now back to your place. You can look at whatever *you* found in the safe. That stuff? For now? Best you tell me *nada*."

"Yup."

And she started pulling the SUV away from Landry's cottage. The night clear. The road ahead empty.

Just a quiet night out on the North Fork of Long Island.

Nice and peaceful, he thought.

But as does happen, he was soon to learn: *that was incorrect.*

20

IN THE MIDNIGHT HOUR

Billy sat with bourbon in his one glass worthy of a quality bourbon. Ice floating to the top, a floor lamp hanging over him. And on a side table, the folders and envelopes from Landry's safe as he went through them.

A quick check for now. Would take a long time to really study them.

But it didn't take him long before he noticed a few obvious things, completely clear from his perusal.

First bank records. Hard copies, in a day when most people just got digital statements. But old guy like Landry, made sense he'd want the actual paper. Especially when Billy saw what it showed.

Money. *Lots of it.* Deposits occurring at irregular periods, to at least three accounts. Massive chunks of cash that went in.

But then also, equally big chunks that went out.

And where they went to . . . interesting.

So many to Stony Brook University Hospital.

Now what was *that* about?

Medical expense? But a man Landry's age would have Medicare, taking care of most things. The amounts were substantial.

Then other amounts, also sizable, were sent to a different bank account. These were also regular as he flipped through the years of statements that Landry had.

Looking at them, Billy now knew something new. Landry had been living his simple life here . . . got lots of money from *somewhere*, deposited it in a variety of banks; Billy was not sure why.

The money going out. For what reason? And those other large transfers? Again, same question.

All very interesting—but what the hell did it mean?

Did it have anything to do with *why* Landry had vanished? Billy had not yet completely signed off on the idea that Landry had some holes put in him like his boat.

So many questions . . .

And then there were manila envelopes. Neatly closed and clasped. A bunch of them bulging with their contents.

Billy took a sip of the bourbon. Getting late. And he did, apparently, have plans for tomorrow.

To meet this Ted Willits and see what he might find . . . *"under de sea."*

He began to unclasp the top envelope. The most recent. Pulled open the flap. Shook out the contents.

And saw envelopes, all addressed to Landry at the same PO box.

Some looked like letters, others cards. Again, the guy was old school in this age when for most . . . *what the hell was a letter?* And who really sent cards anymore?

He started to open one that looked like it might hold a greeting card of some kind when his phone, on mute, rattled. It was late, after all.

But the shaking and buzzing was loud enough that Billy could hear it.

He picked it up from the table, where it sat next to the coaster with a NoFo Eats logo. And before pressing the green icon to answer, he noted the ID, the caller's name.

Deacon Solomon.

The detective was calling. Mighty late too.

And that could mean only one thing . . . something new had come up, and it was maybe, possibly, urgent. Or even bad?

▷

"Detective . . ." Billy said. "Isn't it past your bedtime?"

"Look, Billy, one of my guys called me. Night shift at One Police Plaza."

Billy had a sense that what he was about to hear would not be good.

"So, after you met with Danny Pippo, talked to him?"

"Yeah. Like you said, he was, er, reluctant, but—"

"Um, so Greenport cops found Pippo just about an hour or so ago, some back-alley street. Stabbed to death. Very professional-looking job, they said."

"Oh."

At that, Billy got up and walked to the front window of his rental cottage. Hearing that kind of news? Perhaps a good idea to take a look out your own front window.

Everything was dark, quiet. But Billy knew from past experiences that things *looking* quiet did not guarantee anything.

"Guess he asked the wrong people the wrong questions?" Billy suggested.

"You could say that. But what it means—and I'm guessing no need for me to draw a picture for you here—but *whatever* the hell this is you are looking into? Well, let's say you know now . . . they are playing for *keeps*."

Billy expected what Solomon would say next.

"Billy—I think you should drop this whole damn thing. Try to call whoever it was approached you, this Lisa Cowles, or whatever her *real* name is, and say it's way too hot. That you like being alive, slicing onions and scaling fish . . ."

"I don't scale any fish," Billy said. "The prep cooks do that."

Solomon laughed. "Gotta say, Billy—does take a lot to rattle your cage."

"Yeah, just a quirk of mine. I don't like being intimidated."

"Then you'd probably like being killed even less."

"There's that."

"Look, if you won't back off, I'm going to at least call this local police chief of yours, this Chief—"

"Lola Bristow."

"Yeah. And tell her what happened to Pippo. Maybe *she* can keep an eye on you."

"Think she's already doing that."

He didn't add how Bristow seemed actually to be helping him. Perhaps it was good at this time *to keep things close.*

But there was something else . . . something new to run by his retired friend in Bay Ridge.

"Look, Deacon—I know the names I gave you—"

"Yup—all bogus."

"Right. Well. I found some things. Bank accounts, numbers. A lot of them. Payments to a big teaching hospital near Hauppauge. Thinking they must lead somewhere? And once I can get a scan of the canceled check, I'll send that to you. Maybe—"

"Hmm. Hang on. And—after I have warned you how dangerous this all is—what is it exactly you want me to do now, Billy? Assist with your seeming wish to come to your own unpleasant end, out there at the tip of Long Island?"

Billy laughed. "Come on. You know people, Deacon. Information like that . . . they can track it down."

"In other words, my warning leaves you unfazed?"

"Well, not sure that is the word I would use. But I've already gone this far, and these accounts? The transfers? The cash involved? All kinds of interesting."

"Yeah, interesting and maybe deadly too. Okay. Take some pictures of them. Text them to me. See what I can see. But, Billy?"

"Yeah?"

"Goes against my better instincts. *Detective* instincts."

"Those same instincts where—I dunno, Deacon—I bet would lead you into a case and somehow . . . you simply could not let it go? Even when you were also told to back off, hmm?"

And the detective laughed. "Yeah. Back in the day. Course, it *was* my job."

"Job, pastime. We're not that different."

"Oh, I don't know. You are a far better cook than I am."

"No doubt about that. Okay, thanks for the news. And—seriously—the help. And don't worry—I *will* stay in touch."

"Just stay alive?"

"Always."

"Till you don't. Be careful." Then the call ended, and Billy sat there a moment. Late. Time to get some sleep; busy day ahead.

But as he finished his bourbon, thinking for a few moments about the low-level hood he'd met that day, who was found later killed rather brutally in a quiet backstreet of Greenport.

This place, it's not NYC.

But who knows . . . maybe, might be just as dangerous . . .

21

HUMPHRIES SEARCH AND RECOVERY

Billy felt the deep ruts like craters on the sandy road leading down to the inlet. This spot was sheltered from the open Peconic Bay, the tall reeds and feathery phragmites catching the morning sun.

He had to hope that just showing up really early would be okay. And that the owner of Humphries Search and Recovery—Ted Willits—would be there.

People like that . . . have to be morning people, he reasoned.

But then, what did he know?

As he got close to the cluster of piers—no recreational boats here, only trawlers of different sizes, serious fishing boats—he caught a boat backing out of its slip, doing a slight turn and then steaming east, toward the just-risen sun.

Nice and slow to keep the wake down.

That rule—quite a serious one in this world. A boat kicking up a significant wake could rattle boats in their moorings. Bang them around. Warning signs about it were all over the place.

That did not go down with the locals. Least the ones who made their living on the water.

A few other boats showed signs of activity. Men in rubber waders were moving slowly, about to start a long, hard day of finding and haul- ing fish out of the nearby waters. One of them, long hair in a ponytail, was not a man at all . . .

Every day was probably the same, save for the weather. Today—cool but sunny and clear. Guess that was comfort enough for the workers.

Then as the road turned into an even bumpier driveway of yellow sand and stone, looking as if it had been shelled by a howitzer, he turned right toward a small wooden shack.

The sign outside was big, bold, and looked terribly weathered. White letters on a faded blue background.

Humphries Search and Recovery.

And unfortunately, no sign of searching or recovering, at least that Billy could see.

He came close, stopping the Jeep at the front door where a sign in the ground said "No Parking." Then in dark magic marker below it: "Ever!"

Billy stopped and got out of his car.

He squinted at the sun, which was perfectly aligned to hit the front of the building full-on, showing all the wear and tear of decades of neglect, nobody doing anything to keep it up.

He went to the front door, expecting no one to be there. The place looking deserted.

But as he tapped three times, he immediately heard barking. And no little yaps of a Pomeranian. Heavy, angry barks of one *very* big dog inside.

Billy didn't mind dogs. But when they were really large and came at him whenever he'd jog back in the city, grabbing some quick exercise time in Central Park—*that* he didn't like.

And he always found it little comfort when a dog's owner, just about able to restrain the powerful animal, would say something like, "Don't worry. He likes making new friends."

Billy always thought, *You mean he likes making snacks out of new friends.*

But then he saw the doorknob twist, and the door popped open with a strong tug.

This was—he guessed—Ted Willits.

▷

Willits—mid-fifties?—had a scowl that his gray-and-black beard did little to hide. He had a cap on his head that said "Red Sox."

Out here, it was either Yankees or Mets country, so *that* . . . was interesting.

The interior of the building, even from the door, smelled ripe with years of whatever items Willits had "recovered," with the addition of pipe smoke, a husky aroma that, at least when it came to smoking, Billy didn't totally mind.

"Yeah?" Willits said simply.

"Mr. Willits, I was told I should come talk to you about—"

Which was as far as Billy got.

"Told you? Who the hell *told* you something about me?"

"Lola Bristow."

And that at least made the scowl shift into a neutral position.

"Oh, she did, did she? Well, guess any friend of our local constabulary is, well—maybe not *exactly* a friend of mind—but at least someone I will speak to. Come in."

Willits backed away from the door, leaving it open.

The dog kept barking. Unleashed, tethered to nada, Billy saw. But at least it hadn't lunged at him with what Billy now saw was its one nasty maw, full of teeth. Some very sharp canines.

Yet . . .

Willits turned to the dog and barked back at it.

"*Rufus!* Cut it the hell *out!*"

And with one last growl and then a quieter bark devolving into a rumbly growl, the dog finally became silent as it stood to the side.

As to its breed, Billy wasn't sure. He guessed mostly mutt, a cocktail of a bunch of oversized breeds that didn't play nice with other dogs or people.

There was a cluttered desk and a back wall filled with navigation charts. An old-school diving helmet sat on a bookcase. He could see a passage to a back room. Just visible, serious diving gear. Tanks, dive suits on a rack. Fins.

There was a chair that faced the desk, but Willits didn't make an offer of it.

"Okay then, Mr. . . . ."

"Blessing. Billy Blessing."

And that caused the man to cock his head.

Billy thought, *Okay, here comes that moment.*

"Aren't you *that* fellow. Used to be somebody, on the *TV*?"

Billy smiled at that, but inside he was groaning. Not that line again.

"Yes. That's me."

Willits turned to the dog. "Lookie here, Rufus. We got ourselves a real *tee-vee* star here, or at least someone who used to be one."

Touché.

Then he looked back to Billy.

"Okay, I like the chief. So—if she said I should talk to you, guess it's okay. Now talk. I'm a busy man, in case you didn't know it."

But from the looks of things, Billy didn't detect any signs of busyness. He told the proprietor of this commercial diving operation what he was there for, hoping it made sense.

Willits had sat down. Remarkably quiet, simply listening as Billy explained about the old man who went to sea and never came back.

About his boat, though—for now—he omitted mentioning the bullet holes.

When Billy was done, Willits nodded.

"Let me see if I got this *straight*, Billy Blessing. This man went out to fish?"

"Yes, out to that area I told you about. Not sure exactly, but somewhere, well . . . you can see it on one of your maps over there—"

Billy pointed to a large map of the area, the sea with all sorts of squiggles and markings that he couldn't make out. A serious map for those who worked at sea, Billy knew.

"Yeah. And the weather started getting rough?"

"And 'the tiny ship was tossed,'" Billy said, alluding to the theme song from *Gilligan's Island*.

Willits nodded, oblivious to the pop culture reference. "And the good chief sent you here to . . . what? Take a look-see out there?"

Now Willits got up and pointed to a spot on the map, not far from a big island, last stop before the open water of the Atlantic. "Right about here, you say?"

Billy nodded.

Willits looked away, thinking things over. "You know . . . I can figure out some things you aren't saying . . ."

"Such as?"

"That you suspect that the old man, well, maybe . . . *not* an accident at sea?"

"I didn't say that."

Willits smiled. "I know. But you *see*, my friend, I've been doing this quite a while. And what you are looking for . . . well, means only one kind of suspicion."

Billy didn't respond. So Willits finished the thought.

"A body could be out here, hmm? On the bottom, most likely? A victim of what they call 'foul play'?"

Then, from Billy, a simple answer: "Yes."

Willits again looked away, definitely thinking things over.

"Guess you'd need to use—dunno—those big diving suits, you know, like that helmet you have over there?"

And at that, Willits finally turned to him—and laughed.

$$\triangleright$$

Willits stood up and went to the nautical chart on the wall.

"Okay, you say this here is the general area that the fella at the marina told you this Jack Landry went to, right?"

"Yeah. A guy who kinda works there. Named Will Sharp."

"Okay, well, you go out *here*, past the tip of Gardiners Island, and yes, you are into the Atlantic pretty fast. Hit real depth pretty damn fast."

He tapped the chart.

"*But right here?* All *around* here actually? The bay right there, down to the Peconic . . . depth runs only forty feet, fifty, some places maybe sixty. So—"

And now, as if he was enjoying the demonstration, Willits went to the dive helmet that looked like a replica from *Twenty-Thousand Leagues under the Sea*. Put his hand on it.

"Couple hundred feet down, and yeah, whole different story. Need the hard hat dive suit. A helmet like this. But—you know—*newer?* Sure. The whole rig to work at depth. But where you want to go? Standard dry suit would do just *fine*."

Billy didn't rush to ask what a dry suit was. He figured that, sooner or later, if things worked out, he would find out.

So he moved to the question at hand . . .

"Okay—you can search the area? See if you can find something, maybe on the bottom, let me know what you see?"

Willits put up a hand. And now he paused, enjoying this slow unfolding of surprises to someone who clearly didn't know a single thing about diving.

"Oh, no worry about that, Billy Blessing. See, you will be *right there*. Kind of a two-man operation. And guess you will have to be that second man. Top side, of course—so don't go getting all worried." Then as if to hammer home the point: "If I find something—and it can be needle-in-a-haystack time out there—you'll know. Hell, you'll see *exactly* what I see."

And all Billy could say, this about as unexpected as could be, was, "Sure. Fine."

Not at all convinced it *was* fine.

"Great. Charge you my discounted rate, you know. Since you are a friend of Lola Bristow."

"You, er, can do this soon, maybe tomorrow?"

"*Tomorrow?* Turns out this is your lucky day. This afternoon's not booked. Can start then. But first—"

And finally, Willits returned to his desk.

"You go get us some sandwiches at the B&B Deli. Whatever you want, and they know what I like. Oh, yeah—some Coronas too . . ."

"Um, is beer a good idea if you're going to be diving?"

"After, Billy, *after*. When we are headed back. Drink to our success or plan for another day searching out around Gardiners Bay. By the way, near that private island—they do not welcome visitors."

Billy nodded.

"Figure we can leave . . . little after eleven. I'll get the boat ready. The gear. You"—big grin—"go get the groceries . . ."

And at that, Billy, actually enjoying this character, nodded and turned to the door.

"Back soon. With sandwiches and beer."

"There you go," Willits said, already moving to the back room, where, Billy assumed, whatever he needed to search for Jack Landry—whatever his real name was—would be found.

22

A CHOPPY SEA

Willits's boat—smaller than the fishing trawlers but with the same rugged, no-nonsense shape—rode the choppy water with the determination of . . . well, the only things Billy could compare it to were the sturdy and steady tugs that worked all around the island of Manhattan.

It had a large winch at the rear, which looked solid enough to lift up anything heavy from the bottom of the sea.

A row of dive tanks sat to the side. Two metal ladders were on the back deck, along with a small metal platform that just touched the water's surface.

Willits stood feet above that deck, baseball cap tight, the sun directly overhead. Though the weather was clear, a steady wind made the water spit white curls as the boat bumped along.

For his part, Billy sat at the back, which maybe was not the best place to sit, considering the way the boat—named *Sweet Sally*, Billy had noticed—went up and down. Billy thought he was about to set sail with his own personal Captain Quint. He hoped this excursion turned out better than the one off Amity Island.

As to where they were going—and when they would get there—Billy didn't have a clue. He had seen a lot of instruments up near the wheelhouse that he only got a glance at when he boarded.

The required sandwiches (turkey on rye with swiss and cranberry for Billy and thick pastrami on a roll for Willits) sat in a nearby Igloo cooler, along with a six-pack of Coronas.

For now—Billy had been told—there was nothing to do but enjoy the ride.

And not being much of a boat person, Billy just sat quietly, hoping all that slamming up and down didn't make him queasy—or worse.

Because, if that happened, he was sure Willits would have so much fun pointing it out.

But when they were well away from the small marina that was home to *Sweet Sally* and the serious fishing boats—all long gone with the sunrise—he could see ahead . . . an island.

It looked bigger than he thought it would from the nautical chart.

Not just a small island stuck out in the bay.

And he knew beyond that island was the mighty ocean.

Next stop—Billy had seen from the maps—Block Island and the expanse of the North Atlantic, open sea all the way to Europe.

But as the boat chugged closer, he felt the engine slow. Willits throttled down until the boat suddenly stopped, in neutral . . . or as stopped as it could be as the steady chop of the waves made it rock forward and back.

Willits called down.

"Okay, *showtime*, Billy Blessing. Come on up . . . and I'll show you what we are going to do . . ."

And as Billy got up, taking the stairs up to the wheelhouse, he thought, *There's that word again . . .* we.

▷

Billy had to hold both handrails to make his way up to Willits and stand beside him.

"Okay, my friend. We have a *ways* to go, but I want to show you what will be happening. See here—"

Willits tapped a device with a bright flat screen that showed something that meant nothing to Billy. Some kind of radar or sonar . . . he guessed.

He might have expected an old-fashioned tube device, considering the age of the ship. But this was a very modern instrument, the flat image crisp—whatever it was showing.

Every few seconds something would sweep the screen, showing changes.

Willits tapped it.

"Okay. We're just seeing the seafloor right here. Nice and flat. Actually, the seafloor out here doesn't have a lot of features, you know?"

Billy didn't.

"Occasionally you spot rocks left over from the good old days of the glaciers. Or maybe some garbage someone dumped. One way to get rid of a broken fridge, hmm? And I guess—in your case—hoping we see something that looks like maybe a body? This poor old Landry maybe, that is if that is what happened to him?"

Billy nodded, then saw on the screen a bunch of fast-moving specks flit across the screen.

"Hey—what was that?"

"We call those *fish*. Didn't get a good look but probably stripers, maybe bass. Some of the fishing boats have sonar *sorta* like this . . . but even better. They find where the schools are, plant their boats right over them, and surround them fish with nets. And suddenly—it's Christmas."

Billy looked up, the island to his left. Hard to judge the distance, but a mile away, maybe more?

"We near the spot?"

"Just about. *Gonna* slow the boat down and start a back-and-forth sweep with *Sally*. Mind you, no promises. Could do this for a few hours and find nothing."

Billy nodded.

"So, you keep your eyes on the screen too while I steer and look. More eyes the merrier."

Then Billy—since they were up there, the boat now moving slowly—had a question.

"So, you related to Humphries? I mean, this operation, the boat. Now yours?"

Willits gave him a look.

"Yeah. See, when I left the Navy SEALs . . ."

Interesting bit of information . . .

"Wasn't sure *what* the hell I was going to do. But I was in the SEALs' tactical dive team. Not much under the water that we didn't do."

Billy nodded.

"Someone said . . . well, North Fork. Long Island. Lots of commercial dive operations. Which actually turned out to be . . . not true. Recreational dive boats, sure. Some of that. But that wasn't my thing. Why anyone would dive *recreationally* in these damn murky waters is beyond me."

"So—you came and found Humphries?"

"Yeah. He was, er, getting a bit old when I came. Health not all that good. Had some young fellow who helped him out from time to time. But that kid, well, not reliable. He liked my background. I kinda took over things, at least the real search and recovery part. Stayed like that for a while . . ."

"Until Humphries, what, retired? Got sick?"

"Well, guy like that wouldn't know what the word *retire* meant. But one day, guess, heart attack, maybe a stroke? Came back, and he was sitting in his office, head down."

"And the operation? How'd you—"

"Turned out that he had his lawyer down in Riverhead draw up a new will just a month earlier. Never told me. Guess he had a feeling that his clock was ticking . . ."

"Left it all to you?"

"Yup. That he did."

The boat had chugged so that the island was now behind them. Willits pulled back on the throttle, had the boat do a wobbly turn, waves smacking against the sides, to now head in the opposite direction.

"Right. Nothing on *that* run. But then—we're just getting started, hmm? Could be . . . *a long afternoon . . .*"

And Billy just kept looking at the screen, the bottom showing changes in shape, the depth shifting too according to the window in the right corner. More schools of fish flitting by.

But as to something *there*, obviously sitting on the bottom? *No. Nothing at all like that . . .*

Billy had looked away in the distance. *Sweet Sally* was heading out to the open ocean, a dozen gulls or more accompanying the boat, diving and dipping as if enjoying the awareness that—*what the hell*—they could fly.

When Willits tapped the screen.

"Hang on."

And before Billy could look down, back to the screen he was supposed to be monitoring, Willits had thrown the boat into neutral.

"Well, *there's* something."

For a moment, Billy couldn't see it. But then he noticed the slope of the ground on the screen, and yes . . . something, right in the middle of the screen now . . . but drifting to the side as the boat's momentum carried it farther along.

Indeed—*something.*

"Could that be—?"

"Tell you this, Billy Blessing. What we are looking at—right there— is *not* a natural feature of the floor. Something just stuck there, like it landed in the middle of that gentle slope."

"A body?"

"Ha. Could be almost anything. Something someone dumped, heavy, sunk to the bottom. But—"

Now Willits leaned close, his face floating right on top of the screen.

"I'd *say* the size of the object, length . . . over six feet. Can't really tell the width, but certainly looks wide enough"—he turned to Billy— "for a body."

And this moment, for Billy, was suddenly quite exciting. The missing man was just a name to him. Then a boat riddled with bullets. Could this be him? And if found, what would it mean?

Lots to think about.

Billy asked a question: "What now?"

"Ha. Time to go down and look at it. And see . . . *what we see* . . ."

Willits moved past him, hurrying down the staircase to the boat deck. And not knowing what else to do, Billy followed.

▷

Willits lowered an anchor, saying, "Depth about fifty feet. We probably have drifted a little far from the object, whatever the hell it is. But I'll anchor us here, then get ready."

And when the anchor was placed—Willits testing it by yanking on the thick line to make sure the fluked anchor had dug into the bottom—Billy saw the captain of the boat disappear into the ship's cabin belowdecks.

And in minutes, Willits came out, only now dressed in a puffy red suit, not like any dive outfit Billy had seen from any television show or movie.

In his hand was a small helmet with tubes and wires.

"You're diving in *that*?" Billy asked.

"Yes. *A dry suit.* Keeps me nice and dry and—with the water already getting cold out here—warm as well."

He held up the helmet.

"This has a radio. Up there, you will be able to see what I see—and I can talk to you. C'mon—let me show you."

In a second, they were back up in the wheelhouse. The captain pointed to another monitor, flicking it on, and Billy saw that it showed the wooden floor of the wheelhouse and then, when Willits moved it, the ship's controls.

Right. This . . . the view from his helmet's camera.

"As I said, everything I see, you will too. But got to tell you, water here?" Willits laughed. "*Ain't Jamaica, mon!* I mean—I was born there, so I *know* . . ."

Another interesting tidbit about Willits, but Billy took it to mean visibility would be bad.

"Still. I'll get as close as I can. Oh—" Willits nodded to a speaker over the control panel. "You'll hear me—right here. And the mic on the monitor will pick up any, er, observations you might have."

Billy nodded as he could only think of the expression, perhaps appropriate here, *I feel like a fish out of water.*

Then Willits made his away down again; this time the few steps were a little tricky in the bulky suit.

Billy watched as Willits slipped on a vest where he had placed a tank on the back. He turned some knobs, none of this anything Billy understood. But Willits was treating it like he was getting his twelve-speed bike ready to go for a leisurely ride.

Then, putting the vest on and buckling it, Willits gave it a few tugs to settle it into position. Then he sat down on the bench in front of three tanks.

He already wore booties on both feet, tight all the way up to above his ankles. But now he pulled on a pair of neon-blue fins, each with a dramatic curve, a wedge of bright neon plastic that Billy guessed made them really efficient at propelling someone through the water.

He watched Willits look down at some gauges, nodding to them as if reassured that all was well.

Then he looked up.

"Okay—here we go. Back to the monitor, and *we are off . . .*"

Willits grinned as if this—all looking so complicated to Billy—was just too much fun.

Then Willits put on the helmet, with the clear plexiglass mask showing his full face. More fastening of straps around the neck.

His next words were muffled through the mask. "C'mon. Get into position. Time to go."

Billy went back to the wheelhouse, quickly taking the steps. And when he was up there, he could see what Willits could. He watched as Willits made his way to the back of the boat, near the winch, and sat down.

"Hear me okay?" the voice said through the speaker.

"Yes. Hear you fine."

"Okay then—*down I go.*"

And for this Billy glanced backward as Willits leaned backward, tumbling head over heels into the choppy water. He could see Willits's head bob up to the surface and wait a moment.

And then—the proprietor of Humphries Search and Recovery disappeared below the surface.

Now Billy turned to the monitor, which showed exactly what Willits could see. In the corner of a screen, a small box tracked the descent.

But Billy could immediately see the problem.

There was nothing to see.

Or rather, nothing that he *could* see.

But then he did spot something, barely discernible; Willits was looking down at an illuminated gauge dangling off his suit. Billy could just make that out in the murky water. Looked like it showed the depth and the remaining air in the tank. Willits let the gauge, tethered to his diving vest, fall to the side.

Then, his right hand came up; a look at a watch. Obviously, a special dive watch, redundantly showing the same information. Depth, air—but also time elapsed.

Billy checked the depth reading on the monitor. Twenty feet, then thirty feet, then forty feet. The numbers on the gauge then slowed as Willits must have started easing up on his descent.

He had to admit, this whole diving thing, maybe next time in really warm blue water, with incredible visibility? *Worth checking out.*

Though as *Sweet Sally* rocked on the white-capped sea now, he thought it was not something he'd ever pursue here.

"Almost to the bottom, Billy. I guess we may have drifted . . . twenty, thirty yards or so? Going to have to do some exploring down here. Soon as I can make out the damn bottom."

"Gotcha," Billy said.

He wondered, Was there a special lingo for acknowledging a transmission from someone under the water? Roger? Ten-four?

Then Billy now could, at least, *just* make out some things . . . glimpses of Willits's gloved hands as they paddled slowly through the water. But also, when Willits tilted his head and looked down, the dull brown color of what must be the sandy bottom. Occasionally a broken shell could be seen. Nothing alive, though.

Least not yet.

He remembered that, during the past summer, there had been a bunch of shark incidents reported near the island's beaches. Even a great white or two.

What fun . . .

Billy went back to the small screen on the monitor, which also told the direction Willits was slowly propelling himself—right now showing between north and northwest, heading 330 degrees.

North by Northwest, Billy thought. Hitchcock could certainly pick a good title for a film . . .

But so far . . . nothing popped up on the view of the bottom, and Billy realized that real hunting for whatever sat on that bottom was occurring right down there now, fifty feet below him.

"Hmm. *Thinkin'* . . . we might have drifted a bit farther than I thought." Willits voice came through the speaker as clear and as close as if he were in the wheelhouse with Billy.

"Can you look at the sonar screen, Billy? I dropped a pin with the coordinates of where we saw the object."

Billy had the feeling he was being asked to do something he wasn't at all qualified for. But he *could* see that the screen showed—in the upper right—something that read "Site One," then what must be the coordinates, a string of digits.

Billy read them out.

"Okay, now—look at the monitor. What are *my* damn coordinates?"

Billy did the same. The difference between them seemed incredibly small.

"Okay *good, good.* Gives me an idea. I'll find it. Might take a bit of back-and-forth. But at this pretty shallow depth, got plenty of air, plenty of time . . ."

And then Billy went back to watching the search . . . The whole process was gripping.

▷

Until he noticed . . . the view on the screen, just now . . . changed. Willits looked up. And beside the dull gray of the sandy bottom, something else. A blurry shape. Just ahead.

"*Bingo*, my friend. Got it."

Billy had to lean close. The visibility was so bad, but this—so exciting.

And all he could really see was some dark shape sitting on the silty seafloor bottom. But it could be anything. He wished Willits would get closer since it would take him looking just inches away to really see it . . .

And then—that is what Willits did.

"Okay, Billy Blessing. Think we have something there. Maybe—a little clearer for me down here. But not much."

Then Billy saw Willits extend his hand. Touch the shape. And then begin to move *side to side*, using his hand to confirm what might be inside what—Billy assumed—was a kind of body bag.

Holding Landry? Who had been up to this point . . . just someone unknown, his boat maybe not being the only thing that had taken some bullets.

As Willits hovered over the bag, he edged backward, his hands like tentacles, touching here and there. Not saying anything.

Billy wanted to ask the simple question . . . *Well?* But he waited patiently, letting Willits do what he had to.

Until he could see Willits's right hand move up again, as if double-checking something.

Was there some doubt, Billy wondered? Maybe *not* a body at all? Some heavy trash or junk thrown overboard? In which case, this exciting and interesting field trip under the water would have been pointless.

Again Willits, now with both hands feeling, pressed down hard enough that he kicked up some of the silty sea bottom—which completely obscured any possibility of seeing *anything*.

And then—Willits spoke.

His voice sounding . . . what? Surprised, perhaps? Maybe even shaken.

"Okay, Billy. As they always say, got good news and then, well, whether the other chunk of news maybe isn't good, that will be for you to decide."

Meaning: Willits's examination of the bag had revealed something.

"Yeah. What is it?"

"Definitely a body in this bag here. And some things added for weight. Could feel them too. Rocks, whatever. But you see—and here's the unexpected but, I guess? From your perspective?"

"What?"

"Turns out, right here, fifty feet down? There are—in fact—*two bodies* . . ."

And at that—Billy had absolutely nothing to say. That Louis Prima song came to mind: "'Cause I ain't got *nobody*. Oh, and there's nobody that cares for me."

Well, we got a body and one to spare.

THREE

THE PLAYERS COME OUT TO PLAY

23
UNEXPECTED VISITORS

Willits waited before saying anything else.

The proprietor of the Humphries Search and Recovery operation, when it came to understanding what he found . . . clearly found this discovery confusing and unsettling.

But after a bit, he said, "Look, Billy. I still got plenty of air. Which means *time*, you know? Can do whatever you want me to. This is on your dime. I can come up, though, bring down a line, hook the winch up to this bag containing whoever the two people are inside."

He paused.

"And bring them up. Though—that may have legal, um, implications?"

Billy was thinking, mind racing now. This was *unsettling*, to say the least. And he hadn't really thought through the next step, at least not clearly. Namely: What would he do if Willits found something?

Now this.

But he had to make a decision. After all, there was a person hovering deep down there, waiting for instructions.

"Okay, Ted. Got a question . . ."

"Shoot."

"Can you mark where the—"

First time Billy used the words . . .

"—the bodies are? So you can come find them, get them *at any time?*"

"Yup. Do it all the time. Um. I mean with things I find. Generally, though—*not* corpses."

Some Vegas-style comedy? With bodies in play? Right . . .

Willits here till Thursday, folks, two shows a night. Oh—and try the veal!

Funny guy.

Though Billy was in no mood to laugh.

"Okay. So just come back up. Mark the spot on your sonar, however you do that. So, when the time comes, we can tell . . . dunno . . . Chief Bristow, the Coast Guard . . . whoever will be handling this mess, this—"

He didn't use the word *murder*. Though that word certainly made sense.

"*Gotcha.* Just leave them sleeping here and head back to the dock? That the idea?"

"You got it."

"Okay. Pretty sure that violates some rule or code for people like me. But—never was much one for following rules."

Billy laughed at that. "Me either. Okay—see you in a bit."

And at that, on the camera monitor, Billy watched the seafloor and the body bag with two corpses . . . *disappear.* Now to see just the shroud of the murky water.

Billy thought: *This is important.* But he actually knew nothing about it. Didn't even know for sure that Jack Landry was one of the bodies down there.

But he also knew, once brought to the surface, well then . . . whatever it was he was doing here would be all over.

And this part he didn't really understand clearly—he wasn't quite ready to do that.

So many questions. And well, he had just *started* to get answers. And maybe, *just for a while longer*, he should continue doing just that.

And he realized: it wasn't about the promised money. The hope of getting back some of what he'd lost.

No. This was about people doing really bad things. And Billy—just the way he was wired?—wanting answers.

So, that decision made, that *understanding*—if that's what it was—reached . . . he went to one side of the boat and waited for Willits to bob to the surface.

$$\triangleright$$

For a few moments, Billy thought that something might be wrong when Willits didn't quickly come to the surface.

But soon he made out a blurry shape below the water, and then Willits's head was above the surface of the choppy water.

Willits gave a thumbs-up as he surfaced—Billy guessed maybe that was something divers did. And he watched Willits paddle over to the metal platform on the back of the boat, pull himself up, and sit.

Then he took his headgear off and turned to Billy.

The man smiled. "How about a nice cold Corona?" Billy went to the cooler and pulled out two beers.

When he came back, Willits had his fins off and had also undone his vest, which held the tank; his weight belt was off too.

Billy unscrewed his bottle along with Willits's.

"So, before we get going. Heading back?"

"Yeah?"

"I've been at this a long time."

"And never found a body under the water?"

The man smiled at that. "Oh, no, done *that* plenty times before. You know, boating and accidents kinda go together. Especially"—he tilted his beer bottle back and forth—"when you add a lot of *these.*"

Willits turned, looked at him.

"But, never found *two* bodies, together. Yup, that's a first. And second, well, I *always* bring the unfortunate corpse up."

"You will. I imagine. Eventually. Just now—"

Willits nodded. "Yeah, I *get* it. Right now, all that isn't helpful for whatever the hell you are looking into."

"Kinda."

"But before we get going, I'd be—what's the word?—*remiss* if I didn't tell you. What's down there, all neatly weighted and bagged up . . . ?"

"Uh-huh."

"Think . . . you want to make *real* sure that you don't become just like them. Just a little"—Willits grinned—"um, a little warning?"

To which Billy said, "Getting a lot of those these days . . ."

"Okay. Let me get out of this suit—and back we go."

Willits sat down, unzipping the bulky dry suit as he turned for one more thing . . .

"By the way—for now?—my lips are sealed."

"Good. Appreciate—"

But Willits shot up a hand.

"*For now.* People come asking questions. Dunno. Police. The Coast Guard. Maybe even other people . . ."

Billy could guess who he was talking about. Namely the people who put those bodies down there.

"Well then, may have to eventually say what I saw, you know? Just so you know . . ."

Billy nodded at that. "Got it. I mean, is that even Jack Landry down there?"

"Good point. We can only . . . *surmise.*"

Willits peeled off his suit, sun already low in the sky. The chop in the water was kicking up even more.

But Billy had to think: bullet holes in the man's boat. Body bag down below?

He was a good chef, and while not great at math, he was pretty sure this added up to Landry being one of those bodies.

Yet—two big pieces of the equation were unanswered:

Why? And who was the other body down there?

24

A RIDE IN THE NIGHT

As Billy pulled away in his Cherokee from the small shack housing Willits's dive operation, declining the offer of something stronger than a
beer, the sky had already started showing hints of purple in the west.

And he thought he'd swing by the Northold Police Station. Be good
to tell all this to someone he trusted, namely Chief Bristow, who had
steered him to the dive operator.

He got to Route 25, cars coming at a steady stream from both
ends—whatever passed for a rush hour out here—with this, the main
road from Riverhead to Orient Point, turning really busy.

Looking for a spot to pull out fast, and then to cut left . . . not easy.

Then, a gap, and he gunned his Cherokee—but not before someone heading from his left had seen the gap and (*such a considerate move*)
raced ahead of him.

Lot of aggressive driving out here, he had noted.

But then, Billy had barely driven much in NYC. And in LA—when
he was out there. That place had its own rules and nightmare traffic
scenarios.

So—the bit of dash and dare required here, *not too bad*.

He rolled into Northold, hoping that the chief was still in her office.

▷

He slowed and pulled into a space next to the small post office, just beside Rocco's deli.

Popular place. Which reminded Billy: yup, a little hungry. Maybe a stop there before heading home.

He was just about to pop open the door to get out, dodge the steady stream of traffic on foot, and race to the police station across the street . . . *when he noticed something.*

A car, parked right in front of the station.

Just a moment's hesitation, but Billy told himself . . . *slow down.*

That car looked out of place with all the 4x4s here, the SUVs, the pickup trucks—the mix of suburban vehicles used to ferry kids and the pickup workhorses necessary for the hard dawn-to-dusk work of the farms, fisheries, and wineries out here.

This car was a very large, black sedan. He couldn't—at this angle—make out anything to indicate which brand . . . Audi, Cadillac, Lexus? Other than it was one big and serious car. Windows tinted deep black.

Of course.

And here it was, parked right outside the police station.

Billy, having shut the engine off, lights too . . . simply sat there.

Sure. Curious. About the car. But really his instincts were saying . . . *Something odd about this.*

So—he waited.

He could make out shapes in the window, probably near the chief's desk sergeant.

But then another shape, someone taller. He debated just going in there anyway; maybe it was just a wealthy sometime resident who had missed the signal that, with summer over, it was time to flee back to the big city—complaining about *whatever* to the local authority . . .

And as he watched, he heard someone tapping on the passenger-side window. Billy turned to see an old guy, gray hair sticking out at odd angles as if a firecracker had sent the strands scattering.

The man's beard long ago had turned equally mangy and confused.

Certainly not a customer Billy would have seen at NoFo Eats.

Billy waved him away, guessing the fellow had spent an hour or two too long at the Lighthouse Bar, the one genuine gin mill in town that served those who worked the farms and wineries and those with more "leisure time," who treated it as a second home.

But when the man rapped again, Billy hit a button to lower the window.

"You—you . . . okay, fella? *Been sitting here a while?*"

Billy nodded but also looked across the street. This distraction—and calling attention to Billy—*not great*.

"I'm fine. Just waiting for, er, someone."

The man nodded, digesting this—to him—complex bit of information.

"Just me *seein'* you here, thought maybe you needed some help?" The grizzled man looked up. "Seeing as you're across from our local police station? Y'know. If you *are* needin' any help, bet our chief could help."

The man's persistence was getting more than wearing.

But Billy put on his best smile. "Hey, I do appreciate that. Really! Just need to sit here for a while. You know?"

Billy doubted that the man *did*, but eventually, he nodded, pulled back from the window.

"Alrighty then. Always want to check that people are doin' okay. I remember once—"

Billy kept his smile plastered on, gave the man a thumbs-up, and raised the window, cutting off whatever tale he was beginning.

For a second, Billy looked straight ahead. Not sure if he had deterred any further intervention from this local character, well "into his cups," as the expression went.

But then the man stood up as straight as he could manage, turned, and sailed on down the street. For whatever additional adventures lay ahead.

And when that moment passed, Billy quickly turned back to the station across the street . . .

Where—just now—the station door opened.

▷

A man came out. Billy saw him look left and right quickly, a move that signaled he was checking if he was seen. Then fast—to the big sedan, engine quickly started, lights on.

Billy slumped down a bit more in his seat. The driver of the car— in a black suit, in a town where you did *not* see many people in suits ever—might be curious about someone watching him.

But the sedan eased out and then did a sharp U-turn, an unusual break in the traffic briefly allowing the maneuver.

And then it pulled away fast, heading in the direction of River-head.

Billy sat there thinking . . . *Well—just who the* hell *was that?*

Somebody who looked like they had been plucked off the streets of Midtown Manhattan.

For some reason, here for a chat with Bristow?

So now he tried to evaluate his plan to share with Bristow what he'd found.

Because, seeing this? Was there something *else* going on here, what with Lola Bristow helping him so much?

And whatever he decided, he knew there was a limited time on it. Bristow would want to know what—if anything—was found out in the bay.

Of course, Billy could lie.

But would that hold up?

Willits's promise of staying quiet—not the most secure of guar-antees.

But he knew this: someone very much out of the ordinary had just visited the local police chief.

And as for Billy, his guard was up.

He started his car. Had to be something in his freezer at home that he could cook.

Sure. For now, he just wanted *to get away* . . .

▷

Billy's phone buzzed as he pulled up to his cottage. The place was dark, no lights on, Billy forgetting that he'd be getting back at sunset.

He scanned the name before hitting the green dot on the screen. *Gretchen Di Voss.*

As he unlocked the door, he said, "Gretchen."

"Billy—you sitting down? Think you're going to absolutely *love* the deal they are putting together. I emailed you all the details. Still some things to work out . . ."

Billy turned a living room lamp on and kept moving into the kitchen.

"Yeah. Guess . . . good to hear."

"*Better* than good. But here's the thing: they want to get moving on this thing *now*. The big investor wants to waste no time."

"Now? Sorry. Bit late on the day."

"You know what I mean . . ."

He pulled open the freezer door to see a few chicken cutlets. Quick defrost, bread fry—and voilà—a quick schnitzel.

Glass of white wine would be nice. A chilled Picpoul was waiting. Been a crazy day . . .

Gretchen continued: "Yeah—so they'd want you to come in Friday night. Big network event planned. All the execs, the top talent. A sort of party to get new things launched, and now including all the big plans for you. Cocktails and all that. At the Park Avenue Club. Off Fifty-Fourth Street. Know it? Sure you do, right?"

Billy put the phone on speaker and set it down on the counter as he unwrapped the cutlets.

He thought of what he was involved with here, out on the North Fork. *Hmm. Let me check my to-do list.* Bullets? Check. Bodies? Check.

Mysterious strangers in town? Check. And squeeze in a visit to Manhattan to launch a big streaming network. Alrighty then.

Tempting.

"Yeah. Been to the club a time or two. But not sure I can do that, Gretchen. I mean, all very appealing. Why the mad rush? Thought in the world of TV, everything takes so much time?"

"Nope. Not with this new money guy involved, this Tony Hill? Lots of interest all over the place. He was very specific about wanting you on board immediately, at the event. Anyway, what's keeping you out there?"

Ah—how to answer that? Certainly not the truth.

"I have a few obligations. Look. I may be able to take care of those, maybe I can let you know tomorrow? Gives me time to check the deal that you say is on the table?"

"You'll love it."

"And your lawyer friend . . . ?"

"Larry Schaefer. Yes, sent him the deal memo. He's going over it. On your behalf, of course."

"*Of course.* Okay, so let me see how things go here."

"With your so-called obligations?"

He laughed. "Yes. *Exactly.* Talk tomorrow?"

"Okay, Billy—but please remember: some opportunities you have to catch when they are there. When gone, they're—"

"Gone?"

"*You got it.* Talk soon."

At that, Gretchen ended the call, and Billy went back to his simple meal, starting with a defrosting turn in the microwave for the rock-hard cutlets.

There's something about an uncomplicated meal, he thought.

No amazing sauces. Just some fresh salad greens with a quick vinaigrette, the cutlets breaded and simply crisped to a very nice golden brown. Another glass of the Picpoul, which was —without getting carried away—a perfect pairing for the meal.

Nice and quiet—but then . . . another call.

An unknown caller. But all things considered—since he usually let such calls go straight to voicemail—this time Billy answered.

"Billy? Lisa Cowles."

"Lisa," Billy said, knowing that wasn't her name.

But as long as we are playing, let's pretend . . .

"Told you . . . wanted to check in. You call me, or I call you . . . ?"

"Right. I remember that."

"And so, what have you learned?"

Billy had expected—sooner or later—she would call. Now he had to think: how to give her an edited version of all that he *had* learned.

Since he didn't have a damn idea who this woman really was . . . or even her supposed father, Jack Landry.

So, he told her about the wrecked boat, speculation about an accident, about checking the man's cottage . . . but not about any bullet holes or the wall safe.

For good measure, he added that he had asked someone in Greenport whether there had been any interest in the disappearing man.

Omitting that said man was no longer among the living.

And this bit of information "Lisa" did not like at all.

"You did *what*? I don't remember telling you . . . to get *others* involved?"

Billy took a breath. Not exactly an unexpected response. All things considered.

"I know. But just trying to see . . . what I can see? I mean, you do want me doing all that I can, right?"

That gave the woman pause. Then—she seemed to ease.

"Okay. But no more of that, got it? And we will speak again . . . another day or so? I'm depending on you, Billy Blessing. To learn exactly what happened . . ."

And that made Bill feel weird indeed since he now already knew so much more than he was saying.

But he just said, "You got it."

To which Lisa said, "Good," and then simply ended the call.

Billy took a sip of the still-cool wine.

He was halfway done, catching up with email, texts . . .

Nothing further from Detective Solomon. And as Di Voss had said, the deal—as he saw in the email from Worldwide—was very good indeed.

When he heard the sound of a car moving slowly.

He cocked his head in the direction of the narrow road outside.

The car was barely moving, accompanied by the steady crunch of gravel and twigs as it went down the lane at a crawl.

Until it stopped.

He dabbed at his lips. Thinking: *hmm—a car has just stopped outside.*

And by now, with all that he knew and *didn't know*, the car and whoever was in it could be absolutely anybody.

Not for the first time, Billy thought—especially after seeing the police chief and whoever the hell she was seeing—*Am I now officially in over my head?*

He got up, thinking, *Someone stopped outside.* Yes, a car stopped. Maybe soon a knock, and he'd have to see who was paying him a night-time visit.

But that didn't happen . . .

Billy had stood up and started to the front door when that door was kicked open as if whoever was on the other side didn't know how to use a door handle, let alone knock.

Shards of wood from the frame went flying as the battered door banged against the living room wall.

And two very large men walked in. Each of them, he noted, held a gun, and each gun was pointed straight at him.

"It's open. Why don't you come in."

But one man, shorter, stockier, and with a rough, rumpled face that looked like this was not his first rodeo—least when it came to breaking in and pointing a gun at someone—spoke. His voice like sandpaper.

"Funny guy, Blessing. Just like on TV, huh?"

Well, at least this guy has watched me, so there's that. Of course, he was holding a gun, so might not be a fan.

The short, stocky man—clearly the more verbal of the two—forced a smile onto his craggy face.

His associate just kept his dark, dead eyes locked on him.

Then Billy thought of Danny Pippo, no longer among the living. And then the two bodies under the sea, one possibly Landry, the other— who knows?

And now, *two men with guns.*

And what had seemed an interesting problem to help someone out with, Billy realized, could have—just now—turned personal and deadly.

So, he said, as casually as such a tense moment would allow, "How can I help you two gentlemen?"

The shorter guy took a step forward, but not before signaling to his partner to move to the side, checking the cottage for, well . . . *who knew what.*

Then he said, "You're coming with us. A little ride."

That—did not sound good.

Billy tilted his head back to his unfinished meal. "Ah, right. I was, er, just in the middle of dinner. Wonder if—"

"You're coming *now.*"

At that, the taller gunman went to a coat rack where Billy kept a light jacket. Soon to be replaced by heavier and heavier coats as the North Fork, pointing right to the Atlantic, faced its brutal winter.

The man took the coat and tossed it to Billy.

"Put it on, and let's *go.*"

Billy acceded to the request, zipping the jacket up. Then he turned back to the table, assuming dinner was, in fact, over. Went to grab his phone.

"Uh-uh. Leave the damn phone."

Billy's hand froze as he considered an argument in protest.

The man made his revolver do a small circle, signaling *hurry up.*

"You won't need it."

Then again that disturbing smile on that craggy face.

"And no worries. You'll be back soon enough to get all caught up, call the girlfriend—"

"Don't have one of those currently."

Then, niceties over, the man simply muttered, "C'mon—time to go."

And Billy nodded. When two men with guns said something like that . . . he knew it was best to listen.

▷

The shorter guy nodded to Billy to get into the back seat of the car, a giant Escalade.

Gun still out, of course. The tall guy got in front to drive.

"Ready?" he said, looking to the back seat.

His partner said, "One minute."

He pulled out an eye shade. Handed it to Billy.

"Put it on."

"That's okay," Billy said. "I'd rather see where I am going."

To which the guy sitting beside him jabbed him with the gun.

"On the other hand, who needs the distractions of direction and landmarks." Billy slipped the eye shade on, the fit snug—and then couldn't see a thing.

The car's throaty engine started up, and then Billy felt the vehicle slowly pull away, back onto the narrow lane beside his cottage.

And he thought: *Where are these two goons taking me? Is there anything I can do to change the situation?*

Especially the goon beside him with the gun still pressing against his left side.

And the worse question of all: *What's going to happen to me?*

▷

The car rolled on, the two men in silence, save when the guy up front took a call, hitting a button on the steering column, the voice through the speaker.

"You on your way?"

"Yeah. Heading back now."

The voice was flat. No hellos between these two.

"No stops. Straight here. Got it?"

Billy couldn't hear the other part of the call. Then: "Right," the driver said. "Probably there in an hour and a half."

The call went dead.

Billy started to think . . . an hour and a half, not quite enough time to get back to the city. *So where was he being taken?*

He put his right hand up to scratch his nose.

"Er—don't do that," the guy squatted next to him said.

"My nose itches."

"Let it"—this now reinforced with another jab of the gun—"itch. Don't touch the blindfold."

Billy nodded, sat back, and settled in for the long ride to somewhere. Where something would happen. And he guessed it would not be good.

▷

Billy thought about his childhood, reading all those Sherlock Holmes stories. The great detective could deduce where he was going by feeling the vibrations of his conveyance. The sounds, the twists and turns. A set of railway tracks here; the scent of manure there. And nothing. Sherlock rode in hansom cabs. This was a well-insulated, cushy SUV. So, to try to keep his mind off what was to come, he slept.

But as time slipped by, his tension rose; sleep became impossible. Then, when he just couldn't resist . . .

"Dad, are we there yet?"

And to that classic question, obviously not triggering any fond memories of family road trips in the gunman beside him, the short guy said, "What? Are you freakin' ten years old? We get there when we get there."

Well, thought Billy, *I* did *ask.*

But he knew this: the minutes were slipping away. And perhaps some of the questions he had would be answered. And those answers might be unfortunate.

Then, the vehicle slowed. Made some short turns, indicating that it was weaving its way through some small streets. The guy beside him had cracked his window, lit a cigarette. And Billy didn't protest since he was sure it would fall on deaf ears.

But then, when the smoke was finished, flicked out to the street, Billy guessed, another smell.

Salty. The undeniable scent of the ocean.

And that at least was a clue where they had taken him . . . somewhere on the Atlantic coast.

And if they went far enough along, they would reach the South Fork of the island, a place where rock stars, politicians, and just unbelievably wealthy people built seaside fortresses on the beach to face the ocean.

Eat your heart out, Sherlock.

The car stopped.

The sound of the front window coming down. Then the driver spoke: "We're here."

And—the car still not moving—Billy heard a mechanical sound, a kind of whirring. For a minute, he didn't know what it was.

But then he realized . . . a gate of some kind was opening.

Great. I'm being taken at gunpoint to a place behind a gate. A big metal gate, from the sound of things.

And when the whirring stopped, the car began moving again; now he heard the sound of gravel as the tires rolled over whatever path was on the other side of the gate.

Billy took a breath. He imagined, at least, some of his questions would soon be answered.

Not at all sure he wanted that . . .

25
END OF THE ROAD?

As Billy got out, he was hit again with the strong smell of the sea. He even could hear waves crashing in the distance. This unseen place he was being taken to must be right at the ocean's edge.

Now both the goons, one on either side of him, were each holding an arm.

"Careful. Steps ahead."

Billy nodded. A bit of light hit his eyes from a gap at the top of the eye mask. But nothing that he could make out.

"First step," the man beside him growled.

He thought about making a joke about how considerate his two escorts were being. But so far, they had not shown any appreciation of humor . . .

"Two more," the man said.

Then strangely—since it was night, by the sea, chilly—Billy felt warmth.

A door being opened as his two escorts guided him forward and into whatever place he was being taken to . . .

▷

In minutes, after Billy was guided straight ahead and then to the left, the eye mask was removed. And then he could finally see where he was.

This room . . . like some classic club in London, polished wood everywhere, large leather chairs around a giant coffee table in a teardrop shape, shaped like a mammoth tear. Mahogany, Billy guessed. Dark, glistening.

And paintings on the wall. Again, classic. Ships braving a roaring Atlantic. Then images that—he could be wrong—looked like Gauguin's work from Tahiti.

God—could they be originals?

Someone copying his style? Or the genuine—and priceless—article?

A large brick fireplace with a black wrought-iron grill. Fire on. After all, turning chilly out.

So cozy too. Save for the unwanted ride, and the gun jammed hard against his ribs.

But what made this remarkable living room—this parlor—totally unlike a classic club room from a centuries-old building in London were the windows.

And not just *windows*. These went completely from ceiling to floor. Drapes to the far left and right, but right now, open. Outside, the sea. And in case darkness got in the way of the view on a moonless night, lights from somewhere on this building were aimed *just* at the spot where the waves crashed.

He had to wonder: Could those lights *move*, tracking the rise and fall of the sea, keeping the breaking waves and all that churning white water lit up?

Then a thought . . . *Such a beautiful place but . : . is something very bad about to happen to me here?*

He turned to his two escorts.

"Um, good. Nice place, but a little out of my price range, I imagine."

That—as he expected—had neither of them cracking a smile. But the short goon ordered, "Take a seat."

And, of course, remembering that the two men were indeed well armed, Billy looked around, all the leather chairs oversize and welcoming, and walked over to one with the best view of the sea.

After all, might as well enjoy it.

▷

Then, a side door opened. Actually—a double door, its two panels sliding right and left.

Another man walked out. His dress well matched the room—and Billy imagined, this house itself, wherever it was.

Crisp gray slacks, sharp crease. Polished loafers, no socks. *Is that still a thing?* Billy wondered. A blue striped shirt, with two or three top buttons open.

The sleeves were rolled up to show substantial, tanned forearms, in case anyone thought this was some porky businessman who just lucked into whatever bundle of cash bought this mansion.

"Oh, good. You're *here*. And no one offered you a drink?"

Billy smiled at the man and, gesturing toward the two gunsels, said, "Alfred and Jeeves here didn't offer any refreshments."

"Ah, well. *I'm* here now. What will it be? Did my research. Think you have always been a whiskey and bourbon fan—yes, Billy Blessing? With also a taste for the occasional peaty single malt?"

So, Billy thought, *he knows who I am. And not just my name.* Billy was about to decline but then felt, well, maybe he should just go along for now. After all, what other options did he have?

"Right. A good bourbon on the rocks will be fine. Thanks."

The man nodded, and the short goon went to a cabinet, opened it, revealing an elaborate bar with rows of bottles. He saw the man pick a bottle of Maker's Mark.

Then Billy hazarded a question: "I'm afraid you have me at a disadvantage. You know my name. But I—"

"Right. *Curious*, are we? Well—you see, curiosity and perhaps a touch of greed has brought you to this juncture."

So far, still no name forthcoming.

"Afraid you won't have any need of my name. After all, blindfolded you could be anywhere, yes?"

Billy tilted his head to the sea outside. "As long as it's by the ocean."

The host, at least, smiled at that.

"*Right.* As I said, *anywhere.* And you have never seen me before. Let me give you a bit of advice . . ."

The short goon brought over a hefty crystal tumbler with ice and more than the traditional two fingers of bourbon.

"You *don't* want to know me. Or see me again. But I thought for this first—and last—encounter best you hear from me the way things will go . . . *from here on out.*"

Billy had to guess that this all had something to do with his looking into Landry, the dead bodies, the mystery bank accounts. But what?

He was miles away from having any idea.

"I have brought you here so I could emphasize, without any necessary, um, physical reminders"—a glance to the waiting goons—"what *you* are going to do, Billy Blessing. You see, word spreads fast, especially when it appears there is a lot of money involved. And when I say . . . 'a lot,' I mean a *lot.*"

The man walked over to the bar cabinet himself. Took a red wine glass, examined it, poured a glass.

"So—to begin, I need you to tell me what you have done in this little . . . adventure of yours . . . so far. And I do mean *everything.* I would strongly suggest you leave no detail out."

A big grin was on the man's face. Billy thought, *Yeah, this guy's no successful wealth manager or broker.*

His money definitely came from other means.

"You see, bit of a warning? You won't know what I already know—and what I don't. You got that?"

Billy took a moment. And while the opening was ripe for a bit of banter with this very wealthy and probably powerful, most likely dangerous man, Billy guessed the comedy might be lost on this guy.

And since he had avoided being roughed up so far, best to start talking.

As to how far he got with that, well . . . . *that* he would decide on the fly.

26

THE DEAL ON THE TABLE

"I assume," Billy began, "you mean my looking into the disappearance of that old guy on his boat. Jack Landry?"

As he began, Billy had to remind himself that so far—for anyone keeping score—there had been three dead bodies connected to whatever was going on here.

Two under the water, weighted down and neatly zipped up in a bag. And Danny Pippo, who turned out to have an incredibly short shelf life, least as far as snitches went.

So—the mental note, clear, simple: *let's not add one more.*

And the host, now seated in a matching leather chair, facing him, nodded.

Billy wondered: *Does he know that the name Landry is a creation?* The real identity was still unknown, at least to Billy.

He wondered whether this man sitting across from him knew that real name.

But he guessed, this meeting . . . information would be going *one way* only.

"So, Billy Blessing—we have only two requirements for this little meeting here. *You* tell me what you have found out so far. And do be careful? Then before you leave, I will—"

He looked to the short goon still standing guard at the entryway.

"Bruno, the phone?"

At that, the goon who now had a name—Bruno—slipped a phone out of his pocket, certainly not the latest iPhone whatever. Bruno brought it over to the man in the chair, who still did *not* have a name.

"This is what is called a 'burner phone,' hmm? Disposable. But certain things have been done to it, so it is untraceable, as in . . . who's the owner, where it is located, *anything at all*." The man smiled. "I will give you a phone number. And this will be the phone you use. When you call me."

"Um, to talk sports?"

A look showed he was not amused.

"And here's all that I need from you . . ."

Getting to the point, Billy thought.

"Whatever you learn going forward, *anything, everything*, you call the number I will give you, yes? You may, in most cases, get Bruno. Or me. You tell me, or him, in very clear English, what it is exactly you have found out. Understand? So see—when *you* know something, *I* know something. *Capisce*, as they say?"

"Yeah, got it. What I find out, I tell you."

And Billy had to wonder, once again, just what he had gotten himself into when a lot of people wanted to know about this missing man, now pretty conclusively dead, riddled with bullets like his fishing boat.

Billy knew just one thing: *must be big*.

"Now—you just may be tempted to hold back information. Who knows why? To help whoever has sent you chasing down this rabbit hole? But I need you to realize . . . that would be a *mistake*. Big . . . mistake. Quite frankly, and not to put too fine a point on it, a *lethal* mistake. As in dead? And well—"

The man's grin returned. *The bastard was enjoying this.*

"Oh, I may have to make sure getting dead would be as painful for you as possible. After all, a deal is a deal."

"And what kind of deal is that?"

The man forced a laugh, looked at the two goons with an expression that seemed to say, *Can you believe this guy?*

"Why, isn't it obvious? You do *exactly* what I ask, and guess what, Billy Blessing? You get to live. You can stay out in the North Fork, go on cooking for the local yokels and the tourists. Or go the hell back to New York, though I think things are over for you there, no?"

Billy didn't interrupt to tell him that may *not* be exactly true.

"So yes, a deal. You keep me in the loop with this"—he made the phone wiggle back and forth—"and life goes on. For you."

Billy watched the man stop talking, then extend the phone as Bruno hurried over to recover it.

"But then—sure I can't offer you another stiff drink? Been a long ride. More to come."

"Thanks. But I'm fine."

"You do understand me, yes?"

"*Perfectly.*"

Billy had crossed paths with some tough and dangerous characters, but this guy, well, he might have just taken it to another level.

Because Billy had no doubt he meant every word he said.

"Great. Bruno, give him the number . . ."

And again, the short goon came over and slipped a small file card into Billy's hand.

"Try not to lose it? But not to worry. We don't hear from you, then we'll be sure to 'reach out and touch,' as the great Diana Ross sang."

Great, he's a Motown fan.

"Good to know."

Billy's last line seemed to give the man pause. Any sign of a smile was now fading, eyes narrowing.

Something feral about those eyes, that look.

"You know, Billy . . . I really *do* hope you understand I mean every single word I say. I could give you a little reminder of what might be ahead for you? If you do not play ball, as it were? Right now. A demonstration?"

The man kept his eyes locked on Billy, the threat clear—with Billy having a fairly good idea of what exactly the man might be talking about.

So, he kept his response as clear and to the point as he could. "No need. I understand. From now on, what I discover, what I know, I call you, or nice Bruno here—" He held the card out. "Whoever answers. With this number here. That it?"

"Good. Nice to be sure you understand. So alright, that's for what's to come. About whatever you learn from here on out. Now then . . . no details left out, tell me absolutely *everything* you have learned so far."

▷

Billy had to race ahead as he spoke, editing, thinking about whether he might take a chance to modify any of the information he knew.

But then, as his host had said, Billy didn't know what the man *already* knew. So—this was a dangerous game to play here.

Still, there was one detail that he was sure the man in front of him would have no idea about.

Least he hoped so . . .

So Billy told him about going to the marina, speaking to the owner, Cioffi. And someone who worked there, Will Sharp.

The man nodded, giving no indication that he already had these pieces of information.

Then he got to the part where Will told him where Landry went that day.

That did bring a reaction. Guess in poker-playing terms, a "tell." This information, new. Namely where Landry went that day. And why.

But the man just said, "Go on."

Then on to talking to the police chief. Which brought a smirk from the man. Perhaps signaling, not much—any?—respect for the local top cop.

But the bullet information, holes in the hull of the boat, also brought no obvious reaction. Could he already know about *that*?

This game was making Billy feel as uneasy as he had ever felt.

But then he had a question: "Are you *sure* they were bullet holes?"

"Seen a few," Billy said. "In my time."

"I've heard."

"So yeah. Only one thing makes a hole like that."

"And this police chief . . . what did she make of it?"

Again—all things considered—best to stay nice and factual.

"That someone came to Landry, out by Gardiners Bay. Gunshots. And"—Billy shrugged—"who knows? Landry shot as well? Or maybe just used to intimidate him."

This made the man laugh. "Ha. Intimidate. Go on."

"Anyway, I was able to get into a safe that Landry had in his house. And well, I saw a lot of things."

Billy now told about all the money in and out of so many accounts and the payments to a hospital standing out.

Again the man looked over to his two guards. Billy thought, *This about the bank statements . . . perhaps new information?*

"You have them still? You haven't turned them over to the local authority? Or anyone?"

Now, a first lie. Billy kept his eyes focused. He was used to being on camera. So he hoped that his eyes, his face, his body language didn't indicate that what was about to come . . . *simply wasn't true.*

"No. Had a retired NYPD detective I know run down some of the numbers. But no names attached to the accounts. So far."

Billy tried to keep his breathing normal with that lie launched.

Then the man nodded.

"*Of course.*"

And finally it was time to talk about today. To talk about the trip out to the bay with Ted Willits to dive under the sea in search of a body.

And for some reason, Billy thought: *Maybe* hold this back? No way anyone could know what really happened out there.

For Billy, the reason to do that was very clear. As he talked, he had this thought: that the phone number he was given, the setup of calling it with what he found out . . . could all be a ruse.

To create the false impression that Billy would just walk out of this room. *Alive . . .*

And giving up the idea that two bodies were found, that they could easily be located again, could be dangerous.

As in, *they'd have no more need for him.*

Billy wasn't about to test that theory one way or the other.

He took the gamble and lied about what happened today . . . and what was found.

▷

Finally, it was done.

The man stood up, turned to the dark Atlantic, looking beautiful, albeit threatening with its consistent roar outside the expansive windows.

"Found . . . nothing out there. Hmm? That's too bad. And any further plans with this Mr.—?"

"*Willits.* Well, yes and no. He suggested widening the search area, another trip out there. Different grid maybe?"

The man turned back to face Billy.

"And this is to occur . . . when?"

"Not sure. I mean all *that* just happened today. He's booked. And I have some business to attend to tomorrow. But I imagine, next few days, we'll head out there again. Give the area another look."

"Good. And—well—you know what to do, now, don't you?"

"I call the number. Right away."

"*Precisely.* Good then. Glad we have had this meeting."

The man took steps toward him. Billy felt his stomach muscles clench. Again, not the first time he had been in a room with someone who quite likely was a killer.

Still, this setting, in the middle of the night? Pretty high up there on the scale of . . . *what the hell is going to happen.*

"My men here will take you back now. Eye mask on again, of course. No reason you—or anyone—should know where I live, right?"

"Right."

Billy still wasn't sure whether his being taken back home was still how this would really play out.

A hand from the man on the left fell on Billy's left shoulder.

"You be careful, Billy Blessing. And as they say . . . *stay in touch.*"

Then that hand gave his shoulder a squeeze. Nothing friendly about that at all. The squeeze hard; the man's grip strong.

He wasn't always living out here in this amazing home, with its fantastic ocean views and probably opulent rooms decorated to match the setting.

This guy—had clearly done some serious stuff.

"Okay, guys. Take our guest back to his North Fork 'home.'"

Billy nodded and turned to the two goons, ready for the return ride.

If that was what *really* was next . . .

With Bruno on one side, and the second still-unnamed goon on the other, the eye mask was slipped back into place.

And Billy was once again navigated, this time out of the room, to what was probably a hallway. Then—again steps head. To the big Escalade.

And what would be an uncomfortable drive back to where he lived.

That is, if no lethal detours were planned.

27
TIME TO QUIT

Billy waited till the Escalade had slowly slipped away. Then, unable to sleep, he sat in his easy chair to think things through.

Despite all that had happened that day, he needed to really think about things.

Because there was one glaring realization.

That he was—quite clearly—beyond over his head. And if he wasn't very careful, he would end up as dead as poor Danny Pippo up in Greenport.

But then what, he thought. *Just stop?*

Let anyone he happened to talk to who was involved with this . . . yes, let them know that he was completely done giving a *damn* about Jack Landry, or all that money that went missing back and forth, about who the hell he really was?

Who any of them were!

And worse, after today, seeing Lola Bristow with someone, another mysterious character, he had to accept this question: Could he even trust *her*?

He had instincts. From all that he had done in his life, those instincts said one thing: *get the hell out of this now.*

So then—that decision reached—he was tempted to get a drink. But no, despite being so very tired from the day, best keep his head crystal clear to finish this unbelievably worrisome train of thought.

Namely: *Now what?*

Well, he couldn't stay here. No. How long would it be before whoever the hell it was in that mansion sent his associates—the two goons—wanting to *know* things. Or the supposed daughter, "Lisa Cowles," reappeared, wanting payback for that check?

And then, who knew who else might be involved? Who the hell searched Landry's place? Who tried to rough him up? How many players were there in this game? Which—Billy was now aware—had some very high stakes.

And he was in the center of it.

So again. *Now what?*

Then a thought: *Well—I have an out.*

Would not be perfect. But might render him safer than staying here and carrying on like he wasn't worried about his safety—and life expectancy—at all.

Do what Gretchen Di Voss and the new head of Worldwide and his tight-lipped big-pockets investor, Tony Hill, *wanted.* Go back to the city the very next morning. Take just what was needed to pack from here, then drive straight into Gotham.

Yeah. Get a good hotel with good security. Use the size and teeming hordes of Manhattan for protection.

Maybe even get Deacon Solomon to arrange extra protection, or at least alert the local police in New York.

Hmm. But then, maybe not . . .

Solomon, he trusted completely.

In a local police department, a local precinct . . . well . . . things could happen. These weren't the bad old days of Serpico.

But still, when big money had something to ask, even a pretty straight and narrow uniformed cop might be tempted to assist.

That was just reality.

So—he nodded to himself, glad he took these minutes to think it all through. Make that decision.

He got up, ready to fall into his unmade bed, about as tired as he'd ever been. He just hoped, well, nothing bad would happen between now and morning.

But in that hope, he was due to be disappointed.

▷

"Billy . . ."

He had been dreaming. Surprisingly enough, not a nightmare, not his fears playing out in the surreal theater of dreams.

No. He was back on television.

Some familiar faces. Di Voss's father, the former head of Worldwide, long passed. But in the dream . . . still there, looking on, smiling as Billy interviewed a celebrity chef.

The chef looked rather generic, with a few days' growth of beard, spiky dark hair, fashionably unkempt, and a white jacket with his name embroidered on it, but the name was a blur, unreadable.

The dish, appropriately enough, was some fish, the whole thing, fresh from the day's catch out on Sheepshead Bay or one of the stalls in the fish market, now in its new digs at Hunts Point.

The chef had a cleaver. Held high.

To cut the head of the fish?

But he wasn't doing anything because someone was saying . . .

His name.

"Billy?"

Then the TV set, the chef, Di Voss, the camera crew—all began to fade . . . like a Polaroid in reverse.

And Billy slowly came awake.

With the unsettling awareness that someone was standing over him, saying his name.

▷

And now, again: "Billy, wake up!"

Billy had opened his eyes, this waking up occurring in slow motion.

He could finally see who stood over him. A familiar face, but not one he was so sure he should be glad to see.

The Northold police chief.

Lola Bristow was in uniform, right at his bed. He thought he had locked the door, but the cottage, the door, the lock—not the most secure with the old doorjamb.

"Lola. What the—"

Then he saw someone else—a few steps behind her, also standing in his bedroom, and sending off now some quite serious alarms—a man in a suit. Quick guess: probably the very same man that had been in her police station office last night.

And despite the clarity of all his decision-making and planning from the late night before, he had the definite feeling that all *that* was—right now, in one way or the other—in serious jeopardy.

▷

Lola gave him a small smile. The kind you might force when visiting someone in the hospital.

"Okay, sorry. We, um, let ourselves in. Didn't want to make any kind of late-night scene at the door. Besides"—her smile broadened—"you *really* need to get a better lock on your door."

"Been thinking that myself . . ." Then Billy, aware he was still flat on the bed, head on the pillow, propped himself up.

"Mind if I sit up? Wasn't expecting visitors."

At that, Lola nodded to the man behind her.

"Right. Funny. Okay, how about *you* get some clothes on, then maybe fix up some coffee in your little kitchen outside? And then—we can talk to you."

"'We'?"

Well, that answered at least one question, the police chief and the so-far-silent man in a suit were in this together. Whatever this was.

"Coffee sounds good. The talk, don't know about. But"—he slid his legs out from the bedclothes—"guess I'm about to find out, right?"

To which Lola said nothing but nodded and turned to her companion as they left his bedroom.

Rather bold, Billy thought.

They shut the door behind them.

And all the time, getting dressed, Billy couldn't come up with any theory about what this was about.

He was curious, to be sure. But he also felt genuine disappointment. His neat getaway and stay-alive plan looked like it had just gone *clear out the damn window* . . .

▷

The chief had gotten his Keurig busy, one cup already gushing out, while two more pods waited their turn.

"Got milk, cream, *something*?" Lola said.

The man in the suit stood to the side. Now Billy noticed that he held something in his hands. A manila envelope, clutched in front of him.

Guess that manila envelope is part of this unfolding scene, he thought.

"Um, creamer of some kind. In the fridge."

Lola nodded.

Billy took some steps closer. "If I knew I was having company, I could have gone to that great bakery—"

"Dellasandro's?"

"Yeah. Got you some nice muffins or something."

Lola grabbed the creamer and brought the first cup to the table.

"There you go," she said.

"You are too kind." Billy sat, took a sip of the coffee black, the bitter taste just about right for such a literally rude awakening. Then: "Okay, if you can multitask while the Keurig works its magic, how about you explain why I am being honored by you and Mr. Chatty over there?"

The line did not bring a smile from the man.

Lola pressed a button, getting a second cup on its way.

"Okay, you are on your way to being caffeinated. So—let me explain to you everything we know . . ."

That word again.

Billy thinking: Was his faith in Bristow so wrong? Was she some-how knee-deep in all this?

"That would be great. A good topic for a morning conversation, be-sides what the hell you are doing in my little cottage here . . . uninvited."

To which, Lola's companion finally spoke. "We'll explain all that, Mr. Blessing. Will take some time. *But we will.*"

"He speaks," Billy said.

And now the man walked over to the table, the ominous envelope in front of him, landing on the table as he took a seat.

28

THE ENVELOPE, PLEASE

Billy took a sip of coffee. He gave Lola, still standing, a look, as if asking, *What the hell is going on here?*

But the man started this early-morning meeting. First . . . with an introduction.

"My name is Martin Williams. I'm an assistant district attorney in what is called the Southern District of New York."

"Heard of it," Billy said, thinking, *These days, who hasn't . . .*

The man looked at Lola, who held her cup of coffee between her hands as if warming them. With that glance, she too came over, pulled a chair back from Billy's simple wooden table, and sat down.

"Your police chief here contacted us a few weeks back—"

Lola added, "About the, um—"

"Yes?"

"—the fact that Landry went missing."

"That's right. Because, you see, we had been watching that man for some time, ever since we learned who he *really* was, and what he really did."

There we go, thought Billy. Revelation number one about to come.

"You see . . . the man who lived here quietly as 'Jack Landry' was, in fact, someone else entirely."

"Seriously?" Billy said more than a little sarcastically.

Detective Solomon found no such person. And whoever the man was—getting ventilated via gunshots and unceremoniously dumped in the ocean along with another John Doe meant he wasn't just some nice old guy quietly fishing his way through his golden years.

With that, the assistant district attorney undid the metal clasps of the envelope. Apparently it was show-and-tell time.

And whatever was in the envelope had been organized ahead of time so this Martin Williams could simply slide the first item out.

First up, a photo of a man. For a moment, Billy didn't know who it was. The man was in a suit, in the city, caught by some secretive camera from the look of the photo.

But based on what his now-likely phony daughter had said, it was Landry—whoever he was—from a good number of years ago.

"This man here, the one you call 'Jack Landry,' is actually Paul Steiner. That name mean anything at all to you?"

Billy shook his head. "No, should it?"

"Depends what kinda stories you like to follow in the news. Anyway, he was a key figure in a group of very professional and powerful crime families that were called the 'Associates.'"

"Sounds all aboveboard."

"Yeah. Well, they were very special 'associates.' Basically a gang of high-level mobsters working together in the hidden money, hidden gold, and the free-for-all of the international cash market—stealing it all, wherever they could. Steiner was one of the leads, head of his own group of well-trained and very accomplished criminals. A few killers in the mix too."

"Got it. So goodbye, Jack Landry; hello, Paul Steiner."

"*Exactly.* Now, he vanished a good twelve years ago when a *lot* of people were looking for him."

"You mean—your office."

Williams smiled. "Oh, yeah. But *not* just us. You see—well, this next . . . will be a lot to absorb."

"Try me. I don't have any pressing plans today," Billy said, without adding, *except to get the hell out of here while I can still breathe.*

"There arose an opportunity for a very complicated, very difficult heist mixing inside information, planning—big time—and some very well-placed insiders . . . The details aren't too important, except think of an intricate watch, all those gears working together? For what we can call . . . one *very* massive score."

Billy nodded. This story, so far, was pretty interesting.

"Anyway, that's what this operation took. Lot of people, perfect timing, paid insiders everywhere, airports, offices . . . you name it. Part of it, even loads of cash and bullion that was being moved between off-shore accounts. And here's the thing: there was a very tight window when all of it would be vulnerable."

"Yeah. Sure. *Interesting.* But like you said. Not a story I would generally follow."

"*Got that.* So—I will keep it simple. Millions upon millions of cash and assets . . . gold, silver, and even totally bankable securities were set to vanish down the Associates' rabbit hole."

"Lucky them."

"Not so." Williams looked at Bristow. Billy wondered, *When does the duplicitous chief enter the story?*

"My office, NYPD Fraud, FBI—all had gotten wind of it all. Lucky breaks. They happen. And we were able to round them all up just when all those gears started moving. I was brand new at the time. Low-level attorney. But everyone hustled to get the cash and bullion about to be stolen, stop all the incredible wire transfers, protect all those bankable assets."

"Sounds difficult. And like you did a good job."

"You know, Mr. Blessing—I imagine you are sitting here, thinking, *Sure, interesting story. But what the does it have to do with me?* Hence your—let's say—demeanor now?"

"That what it is?"

"Yeah. You're a TV guy? An ex-TV guy?"

"Ouch."

"So bantering, comments you're making . . . all barely amusing. But just have a little patience."

Williams nodded as he said that, as if he had some very major cards to play.

"Trust me. Does any of this matter to you? It *does* . . . and you had better believe it."

▷

With that, Billy looked at his coffee cup. "I, er, could use a refill."

He stood up. But then again, not sure what was going on here, he said, "I mean, is it *okay* if I get another cup?"

Williams, in charge: "Sure."

Billy put another K-Cup into the machine, pressed the top down, and started the brewing process.

"You can go on," Billy said. "I'm listening."

"Right. So—we caught them, protected the cash—so much of it. Crates of bullion. Can you imagine? And so much damn cash. Like I said, one incredible heist. But see—and this you may find indeed even more interesting—all along, one of these mobsters, one of the so-called Associates, was planning to double-cross *all* the others."

"Really? Sounds dangerous."

"Oh, yeah. And it's not clear whether he or someone he knew helped set all the others up. May never know that now. But he was going to take a really big slice of this cash and gold pie—*and then vanish.*"

The coffee machine started shooting out its dark elixir.

"Easier said than done? Just speculating . . ."

"Oh, yes." Then: "And a very deadly move to make. Did he know that NYPD and the Feds were ready to corral everyone ahead of time? Then plan his solo bold move? Don't know that."

"He got away with it?"

"Oh. Really interested *now*, are we? Well—he went totally off the grid for a while. Dunno. South America? Maybe the DR? Anywhere he might have felt safe. But there was a small hitch in that plan of his."

"Isn't there always?"

"Yeah, sure. See, he had a daughter, not that he saw her much at all. And while this score, absolutely gigantic, would allow him to vanish—new identity, relocation, cash to do anything, pay people to keep quiet—he may have made a mistake."

"Mistake?"

"Missing his daughter, wanting to at least see, if not contact her . . . *he came back*. Time had passed. Maybe thinking . . . still kinda remote out here? But remote enough to feel safe? *Be* safe?"

"Apparently not?"

"*Right*. Anyway, well, this is where you come in. See, those records you found with Chief Bristow's help?"

"Yup. Fun fact—you may not know this? Our chief here was quite good at safe cracking." He smiled at Lola, though, despite their pleasant dinner at Touch of Rome, he now felt he couldn't really trust her at all.

"We guessed that what Paul Steiner was doing—and had done with his big score—"

It was hard for Billy to get used to that new name.

"—would be somehow buried in those papers, the bank documents, whatever else was found."

Billy didn't say anything.

"And, well—sorry. It's our job. But we *also* know you asked retired Detective Deacon Solomon to do some digging."

Now Billy was genuinely shocked. Deacon was working with this DA guy too? *When did that start happening?*

But with that card on the table now, Billy simply said, "I did."

"But see, we wanted to tread lightly. Not barge into Steiner's place. People watching. Rip it apart. Scare others away? So your appearance has proved very helpful."

"That's me: the working DA's friend."

Williams paused, a look of annoyance on his face. But pressing on: "And now, well, the first thing we need you to do this morning is tell me everything you found."

First thing, Billy thought. *Means more things to come?*

And then he realized that maybe now was a good time to tell them that he was—*sad to say*—done with all this. *Leaving Dodge*, back to the big city. Back to the lights, camera, and action of a less lethal sort.

And no better time to tell the two people in his small kitchen . . . *than right now.*

▷

"Okay, I have some things to say. First thing, before we go any further with this?"

Neither of his guests said anything. Could they suspect what was to come?

"So, in the past few days, I have had enough, um, experiences to know that what seemed like an intriguing mystery to look into, for some very useful cash—an old guy disappearing at sea—well, seems it could be mighty unhealthy . . . for me."

Still nothing from them.

"Why unhealthy, you ask? Not that you did, and thanks for the concern. For starters, there are, at least, two different new 'friends' I have met—not sure what to call them—who have made it clear that if I *don't* do precisely what the hell they say, share what I learn, then well—"

He stopped. Looked at Chief Bristow.

"I assume our police chief here has told you about the boat, riddled with bullet holes?"

The assistant DA nodded at that.

"So, I can easily imagine what could happen to me. That is, if I continue doing what I have been doing."

Billy took a sip of the coffee, now turned a little cool. Kinda like the vibe in the room, he thought.

"And now I have this opportunity to go back to the city, could go today. *Kick-start* this whole 'Billy Blessing' revival they got planned. Big event on Friday night. Meanwhile, I can hide away in some luxury hotel with really, *really* good security."

Martin Williams scratched his head, looked to the side.

Looking—Billy imagined—real displeased at this.

Oh, well . . .

"Yup. So—soon as we're done here, that is exactly what I will do."
Billy nodded as if confirming that this decision was made.

"I do, though, have a few things to share before that happens . . .
things"—a look to Lola Bristow—"things even the chief here does not
know."

"How thoughtful," Williams said.

Yeah. *Definitely displeased.*

"And once I've done that, well, I'll lock this place up—though, from
your arrival, I can see the lock's not much good in this old place. Drive
to Manhattan as fast as I can. Leave the life and the bullets here . . . all
behind."

To which Attorney Williams actually sniffed. A glance at Bristow,
who, Billy thought, also looked uncomfortable. Guess . . . she hadn't
been expecting this?

*But she has to realize I'm no private detective walking around with
whatever gun those guys carry. Or 'pack.' That the word? A Smith and
Wesson something or other?*

No, Billy thought. *I'm just someone who got involved in a few murky
cases before, maybe helped the local authorities out, here and there.*

*Just a matter of having good instincts and maybe asking the right ques-
tions.*

*But this? Way over my head. And I would like to keep that head intact,
right where it is.*

So, before revealing a few secrets of his own, he finished (this part
of the dialogue, at least) by saying, "Anyway—that's exactly what I'm
going to do."

Which finally triggered a surprising answer from DA Martin Williams, his voice signaling there was no doubt about the message to
come—and how much he meant it—when he said, "No. No, you're not."

29

A CHANGE IN PLANS

Billy looked right at the DA. Those very direct eyes. *Piercing* might be the apt word? And, well, he could easily imagine a jury buying every single word this Martin Williams had to say.

"Excuse me?" Billy said.

Williams nodded. "Look, I *get* why you feel that way. Makes sense, as we say? Who *wouldn't* want to pull out of this before it's too late?"

"Exactly, since I—"

Williams cut him off. "But *that* simply cannot happen. You are, unfortunately, in too deep with these people."

"Not by my choosing . . ."

"No matter. See—my office is very interested on what you have *not* shared with Chief Bristow here. But you have become too close to some very important—and yes, extremely dangerous—players."

"Players?"

Williams patted the envelope still bulging with as-yet-unseen items.

"Yes. That's all to be explained to you."

"Well, now, you don't have to do that because—"

Again, Williams cut him off at the pass. "You see, Billy—if you did what you say, just now? What you think you are going to do . . . walk away? With these people, there's no hotel big enough, no security tight enough, no city huge enough for you to ever hide from these people.

They'd find you. They'd come for you. And as you might imagine, that would not be pretty. And if you, well, really bailed on this? Not sure what kind of protection we could then offer you."

"That sounds like a threat."

"No. Just a statement of fact, Billy."

And as if he were standing ankle-deep in the surf with giant waves coming, Billy could feel the sand being drawn away from his feet, as if the water itself wanted to send him tumbling down, drag him out to sea. *To drown . . .*

Lola finally added something. "Billy—listen to the DA here, hmm? He *knows* who these people are. He knows what they can do. In fact, my guess is"—she shot a look at Williams—"your only shot at staying alive is seeing this through."

Billy sat back in the simple wooden chair. The air in his small kitchen suddenly tasted close. He wished he had a window open to let in the fresh salty morning breeze.

"'Seeing this through'?"

"Yes," Williams said, jumping back in. "*Continue* doing what you are doing. I mean, once we hear what you were going to tell us . . . then we'll all have a better idea of precisely what that means."

The way Williams spoke now sounded all very cozy. Like fraternity bros working out a kegger. Just have to get the pledges all together.

No way out at all but to see this damn thing through.

And what would that look like at the end of the road?

Billy tried to think. He was always an "options" guy. Always good to have, whether in his TV career, running his restaurant, in relationships, or anything he did. Have as many damn choices as possible.

But this—what was on the table?—was only pointing in one direction. Namely: if he wanted to say alive, if he wanted to have protection—somehow, someway—then he had to continue.

That was option A. And option B? End up like good ol' Jack Landry or Paul Steiner, or whoever the hell that was down below.

Some seconds went by, and everyone was quiet until Williams said, "So then, Billy . . . *Blessing* . . . what will it be?"

He had said his last name as if he knew before "Blessing" there had been the other, real name: Blanchard. And that person had been gone for some time.

Not a lot. *But some.*

And now it was apparently time to make a deal, which—in this case—was no deal at all.

Billy said, forcing a smile at this unpleasant outcome, "Okay. You got it. I'll keep on . . . *keeping on*, as they say?"

"Excellent," Williams said. "Now then—how about you tell us both what you have not shared yet? I mean, now that we're all partners in this?"

Partners? Except, I'm the only partner with his neck on the chopping block!

"Okay. Yesterday when Ted Willits brought me out to the spot Landry—sorry, I mean *Steiner*—vanished, he did a dive, searched . . . the whole area."

"Found nothing, you said?" Lola added.

He had their attention.

"Well, not quite nothing."

▷

Billy realized that what he was about to share was, well, somewhat unexpected.

"Willits found something on his sonar, then went down. Did a search. Wearing something called a dry suit."

"Yeah," Williams said. "Water getting chillier out there."

"I guess. Anyway, he could talk to me topside, and I even got a video feed of what he saw."

"And?" Williams said.

"Well, visibility really sucks out there."

"It's not the Bahamas."

"So I heard. But there was a shape. Saw his gloved hand reach out. And he felt all around."

"A body in a bag?" Williams said, giving Lola a look. This report of a grisly demise was actually useful news to the DA.

"Well, you see . . . and this is what was interesting . . . Willits said he felt *two* bodies."

"Two?"

"Yup. I assumed one, based on how his boat was shot up, was your Steiner. But who was the second one?"

"And you left it there?"

Billy nodded. "Willits said he could pin the location, so easy enough to come back to. So I said . . . leave them there for now."

"Good thinking," Williams said.

"How come?"

"You bring them up, someone sees, notices? And you and your diver friend—"

"Hey. I don't really *know* him . . ."

"—could be in a lot of trouble." Williams turned to the chief. "Chief Bristow, this is, well, good for the case. For now. We know something that the others don't . . ."

Billy guessed the others included people wanting Steiner—but not whoever had put those bodies in a weighted bag . . .

"Yes," she said. "For now, I'm getting really worried about Billy here."

About damn time, Billy thought.

"Yeah. But for *now*. I imagine that they think he came up empty-handed."

"*For now*," Bristow added.

"You said there is a Coast Guard lieutenant? Came to see the fishing boat with you?"

She nodded. "Yes. Lieutenant Jerry Talbot."

Billy watched as the DA wrote that name down.

"Good. I will reach out to his supervisor. Tell him what I'd like him to do."

Billy, based on his brief interaction, wasn't so sure involving the lieutenant in any of this was a particularly good idea. So he asked, "What for?"

"As I said . . . bad things can happen with these people. Best you and this Willits guy don't go back there. The Coast Guard can take that over."

"Yeah. You know—about bad things? I kinda got that feeling on last night's road trip to wherever that—"

"Oh, hang on. We'll talk about that. Anyway—"

He turned back to Lola. "I'll get this Lieutenant Talbot to go out there. With a crew, dead of night, recover the body bag. Once they have the location, should be fast. No one to see, or really suspect anything."

Lola nodded at this. *Funny*, Billy thought. *She came out here maybe expecting a lot less excitement compared to being a cop in New York.*

And now look what she's dealing with.

"Meanwhile, Billy—well, I have something that I want you to do."

"Oookay." At this, the smallest smile. The DA, now clearly in charge here seemed to be loosening up a bit.

"Right. Well, first. Let me show you what else I have inside this goody bag here. I think . . . you'll find it all very interesting."

Interesting. That word again. In Billy's experience, that word didn't presage the best of things to come.

Especially with a DA basically in charge here, and multiple major mob members in play. One of whom probably made sure Danny Pippo never talked to anyone.

His sad-sack dead body left on the street as a warning. And not to mention the two bodies hanging out in Davy Jones's locker. Billy didn't like how the addition was going, but he didn't have a choice.

Let's see what's in the envelope, behind door number one, Johnny, and what our contestant's going to have to do to.

And that contestant?

As they say on *The Price Is Right*: *Billy Blessing . . . come on down!!!*

30

MEET THE MOBSTERS

Williams slid a glossy black-and-white photo toward Billy.

"See anyone you know?" he said.

Billy leaned over the photo. It showed people at a fancy restaurant, guys in suits, a few with cigars looking classically mobster-ish. But some younger people as well. And at first, he didn't recognize any of the faces . . .

Until he saw a woman standing at the back, martini glass in hand. Her face slightly turned, but in a second, he knew . . . *that he had indeed met her.*

Once.

Billy pointed to her.

"Okay, this woman here? Lisa Cowles. Who gave me the check and said she was Landry's—I guess—Steiner's daughter."

The attorney spun the photo around for a quick look for himself, then a spin back to Billy.

"Anyone else?"

Billy scanned the picture.

"No. Looks like a nice bunch of guys. *Not.*"

The Assistant DA grinned. Billy thought, *Hey, he is loosening up a bit . . .*

"Okay, that is—real name—Celia Kole. Daughter of one Max Kole, the fellow at the head of the table. *This* guy."

Billy could see that this Max did seem to be the king holding court.

"His brother Sal was one of the Associates that planned the giant heist over a dozen years ago with Steiner. Said brother Sal was sent to prison. Unfortunately, with some health issues, Sal soon died there."

"Ah, too bad."

"And Max, the brother here? Well, he has always wanted to find Steiner and the money and assets ever since. *Real bad.*"

Billy looked up. "And so he had his daughter come to me . . . ?"

"Well, if he or any of his boys are involved, yes. Make sense, no? So they could find those who killed Steiner and made him vanish. Guess . . . that is why they used you—"

"As a stalking horse?"

"Pretty much. With Celia having a big check and knowing the strings to pull with you? She actually is an attorney. A mob attorney, but still. All these mob guys have a bunch of them. Always good to have one in the 'real' family. Hear she's good. But my guess would be they clearly did not kill Steiner, nor did they learn—yet—about the hidden money."

"Time for more pictures then?"

"Yeah. Okay—ready for another one?"

"Be my guest."

Williams slid another picture out from the packet; also large, eight by ten, but in color.

And the setting was so different. A lush green lawn rolling down to a sandy stretch near a dock. A few really big yachts tied up. A classic Long Island mansion in the back, or maybe more of a Cape Cod look. People in crisp white dress shirts, sleeves rolled up, champagne flutes in hand.

Just a nice party being held by some billionaire.

"Look at this one *really* closely."

And Billy did just that. Again, a lot of people he didn't recognize at all. Envy maybe, yes. For a setting like that.

But then—toward the back . . .

"Hey. Those *two* guys. Looking like they're not part of the party? Like guards or something? *They* are the two nasty goons who came to pick me up last night for a ride."

"Yeah. Just two punks, but real close to their boss. But the others . . . see anyone?"

Billy turned back to the rest of the party. Most were in sunglasses, making any identification hard. But then—he looked at one guy. Surrounded by people listening to him. Sipping, smiling . . .

And even though he wore such dark and trendy sunglasses, Billy thought he knew who it was.

"Okay. Not one hundred percent sure . . . *but I think* . . . this here is the guy the goons brought me to see last night."

Williams nodded and fired Lola Bristow a glance, perhaps pleased that this game of *who do you know* was going so well.

"That would make sense. That is Marco Pierce. Last name was changed from Kozalka. Go figure. His father came to this country from Eastern Europe when he was a kid. Wasted no time setting up a crime operation similar to the one he had run in Romania. The usual. Drugs, gambling, loan sharking, et cetera . . . Did quite well. And he too was—"

"Let me guess—was one of the Associates? Involved in the heist?"

"Right. Well, actually his father, Andre, was. But though powerful, ruthless, Marco Pierce's dad was—at that time—an old guy when that went down. Did some time, but then was let out since he had only months left to live. The DA back then tried to nail the son, Marco, who—thinking was—had to be involved. That didn't work."

The agent pointed at the mansion.

"You can see in the picture here all he inherited from his old man? But so far, Marco Pierce here has evaded charges. But does he want that big chunk of money and assets that Steiner made off with? You bet."

"Needs it that badly? Dunno—he looks like he's doing okay."

"Guys like that—*never* have enough."

Billy nodded. "This is all . . . very interesting. Nice to know who I have been dealing with. *Gotta* tell you—lot of names to remember. And actually, all things considered, rather surprised I am still alive."

"Yeah. Let's aim to keep it that way."

The ADA stopped, put the photos back . . . though it looked like there had to be more inside.

"Okay," Billy said. "Who's next?"

"Next?"

"You said . . . Steiner did this massive score with heads of other crime families? By my count, you have shown me *two*? Any more to come?"

"Oh, yes. And well, in this case, the third, well—we can't be sure. I mean. We're clearly talking about the person who shot up that boat, probably tried to get Steiner to talk, then sunk his corpse in the ocean."

"Yeah. So *who* is that?"

The ADA looked at Bristow. Something about this . . . a little tricky for him.

Then: "We're not totally sure. Could be any number of people. One little piggy escaped—and is unknown. Nothing the DA back then could nail down."

"Not even any likely candidates?"

Williams nodded. "Well, yes. A few. Dunno. How about I show you a few more photos. See what you see? You never know . . ."

"Yup—that's what they say."

And then the ADA pulled out the rest of the photos.

"Anyone you recognize from anywhere—just say the word."

"Got it."

Slowly Williams began to slide photos to Billy.

▷

Williams was down to the last photo.

So far the pictures all looked like snaps from a bunch of overblown and garish weddings Billy hadn't attended nor—from the looks of some of the gentlemen in the photos—would he ever wish to.

Then . . . that last photo.

This one was outside a place Billy knew well. One of the best steak houses in New York, historic even. The Palm.

Someone was at the head of a table—and if Billy wasn't mistaken, that was the famed Babe Ruth table. Where . . . well, the great Bambino had held court, devouring tons of beef with stiff drinks to match.

A man in the photo had turned, as if surprised by someone taking a picture. Not happy at that.

And it was someone Billy knew.

Well, *knew* might be too strong a word. They had crossed paths.

Billy looked up. A smile. "Okay, this guy here? This guy looking at the camera like he's going to tear someone's throat out? *I met him.*"

Williams looked to Lola. Billy guessed they had gone over the photos together . . . After all, Bristow could have crossed paths with any of them if they had somehow wandered out here, looking for hidden millions.

"Yeah. Just a few days ago. Name's Tony Hill. Well, that is what I was told. Kinda quiet at the meeting, but apparently he's the big money behind some of the projects to get me to come back to NYC and all that jazz. Yeah. Tony Hill . . . of Hilltop Entertainment."

To which Williams, with a quick glance back at the photo and a smile, looked at Billy and said, "Well—no, it isn't."

▷

Now it was Billy's turn to see what last rabbit the ADA was about to pull out.

"It's *not?*"

"Nope. His real name—as much as we have been able to work out—is Sammy Rose. And his company, Hilltop? Imagine it's nothing but a front. One of dozens. Place to move money in and out of."

Billy had to laugh at that. "Nobody ever uses their real names in their line of work? And I can kiss my big revival goodbye? No *Blessing's Back?*"

"Oh—I am sure that Rose really wanted you back in the city. For his own purposes, I imagine. When did you say your old boss—this, um—"

"Gretchen Di Voss."

"—want you to come back to get things going?"

"Friday night. The Worldwide Industries Fall Gala, at the Park Avenue Club. Apparently, it was a stipulation. Like, you know—a *demand?*"

"Okay. Well then. I'm now going to tell you want I think—and what I hope we can do now. Together."

Billy suddenly said, "Show of hands. How many people want this guy to back out now, while he still can?"

"You *can't*. My guess is Rose and his people discovered where Paul Steiner was. Then with some local help—"

"Yeah—and I'm working on where that info might have come from out here," Lola said. "Have some possibilities."

Billy immediately had one idea in that department for himself . . . but for now, he held that thought back.

"So—they track Steiner out there for fishing, if that's what he was really out to do . . ."

"You mean he *wasn't* out to go fishing?"

"Not sure. But they find him. And well, grab him. Sink his boat, and—just speculating here—make him talk. The classic offer on the table?"

"Right. Think I can even guess at the nature of that offer? Namely, he tells them where all that cash and liquid assets are hidden. Or they kill him. But—and maybe, possibly—he lies."

"*Bingo.* Though I imagine someone with Steiner's history had to know . . . soon as he told them that, why they'd just as easily kill him anyway. Which is probably what happened."

"Least they don't get his money, right? And the second corpse?"

"Ah. That we don't know yet. But after tonight, we will."

"Yes. Coast Guard getting the bodies tonight. Got it. Okay then, so why does this mobster Sammy Rose put money into backing me, a show, restaurants . . . ?"

"Well, would any of that really happen? Who knows? *Dubious.* But he definitely wanted you to *stop* rooting around in things. Probably knew the other two Associates would most likely be watching you, using you."

"I get it. Get me back to the city, under his careful watch?"

"For a time . . . until, well—"

Billy guessed he knew what *that* meant. Talk about getting your show canceled . . . permanently.

"But hang on—that means they *have* recovered the money?"

"Oh, we don't know that. It is possible. But if Steiner at some point shared its real location, somehow, to someone—who knows why?—then he could have told Sammy Rose's people the wrong information. Which, if that happened, makes what *you* know, or may know, even more valuable. If you follow . . . ?"

"Um. Not sure. But this sounds like I'm in an even deeper mess than I thought I was."

"Could be."

Well, that's reassuring, Billy thought as he sat back in his chair, not at all comfortable in the corner he was now firmly painted into.

But as much as he hated that, he thought it best to ask the big question . . .

"Okay. Think we know what we all know. Also—what we don't. What am I supposed to do now? I mean—*hello*—to stay alive? If that's even possible?"

The ADA smiled. "Good question. And fortunately, there we have a good answer. 'Cause, if we are right here, *if* we all play this correctly, it will all be over for you in—oh—about forty-eight hours."

Again Billy laughed. "You might want to rephrase that. It doesn't give a brother much confidence."

Lola Bristow laughed at that. And with that bit of levity—it was time to get serious and learn what could be done . . . *had to be done . . .*

So that this didn't turn into the end of the Billy Blessing story . . .

31
THE PLAN

Williams got up, went to the Keurig, fed it another plastic cup. And as the machine went to work . . .

"Okay. As you said, we spoke to retired Detective Deacon Solomon . . ."

"What? He came to *you*?"

"No. Not really. He was concerned. About you. Called Chief Bristow here. Then he talked, once he knew what was at stake. So—we got a look at all those statements you found."

"Okay. So much for his discretion."

"Yeah. Well, a lot of them are hard to figure, money going here, there. But clearly Steiner sent a lot of money to that medical center. Gifts. So many of them. But here's the thing—he also funded someone's tuition, completely. 'The full ride,' as they say. That person unnamed."

Williams came back to the table.

"So . . . our thinking in the DA's office—the key to this is this hospital. Those statements show how much he sent to that medical school. But also, exactly whose medical education and training was fully supported? Find that person, and maybe, somehow, find the clue as to where Steiner hid all the cash and assets?"

Billy watched Williams grab his cup. Taking it black. It was clear that the assistant DA had, with his compatriots, thought this all out.

"You make it sound easy," Billy said. Thinking, in fact, it sounded impossible.

"Took some pressure, squeezing hospital admin people—hard. But we got a name. Who that person is. *Dr. Katie Brennan.* Heads up something called pediatric oncology? She took her mother's last name. And well, this is where you come in."

"What?"

"For what we are planning, needs to be you, just following up on things. Meet her. Talk to her. Just like you've been doing . . ."

"And everyone—all those nice people from the photos—I imagine they will be watching you. Whether you know it or not," Lola said.

"Which," Williams added, "we can assume that, with everyone seeing you go to the hospital and all of them still wanting to follow the yellow brick road to the cash?"

Williams paused. Billy thought . . . *Not liking this next bit—at all.*

"So, yeah. They will be ready to pounce on you hard if they think you have learned any possible new information. Whether you actually *have* that information. Or not."

"At which point, let me hazard a guess," Billy said. "I will become disposable?"

Lola responded to that. "Billy—we are going to do absolutely *everything* to keep you safe. Me, ADA Williams, and his team here. You may not see all the people watching out for you—but they *will* be there."

"Good to know. So, I go to the medical center like, um, when—?"

Williams smiled at that. "Oh, I'd say in about five minutes. Call Chief Bristow the minute you learn anything. And, Billy, I know from what you've done in the past, in New York, LA, Chicago. You're really smart. Use *all* of that to learn what the hell you can."

"Since I do not appear to have a choice, I guess I will indeed do that."

"Then, well—you go to the event tomorrow night at the swanky Park Avenue Club. As if you are all set to jump into bed with this 'Hilltop Entertainment.'"

"And guess I'm not?"

Williams bypassed that question . . . "You will contact all those nice people who have reached out to you, say you have, yes, indeed learned something; tell them to meet you *there*. At the event at the club. Nice and public. They will know what strings to pull to get into the event."

"And if I haven't learned anything . . . if *we* haven't?"

"Let's just hope we *do*. Either way, you won't be alone at the event. And if all goes well, this all ends for you, for them, for this whole damn case . . . tomorrow night."

"Nice. Hors d'oeuvres. Champagne. Live music. And a dead man dancing. Sounds like a fun evening."

The ADA, ignoring the remark, continued, "Yeah. So, the key thing is act as though you have never spoken to anyone about all this but Lola here. Certainly not me. Or anyone in the DA's office."

"Got it. Guess—I better get going." Billy stood up. "Um, you're sure this, Dr. Brennan—most likely Steiner's daughter—at the medical center in Hauppauge will even speak to me?"

"My office set that up. No details, no whys or wherefores given. But we already called. She will be expecting you. On alert too, I imagine. But, Billy—she won't really know at all why you want to see her. So tread lightly?"

"Got it. I mean, what about her—*maybe*—father being dead? I could do without delivering that news."

"For now, leave that out. With luck, Dr. Brennan will speak openly to you. And with luck, share some interesting information. It's our best shot."

"Right. About Paul Steiner's big money gifts and the mystery donation for her training?"

"Yeah." He took a breath. "You need to find out if that person knows something. Maybe, without even knowing she does."

At that, Lola also stood up. Williams put his coffee down on the table, half-done.

"And Billy," Lola said, "be really careful, okay? Thinking—I'd like you to survive this."

"Oh, good. That makes two of us then."

To which Williams added: "*Three* . . ."

I guess he likes me.

And with that, they left, with Williams first doing a scan of the sandy road outside, making sure no one was around there in the early a.m. Then Billy watched the two of them disappear.

Some mighty big plans in place. Probably—dangerous plans.

And all about to start now.

▷

With an early start, Billy found the Long Island Expressway busy, but moving along at a good clip. He had Sirius Radio on one of its channels devoted to baseball.

The Yanks were still in the running for the series. *They certainly should be,* Billy thought, *considering how much they paid for their roster!*

But somehow that news—that hope of playoffs and a series for the damn Yankees—made the day better.

Nothing like October baseball.

And the nice maps lady, who sounded an awful lot like Siri, kept giving him clear instructions as he hit the Hauppauge exit, toward the town were the medical center was located.

This area was someplace he had never been.

But then the navigating turned tricky as he was directed to a side road, past some chain motels with matching restaurants, a Red Lobster, an Olive Garden, then a few sharp turns, before—avoiding the town of Hauppauge completely—he suddenly came to the sprawling hospital and campus location.

A mammoth site, and he was soon faced with one of those signs that was an attempt to tell you where each different facility was located: the emergency room, the Rupert Thomas Cancer Center, administration, the hospital's main entrance, and a host of other divisions and departments dotting the massive campus.

But he saw the one he needed—pediatrics—and it showed an arrow pointing straight ahead.

Then, going slowly over the speed bumps, he saw another sign that said Pediatrics, and below that: Pediatric Oncology.

For the first time, Billy thought of the weight of those words. Thinking . . . he best steel himself for the visit ahead.

He turned and soon saw the parking lot, where he'd get a ticket and probably have to pay inside to get his car out.

He stopped.

And just for a moment, he looked behind him.

ADA Williams had said "they" would be watching him.

But so far, now only a little after 9:00 a.m., it didn't seem like anyone was following, or if they were, they had to be *really good* at not being seen.

He found a space, jumped out of his car, and started for the administrative building entrance, with its twin gothic pillars making for an imposing entrance. Up the stone steps, to a security guard with his wand.

A check with the wand, then Billy went through the metal detector; then he was cleared to approach the reception desk, staffed by a trio, all with paper coffee cups in front.

Billy smiled as he came close to them.

They didn't smile back.

Does nobody remember me? he thought.

He got right to the point, hoping that Williams was as good as his word about "arranging" things.

"Hi. I'm here to see Dr. Katie Brennan?"

Three sets of eyes looked at him while the burly man in the center picked up a phone, pressed some buttons, and said, "Name?"

"Billy Blessing."

No reaction to that. *Oh, come on.* Too young to have seen him on TV? Oh, well—maybe that was all to change. Unless all those plans of *Blessing's Back* being organized by Gretchen and Worldwide would also disappear as soon as this was all over. Just as long as he didn't.

He waited. The man nodded as he said Billy's name. Then he hung up, looked at Billy. "ID please. Oh, and past this desk, you will need to wear a *mask*. Still required here."

One of the reception people pointed to a sign on the counter informing visitors of that fact.

Billy nodded. "Right." Funny how masking was once normal every-where . . . now, really just in specialized medical places like this.

He took out his wallet and grabbed his driver's license.

The third receptionist of the somber trio pointed at a box filled with masks.

Billy took one. "Thanks." Slipped it on.

In a few minutes, a machine spit out a badge with a blurry copy of his photo from his license, as well as a barcode—the "open sesame" that would allow him entry.

The man in the middle handed it to him. "Third floor. She will still be doing rounds . . ."

"Why thank you," Billy said as he looked around. Spotted the way to elevators, barred by security gates.

"Just scan your badge."

Billy nodded and headed to the plexiglass gates.

32

WHAT PAUL STEINER DID

Upon his arrival at the Pediatric Oncology Center, a young woman appeared at another desk, with an easy smile, and simply said to Billy, "Mr. Blessing? I will take you to Dr. Brennan. She's on the floor. Doing morning rounds."

Billy nodded. "Thanks."

And armed with another just-issued badge, he followed the resident through a maze of corridors, then elevators, and more hallways . . .

Until the woman slowed as they entered a final hallway, the destination close.

He stopped.

The door opened.

And Billy, from the hallway, could look inside . . .

▷

To see a woman, medical coat on, standing beside a bed. A young girl sat up. Eight . . . maybe nine years old? Smiling, grinning. Bandanna on her head. Then the sound of both of them laughing.

He waited a moment as the doctor, the head of this whole department, patted the girl's hand, then turned to leave the room, when she saw Billy at the doorway.

She kept walking.

"Yes, um, how can I help you?"

Billy nodded, all this feeling intrusive, awkward . . .

"Dr. Brennan, you were told . . . I would come? Have a few words with you?"

The doctor came to the doorway, and Billy backed up as the woman shut the hospital room door halfway.

"Oh. Right. Told? *Ordered,* more like it. Anyway . . . Busy morning here. So—damn. Hold on."

And she slid out a phone. Read whatever message was there.

Then she looked back to Billy. He could see her full name on the ID tag on her jacket pocket: *Dr. Katie Brennan, Director of Pediatric Oncology.*

For a second, it seemed like she didn't know what to say. And certainly Billy was unsure how to begin this.

"Billy *Blessing,* is it?"

He nodded.

"Why don't we . . . go to my office? And I can see what it is you need to speak to me so urgently about?"

And as he nodded, she led the way forward. Billy had to wonder . . . this woman, so young for such an important position . . . *does she have an inkling what this is about?*

He guessed he would learn that soon enough.

▷

Dr. Brennan gestured at a chair facing her desk, loaded with stacks of paper and books in haphazard piles. Next to it was a side table that held a computer and a keyboard.

Billy got the feeling that the doctor didn't spend a lot of time in here. That she viewed her job to be *out there,* among the children.

And this thought: *What amazing work that must be.*

Dr. Brennan shut the door, then hurried to her desk, sat down. A quick smile.

"Okay, Mr. Blessing—"

"'Billy' will do," he said.

"Right. You needed to speak to me about—?"

Billy had considered how best to do this. But now—facing this formidable woman—that plan didn't seem all that well thought out.

"I have been, well, helping some people look into a man's disappearance?"

He felt her eyes trained on him, unwavering.

Billy rattled off the bare bones of the story, omitting—for now—key details . . . namely about the bullet-ridden boat, the bodies buried at sea.

To get to the essential point.

"Among the documents, I found—"

But the doctor started shaking her head. "*Excuse me.* I am seeing you because the Manhattan DA's office asked me to, *yes*? But—correct me if I am wrong—you *are* a TV celebrity? Or were? And now you have a new line of work? Detective?"

She was sharp, Billy could see, getting to the point in her own direct way. "No. Not a detective. Just that, well, it is a complicated trail how I got caught up looking into this . . ."

Katie Brennan didn't need to hear anymore. "And you have brought this information to me. About this man, missing, now . . . maybe dead? Because—let me hazard another guess—because you think there is a connection to *me*?"

And he pulled out from his jacket pocket a small sample of the bank documents that belonged to Paul Steiner.

"See these here?" Billy stretched out his hand, offering the papers.

A moment's hesitation, then the doctor took them.

"They are, Dr. Brennan, bank records of rather large sums being transferred from a number of bank accounts . . . some here in the states, lots offshore."

"Right. As I said, this ADA asked me to cooperate. So I will—*to an extent.* These funds, well, look like—yeah—grants to this institution. And they had major impact. For example, this new Pediatric Oncology Center? World class, and it wouldn't have been possible without all this . . . money."

The next thing was hard for Billy to say. This rather remarkable woman and his questioning words . . . nearly embarrassing.

"Yes." Billy took a breath. "And your tuition, for all your education, training . . . ?"

Billy looked at her. *Not pleased.* Because he knew . . . the issue of the tuition?

Dr. Katie Brennan would know full well all about that . . .

He detected a shift in her face, as if this was something she didn't want to think about *at all* . . . and yet here it was, right there in the room with them.

"This man, Paul Steiner, seemed to support your education all the way through medical school and was so generous to the hospital. So, I'm guessing—"

Billy had not been sure at all that he was going to suggest this next bit.

But now it seemed so clear—so he did . . .

"I'm *guessing* . . . that this man—this Paul Steiner—now missing, *was your father . . . ?*"

▷

And at that, Katie Brennan sat back in her chair. She looked out her office window. At the same time, Billy scanned the shelves behind her. Books with dark covers, embossed letters. Serious medical books . . . except on one shelf.

At one spot—a photograph.

A little hard to make out from here, but it showed a man holding a baby. Considering what Katie Brennan did here, it could be anyone.

The doctor turned to him. Took a breath.

"Okay. Just, well—all this . . . a lot to absorb? But if your 'trail' led you here, I might as well fill in the gaps . . . least the ones I know?"

"Good. That was my hope."

He didn't add that he also had a fear that if he found this woman—who was indeed really Paul Steiner's daughter—then others could.

And that could be so dangerous.

"So yes. He was my father. But I did not know my father growing up. Oh, I remember a very few times he came to see me. He supported my mother, but they didn't have anything to do with each other."

Another look away. Then: "When I was a baby, then again, a young girl . . . a handful of times. My mother had kept her maiden name. Were they even married? I don't know. Because—well, I assume you know *all* about this—about who my father really was? What he did. So those visits . . . rare."

"But . . . he cared for you?"

Another smile. "*Guess so.* I mean, made sense, his keeping distance. And then—well, after that big robbery where he was one of four involved. A massive heist. Meticulously planned. Successful. After that—he somehow vanished, while all the others were caught."

Billy nodded. "Yup, all that I know. Have crossed paths with a few of them or, at least, their relatives."

"*I am sure.* The others all went to prison, at least one dying there? And all that money that they worked so hard to steal—the money, the bankable assets—gone. Just like my father."

Billy guessed . . . *best not to interrupt the flow of this.*

"I never saw him again after that."

"But—there was *contact*?"

A pause from her.

"Of a *sort.* My mother kept my eyes looking forward. To the future. Education. Making something of myself. And somehow, the money for the tuition . . . a good private high school, NYU, then getting trained here . . . all completely paid for."

Billy had to ask: "Did you feel conflicted? All this support from money, well, ill-gotten gains?"

At that she laughed. "That what they call it? Look—I have attended enough galas for the big donors to know . . . all those wealthy people? With their hundreds of millions . . . did they all come by it doing good deeds, simply working hard?"

"Fair point."

"So—I spoke to a few people. A mentor in college—actually my

English literature prof, an ancient, white-haired man who had a lot of wisdom. And then, well, other mentors I met on the medical staff here. People I trusted. Heard pretty much the same thing . . ."

"Which was?"

"Let the loss of your absent father, and that money for which everyone paid a price . . . let it do some *good*. By doing what I could do. So—I made my peace with it. As, I imagine, so did this hospital . . . asking no questions."

"Seems to me, from what I can see, that was a good decision."

And Katie Brennan nodded in agreement. "Good. Glad you do. Tell you—there are moments I really doubt the way I got here. But I know the good I am trying to do, that the Pediatric Oncology Center does. So—my 'questioning' doesn't last long."

Then Dr. Brennan stood up.

"So, now you know what happened—and I can get back to my life. And you to yours. Since—"

Billy cleared his throat to interrupt. "Um, for what you have told me . . . *thank you*. But I'm afraid there is more going on. And I won't lie, some people—the Manhattan DA's office, for example—thinks it is dangerous. For you."

"For me? How on earth? I told you I *know* absolutely nothing about my father from that time, not even where he lived. Never saw him. I'm as clueless as anyone else about my *disappearing* father."

"Yeah," Billy said. "That may be. But could be, other parties may not be so sure about that? And if, well, you're to be protected—there is one other question I need ask you. For you to think about."

Brennan, still standing, seemed surprised that this meeting wasn't over.

"And that is?" she asked.

"Did your father *ever* say something, give you something, *anything* at all . . . that might have been his way of telling you his secret?"

"*Secret?* Sorry. I don't follow?"

"The money. A lot came here. But there is a *ton* still missing. Or so people think. Nasty people. Trust me on that one."

"Go on . . ." Her voice was tight.

"Could you know something . . . that perhaps you *don't* realize you know?"

And for a moment, another pause. The answer to this question Billy knew . . . so important.

33
THE CLUE

The doctor laughed. "Well—so you *think* I could know something that I don't know?"

"Okay. Perhaps I said that a little awkwardly. But is there anything that your father—though such a distant figure in your life—gave you? Something that could, in some way, be important?"

Dr. Brennan started shaking her head. "No. Nothing." But then she stopped. "There's just . . . *that . . .*"

She pointed to one of the bookshelves behind her. At the photograph. *The man with a baby.*

Billy stood up and walked over to it.

"May I?" he said, turning back to the doctor, who nodded.

Billy took the photograph down.

"I'm guessing—"

"Yes. My father. And me. The only photograph I have of him. He gave it to me when I was in high school."

"In person?"

A shake of her head. "No. He mailed it to me, with a note . . ."

"Do you have the note?"

"'Fraid not. But kept the picture. Guess, it is kind of important. At least one time, long ago, he held me."

"Yes," Billy said, studying the picture. "And do you remember what the note said?"

"Um, not really. Something like . . . well . . . '*Wish I was a better dad. More like the person in this picture.*' Something like that."

Billy had hoped that the picture, important to Dr. Brennan, could actually be of help in figuring out the mystery of Paul Steiner.

"Just that note then? And the picture?"

Another nod. "And well—there's something on the back of the picture. Didn't seem to mean anything."

At that, Billy froze for a second and then turned the frame over. But to see what was on the back of the photo, he'd have to take it out of the frame.

"Do you think I could take it out? See what's there?"

"Sure. Doubt it means anything. Least, it didn't mean anything to me."

Billy carefully slid the backing of the frame down, taking care to hold the glass of the frame and the picture in place.

Until the black felt-like backing was off, and he saw what was written on the back.

There was a name. *Luis.* Then a series of numbers that meant absolutely nothing to Billy.

"This 'Luis' . . . that mean anything to you?"

"No. Not at all."

Billy nodded. "And these numbers?"

"Not them either. Maybe went to a combination lock or something? Maybe just a note he made to himself . . . before he decided to give me the picture?"

Billy wasn't at all sure about that.

Was it just sentimentality and regret of all the time lost with his daughter . . . was that all that this represented? Or did it mean something else?

He kept staring at the two rows of numbers.

411525704

And below it:

72153947

Meaning absolutely nothing to Billy. Until—

They did.

Amazingly . . . *they did.*

"Do you mind if I take a picture of the photo of what's written here?"

"Sure. And if you have nothing more—"

Billy used his phone to take the pictures.

"Okay," he said. "Guess I'm done. But thank you for talking with me. I think that your father, whatever his failings, would be so proud of you. The work you do . . ."

Billy was tempted to tell her what was likely the fate of her father. But that—would be best left till he knew for sure.

"The work you do here—that he made happen? Guess—good can come from some odd places."

And at that, Katie Brennan turned to the office door, and Billy slid the frame's backing up again, replaced the photo on the shelf, and then hurried to leave.

But Dr. Brennan had some final words: "Stay safe . . ."

Billy nodded. That was the goal, of course.

And he sure hoped it was possible.

▷

Driving back to the North Fork, Billy used the Jeep's Bluetooth setup to make a call.

"Lola Bristow," he said, and Siri heard and confirmed the call to be made in her no-nonsense voice.

"Calling Lola Bristow."

He waited while it rang . . . once, twice, then again. Maybe she was out somewhere, out of range? The North Fork did have many dead spots.

But then—

"Hello, Billy! Where are you?"

"Heading back."

"Did you learn anything?"

Billy told the Northold police chief about the grants to the hospital and how Steiner had funded his daughter to do the amazing work she was doing.

"And that's *it*? Nothing that can help us with what's going on here?"

"Well. I think . . . I saw something. A photo. Katie Brennan as a baby, with Steiner. But there were things written on the back."

"Things? Such as?"

"Two series of numbers. First thought—they could be anything, or nothing. You know, maybe a combination lock? But then—something *clicked* . . ."

"Go on?"

"The numbers. Realized I had seen something very close to them, arranged in just the same way. See, not sure. But I think . . . they aren't *just* numbers? I *think* . . . they are GPS coordinates."

"Coordinates? I don't follow?"

"A location. I was seeing numbers just like these when I was on Willits's boat. Marking a specific location."

Then a pause. And he guessed that Bristow understood what that might mean.

"Wait a minute. You're thinking . . . maybe . . . the money, the bullion . . . maybe *there*?"

"Wow. Bingo. Or being cautious—*hopefully* bingo? Only one way to find out."

There was excitement in Lola's voice. "Go to wherever they indicate, right? I'll set that up. You want to come as well? Will bring in Talbot from the Coast Guard. Time we did that . . ."

"Good. Sure. And oh, there was one more thing written on the photo. Probably doesn't mean a thing. Right above the first row of numbers."

"Uh-huh?"

"A name. Luis."

And at that, he heard Bristow laugh.

"Well, Billy Blessing, my turn to tell *you* something. Does that name mean something? *You bet it does.* But why not wait till you are back? Come direct to the station. Meanwhile, I'll start making some calls."

Billy was tempted to ask her to please tell him now but then thought: nah, a little bit of suspense would make things all the more interesting.

So he said, "See you soon."

"You too."

And the call ended, Billy wondering: *What does Lola know about this name, Luis?*

34
TONIGHT, TONIGHT

Billy took care to park down a couple of streets from the small police station. And after he did, he sat there, looked around.

Of course, he now had the constant feeling that he was being watched. *Is that true?* he had to ask himself.

And if so, which of the various parties were watching him? And what were they thinking?

As he sat there, he took a few breaths. Been a while since he started his day with some meditative breaths; when one gets busy and preoccupied, *out* goes such things.

But now, sitting here, just to gain a smidge more composure, it was well worth doing.

Then, after one more look around, he popped open the Cherokee's door and got out. He walked in the direction of the station.

Lot of places he could be going to now . . . maybe the deli for a sandwich. Post office still open. Or the small drugstore, where he knew from personal experience one often had to wait a few days for whatever med was ordered since their stock was not at all close to a CVS.

But he walked past all three. Then, after a Ford pickup roared past, he dashed across the street.

Straight up the few steps and to the Northold Police Station door.

Opening it and walking in, he felt as if he had just broken into the Bank of London, safe and sound . . . *for now.*

▷

Lola was alone, standing by an open file drawer.

"Oh, good. You're here."

"Un, where's—?"

"Edgar? Told him to go home early. Said quiet day. I'd finish the filing, whatever. Didn't want him here when you came."

Billy nodded as if that made perfect sense. And he guessed, in a way, it did. The fewer people who knew what was happening here, the better.

Then Lola turned to him.

Big smile on her face.

"So let me tell you who I spoke to, what we have found out while you went to the hospital. And then what's ahead . . . *for tonight.*"

And Billy had to say, thinking that the day was pretty much coming to an end, "*Tonight . . . ?*"

▷

"I spoke with Martin Williams in New York. Told him of your discovery. He was impressed. If you ever want to give up the *cheffing*—"

"Um, nobody calls it *that.*"

"Then whatever it is you call it . . . I think there's a slot in the Manhattan DA's Office of Investigation for you."

"Good to know."

"Kidding. But then he did feel that those numbers, the coordinates? Definitely something to be followed up on *fast.* 'Vital' was the word he used. Oh—and also maybe a breakthrough."

"Thought it was pretty amazing myself," Billy said.

"Precisely. But then there was this name . . . Luis?"

"Though no way to tell who that was. But you said—"

"Yes. Well—guess what?" Bristow took some steps and sat on the edge of her sergeant's desk. "Turns out, *there was.*"

Billy nodded, waiting. He had discovered that name. God—he may have even discovered a place—somewhere—that had to be important.

But right now, Lola Bristow was in charge of the surprises.

"Fingerprints on record helped. Another person, maybe, well, who knows what citizenship . . . or immigration status of this Luis? Probably no way to identify who it was. And the people who sunk the two bodies could have comfortably assumed that both bodies would never be seen again."

"But?" Billy said.

"Yeah, *this* Luis, turns out did a bit of time for a few penny-ante things. Not recent, but his info, last name, last location, are all in the data records. So we know, right now, a good deal about this Luis."

While Bristow talked, Billy still remembered the word she had said, which was now reverberating in his mind. *Ominously as well,* he thought.

The word: *tonight. What the hell is happening tonight?*

"Luis Rivera. And he had a green card at one point in time, but I guess, since moving out here, he hasn't needed it. Supported himself doing a bit of this, bit of that. Helping in the boat yards. Working the fishing trawlers when they were a man down. Small construction projects."

"Lived here too? North Fork? This town?"

Bristow shook her head.

"Nope. Lived on Shelter Island."

"Really? Been meaning to go there."

"You should. Quite nice. Ferry out of Greenport. Good for a day trip. Between the two forks. Anyway—he lived here doing those kinds of things. But the Shelter Island police asked around, found out one other thing he did. Regularly. Guess it was no secret. No *apparent* reason to keep it secret."

"Which was?"

"Turns out there was this old man who, from time to time, would show up in his small fishing boat. Luis would be waiting on the dock.

Get in, and *off they'd go*. Like I said, a regular thing and, well, you know by now, out here? Small things get noticed."

Billy smiled. "I have, indeed, seen that."

"People assumed . . . the old man going fishing. Luis was hired to help, et cetera, et cetera. But listen to this: the same time, the very same day that Paul Steiner—the former Jack Landry—disappeared, so did Luis."

"But why? Why kill someone like that?"

"Well, one reason might be if you are going to kill Steiner after making him tell all, and he has this Luis with him? Then well—rules of the road, or the sea—better take them *both* out and dump the bodies in the drink."

The chief did have an effective way of expressing herself.

"But—that's not what happened?"

"It isn't."

Bristow shook her head. "No. You see no one *remembers* the old man and his boat coming that day. No one remembers Luis waiting on the dock for him. Which makes sense if Steiner did *not* come to pick him up."

"You are really losing me . . ."

"So, okay. What if . . . whoever killed Steiner had—somehow, some-way—already picked up Luis? Maybe even tricked him? Luis thinking he would be doing some work. On whatever boat those people were on. And then, somehow knowing where Steiner was heading, they cornered Steiner. Already had his helper, a prisoner, who did something together on a regular basis out on the open sea."

And finally . . . that all sort of clicked together for Billy.

More or less . . .

"So," he ventured, "they *what*? Questioned Steiner? This Luis? And when done, after—I assume—the two men spoke, maybe told them what they wanted to know, *killed them both*?"

"There you go. That's what I thought and the team in Manhattan agrees as well."

"Okay," Billy said. "That means they learned where the money was, right? All that cash, the gold, silver, whatever? Then—"

But Lola was already shaking her head.

"No. That is *not* what we are thinking right now . . ."

And Billy waited to hear what the current thinking was.

The ominous word uttered earlier . . . still front of mind . . .

Tonight.

▷

He saw Lola look at her watch.

"Got some place to go?" Billy asked.

But no answer, just a smile that he would have labeled *enigmatic.*

"ADA Williams's current thinking is, well, those people who picked up Luis? Who also picked up Steiner, made them both talk? Sure. They talked. Only like we said . . . what if Steiner *lied* to them? And Luis, not sure what to do, supported the lie?"

"You mean told whoever . . . where the money and assets were? But told them the *wrong* place?"

"Yes. Maybe Steiner thought they would let him go. Maybe he didn't care what they did. He just didn't want them to get all the money. And maybe, that is why he had those coordinates on the back of that photo. Thinking someday, well, the stolen money could maybe continue to be put to good use."

"And so they killed them?"

"Yes. Most likely. Williams says sometimes these guys think they got what they needed . . . only to discover that they didn't. Probably went to wherever Steiner directed them to, and found nada."

"Okay, that . . . kinda makes sense. But back up. Why not keep Steiner alive? Take him to the place?"

"Yeah. That—is a very good question. And I asked Williams. Whose thought was that, if they did *that* and Steiner didn't get back to the marina, people—the Coast Guard, I guess—would come look for him, his boat."

"So easier to just make him *disappear*? The prize apparently at hand?"

Bristow nodded. "So—that's the thinking."

For a moment, Billy said nothing, thinking this through. Sun down, and getting dark outside. Maybe they were done here.

But: "You mentioned something about tonight? Appears night is arriving."

She nodded. "*That I did.* And well, not only about tonight. Tomorrow night as well. The event at the club? Busy nights and day ahead for you, Billy. With luck, you may be alive at the end of it all."

"I love how you and the ADA always paint such a positive picture."

"So here you go. Here's what's going to happen, what you will do."

"No choice in the matter I am guessing?"

"Not if, as mentioned, you want protection, if you want to stay alive."

"That I do."

"Okay. Here are the plans . . . for tonight . . . and tomorrow as well."

"Tomorrow too? Should I take notes?"

She grinned. "Oh, I think you will remember *just fine* . . ."

35

TREASURE ISLAND

Billy watched as Lola went to the coatrack and grabbed a leather jacket. He could see a skullcap sticking out of one pocket.

"Tonight? Well—we will go to the place indicated by those coordinates you discovered. To see what we can see."

"In the dead of night?"

"You do remember me mentioning that you *are* probably being watched? Would be a very good idea to do this at night. So—you, me will drive to a spot not far from the marina—"

"In separate cars?"

"Of course. And meet up with Ted Willits, who will pick us up. Just a little beachhead, a cove, I guess they call it. Then—*away we go.*"

"And I am going because . . . ?"

"Because, Billy Blessing . . . I need *help.* That is, finding what we hope to find."

"Isn't this the point in the plot that the Coast Guard gets involved?"

Lola rolled her eyes. "Then, well, we come back. Same spot, dropped off, you home, hopefully no one seeing any of that."

"And isn't this the point in the movie you give me a spare gun? Might come in handy."

She ignored that question.

"Now then, when you are back to your place, you reach out to who-ever has been interested in what you have been doing. Tell them—and be *very* careful here . . . this is exactly how ADA Williams said it has to be—*tell them* you are ready to meet whoever it is. Think there are, at least, three players in motion with this thing?"

"If you say so . . ."

"But—meet them in Manhattan."

"Really?"

"Yeah. But let's get a move on. Tell you all the rest in the boat. Hope you don't get seasick—looks choppy out there."

"Oh, I think I might."

She opened the desk sergeant's drawer, took out another skullcap.

"Choppy and chilly, so put this on. Suits the activity quite well."

Lola wasted no time getting to the door, killing the lights.

"I'll go first, you follow. I'll text you the location; then you just nav-igate there, not far."

All this is going so fast, Billy thought. *Crazily fast.* And he realized that he had long passed the point where he felt he *might* be in danger.

Yes, going out to sea in the dead of night, and now whatever the hell was planned for tomorrow night at the big TV event, one where he now knew that "Tony Hill," also a member of this big-time mobster club, would undoubtedly be there.

And he knew one thing.

No *might* about it . . .

He was in danger.

▷

Willits stood on the sand near his boat, pulled tight to the shore.

"*Yer* late," he said.

"Apologies," Billy said, not sure the sarcasm would find its mark. "Our police chief here had some *'splaining* to do."

Willits ignored that.

"Gotta say—Chief Bristow, Billy Blessing—this here is *all* new to me."

"Hey, me too," said Billy. "And hoping first time, last—"

He watched Lola hop into the boat.

She looked at him and said, "All aboard."

He followed suit, and Willits came behind him, clambering up to the wheelhouse to quickly back *Sweet Sally* off the sandy beach and away from the cove.

▷

The coordinates had been entered into Willits's GPS. Lola sat next to him as this strange adventure began.

And yes, the sea was choppy, the boat riding one crest, then slapping down *hard* in the trough of another.

And Billy did actually start to feel a bit green around the gills, if that was the expression. Glad he had not yet had any dinner.

Lola Bristow, though, seemed as steady as a rock.

"Okay. So later, when you call your lovely mob contacts. Tell them you have discovered some information. They won't be surprised at that. But that's when you say you need to meet in a safe place."

"Such as?"

"The Park Avenue Club. You know. Where the TV event is tomorrow night?"

The boat hit a particular big swell, was forced up, and then slammed down like it might break in two. Willits leaned out from the wheelhouse just above them. "Sorry for all the chop. Sea's a little angry tonight. Hope you can handle it?"

"We're just *great*." And then Billy turned back.

"Really? Speak for yourself," Lola said.

"Okay. Back to your plan. So—all these people who want this stolen treasure, hidden for all these years and used by Steiner—"

"To do *good*."

"Yeah—but still, you know, still stolen. You want *me* to have them converge tomorrow at that building? Where Tony Hill will undoubtedly be since he was pulling strings to get me the hell out of here, right? All of them at the club. That what you are proposing? To speak with me? And this is going to help keep me alive *how*?"

"Told you. You will be watched, protected. You might not see them. I mean, you will see me. I'll be there too. But there will be detectives, people from the DA's office, and New York's finest in plainclothes. *Lot of protection.*"

"As I recall, ADA Williams told me there's no security tight enough to keep these guys from getting to me."

Lola gave Billy a hard stare.

And he returned the gaze with a smirk, adding, "And regarding the plainclothes cops and the club's dress code, best maybe not *too* plain?" Billy said. "Quite the glitzy affair, these things."

"Right. I will pass that on. So, you will set a time and a location. Do you know the club well? The layout and all that?"

"Been to a few fancy events there."

The boat hit another swell, and this time, Billy felt his body actually levitate inches off the port-side bench. The nearby air tanks rattled as if eager to escape the rack that held them.

"*Jesus.* Great night we picked for this little hunting expedition."

"Didn't actually *pick* it. You had a breakthrough. And it was time to move."

"Right . . . all my fault," he said with a grin.

"Look, Billy—despite your *colorful* background . . ."

He guessed she knew pretty much all that he had done, from jail, the name change, and his previous encounters with murders—and all that jazz . . .

"This, still—I know—more than a little scary? Pretty damn tense? But hold on to this—not a one of them would dare hurt you, *not* if they all think they need what you have."

"Good to know. I will try to remember that, even though that didn't work out for Paul Steiner and Luis."

"Okay. Point taken," she admitted reluctantly. Lola continued, "So, I said you tell the time, the place. You know the outdoor roof patio, connected to the main ballroom?"

"Do indeed. Quite the spot on a beautiful New York night."

"Oh—and I checked that out, tomorrow night will definitely be one. Temps not too bad for mid-October. But chilly enough that you should be able to find a spot all to yourself."

"And what? Just wait for all my new pals to show up?"

"Pretty much. But—oh, forgot one important thing."

"I will be carrying that spare gun you forgot to give me to protect myself?"

She laughed. He decided he *liked* that sound. He always enjoyed making people laugh.

A nice random thought . . . before back to the business of this—to him—so far nearly insane plan.

"Nope. No weapons for you, I am afraid. One of the parties will undoubtedly have you patted down very fast anyway."

"Makes sense. So, they show up and demand—I imagine—to know what I know?"

"Yes, and well, here—you've done a lot of TV? A lot of ad-libbing at times, when needed? What do they say to each other, to you? *Not sure.* But what I have been told is that the DA's office hopes they all will incriminate themselves."

Then—it dawned on Billy. "Hang on. I'll be wearing a wire?"

"Yes. Compact, undiscoverable even if you are patted down. Remember, lot of eyes on you out there too . . . in the building. In minutes, with luck, should be all over."

"The 'with luck' part doesn't sound too reassuring."

Then—and he did not expect this—she leaned close, only inches from his face.

"What—a man like you? All you've done? Oh, I think maybe"—a grin—"luck will do? My guess is you have always depended on taking a chance. Flip of the coin?"

Did she just close that distance between us a bit more?

This was getting interesting in an entirely different way.

But then, from above: "Okay, folks. We are *here.* Might need some help beaching her. Gotta watch the sonar . . . damn hidden rocks all over the place. But the small island is just ahead. And whatever the hell it is you are looking for."

And with that, the moment over, Lola moved away.

Billy stood up as Willits slowed *Sweet Sally* and prepared to beach the boat on the small island.

Billy held the railing, the boat rocking as Willits nudged it ahead ever so slowly, hitting the shore; then he gave the engine a quick burst to jet it forward onto the beach.

Then Willits hopped down.

"Now just hope I can *unbeach* her when we leave."

Lola meanwhile showed up with three shovels, handing one to Billy, then another to Willits, who took it, as if not knowing what to do with it.

"Um, I believe I am the captain? Get you two here, then back? As a favor to our local police?"

"Could use the help, Ted."

She waited. And the man grinned. "Yeah, and hell—maybe I could use the exercise."

Billy had to ask: "And the coordinates. The spot we are looking for?"

Willits turned to face the small island. "About fifty yards that way, into the brush, near the trees."

"And we find it—how?"

"Oh, I have an app that goes on my phone. Connects to the ship's satellite GPS. I'll find it alright."

Then he waved his shovel. "Whether we will find anything there . . . remains to be seen. Anyway—shall we get going?"

And Willits walked to the bow, stepping up to the railing. "Bit of a jump," he said. Then he hopped down, a small splash, onto the wet sand as water lapped at the edge of the beach.

He shouted back as Billy went to the front as well.

"Ha. Got a bit wet. But no worries . . ."

Billy watched Lola toss her shovel off to the side of the beach.

Step up to the front railing. Look down. With just a bit of hesitation.

She turned back to Billy. "Tell you . . . this is a long way from Bushwick, Brooklyn, Billy Blessing."

Then she too jumped, leaving Billy now to jump onto the sand. He could only agree with what Lola had just said.

What on earth was he doing here?

▷

Willits acted the part of the great expedition leader, one hand holding his flashlight, the other his phone, giving him a constant readout of the coordinates.

"*Okay*—should only be a few more yards this way."

And Billy followed the light, Lola next to him. He spotted crabs scooting away as Willits's light hit the sand, probably not used to any nighttime intrusions. A light breeze blew off the water.

Billy turned around and saw—in the distance—some lights. Looked like a big ship, out there somewhere. Maybe heading east to cross the Atlantic.

It only reinforced how alone they were here.

Willits stopped and turned to them.

"Okay. Um, according to this, we have *arrived.*"

Lola wasted no time. She handed Willits back his shovel.

"What? I'm supposed to—"

"C'mon. Will go faster if you help. Besides, haven't you ever wanted to dig for buried treasure?"

"No—I haven't. Do enough of that under the water."

Billy went to the spot Willits indicated and started digging. The sand was surprisingly heavy.

"Digging for goddamn buried treasure. On an island. Who'd believe it?"

And they all laughed at that.

▷

But when they had gone pretty deep, they stopped . . .

Willits first, then Billy, who had built up a sweat despite the cool breeze. Then Lola.

"Um, think we have made an unfortunate discovery," Willits said.

Lola nodded. "Yeah. Nothing here. Could your GPS-coordinate device . . . be *off*?"

Willits shook his head. "No—and that's from years of using it marking dive spots, *down to the foot*. 'Fraid there's nothing here, Chief."

Billy had a question, though he feared it might be a stupid one. "Should we try some other spots?"

Willits laughed at that. "Kind of a big beach, Billy Blessing. Any spot in particular strike your fancy?"

Billy nodded. Willits certainly had a point. If the coordinates indicated here, and now, with this big hole, nothing here? Then where the hell else?

Then he had a thought—simple but obvious: *they were missing something.*

But Willits stuck his shovel into the sand so it would stand upright. Then walked over to him.

"You said . . . you had a picture of the clue? The coordinates leading here?"

"I do."

Another step closer.

"Mind if I—"

And Willits came close enough so he could look, as Billy opened the Photos app, scrolled, and found the picture of what he'd found—just today—on the back of the photo of Steiner with his daughter as baby.

Willits took his time looking. Lola had also come closer, looking at it.

While Billy waited.

36

A MISSING CLUE

Willits hadn't said anything. Least not yet.

So Lola prompted: "Hey, Ted—see something?"

A pause, but then he looked up, his face quizzical. "*Maybe*. See, um, those coordinates are, well, right *here*?"

"Yes. Um, so we don't have them wrong then?"

"No. But, well, why that name here, right above them? This *Luis*?"

"It's the name of the guy we think Steiner used when he came to make his 'withdrawals.'"

"Not from this spot here, he didn't. But I do see something. Not sure. Could be nothing."

Billy now also looked down at his own phone, the string of numbers, the name above them.

And Willits tapped the name. "This Luis? Why is it here, next to the supposed clue? You know what I'm thinking?"

Actually, Billy had no idea.

"That is . . . because maybe it's *part* of the damn clue."

Billy looked at Lola, her face catching the light, eyes wide—excited because, no matter how you sliced it, this might be important.

"Just a name, right? But see the marks, those two dots between the *LU* and the *IS*?"

"Yeah," Billy said.

"Right, and then . . . almost hard to see, the little mark after the *S*, one of those, what do you call, them?"

"Apostrophes," Lola said.

"Yeah. Well, notice anything when you just look at them, then down to the string of numbers, the coordinates below it?"

Then Billy saw it. The last four digits of the coordinates had the same markings as seen in the name. The two dots of a colon, the small apostrophe at the end. But then—what did that mean? Weird. Interesting. *But what the hell was it about?*

Lola kept her eyes on the screen. "Hang on. Maybe the name with the symbols indicates that—somehow—*they* should be the last four digits of the coordinates? Meaning the name is somehow a clue to the right spot?"

Willits finished the thought: "And if right—we've just been digging in the wrong damn spot. But hang on—and correct me if I am wrong—those are letters, *not* numbers?"

Then something else clicked for Billy. "Wait. In any clue—I mean I am not a cryptologist—but letters can sometimes stand in for numbers, right? The *L*, the *U*—"

"Holy shit," Willits said. "Excuse the French. I've heard of that. In movies, books. Sure. That's really cool. But, er—do either of you two smart people know *how* to do it?"

"Do what?" Lola asked.

Another tap by Willits on Billy's screen. "Change those letters into numbers?"

Lola was quick to shake her head. "Sorry."

Willits quickly turned to Billy, who had to add: "Me either." But he did have an idea. "We have internet here, off your boat's satellite connection?"

Willits nodded.

"That means we can hit the internet, and—this day and age—must be an app or a website that can do just that?"

Lola looked up, warm smile on her face. Billy liked that smile in this reflected light as she said, "Then—what are you waiting for?"

And Billy brought his phone close and began tapping at the screen.

▷

Amazingly, it took almost no time at all.

Billy, who had thought this was all quite eerie and exciting before, was feeling that way more now.

"Okay," he said. "According to this app, we have four possibilities . . ."

"Four?" Willits said, losing some of his enthusiasm.

"Yup for the *LU*, could be twelve or twenty-one. And *IS*, nine or nineteen."

Lola nodded, catching on what that meant. "That means . . . we may have new coordinates?"

"*Four* new coordinates," Willits said grumpily.

Lola nodded. "But all near here, yes? We just have to go to each spot, dig . . ."

"Dig we must," Willits said with a laugh. He brought out his phone, and then he entered the first possibility, with the new final digits of 12:19′.

Then he led the way again.

As he did, he said, "You know . . . those pirates, back in the day? Must have been real tough before all this technology!"

And Billy laughed.

▷

They were on the third possible combination after creating yet another new set of coordinates.

This spot was some distance from the boat, more inland, and there even seemed a path of sorts where the grasses had been pressed down. But Billy also had the feeling: What if *none* of the four places to dig revealed anything?

Then the wild goose . . . will not have been caught.

Willits stopped. "You know, at my age . . . not sure all this strenuous exercise is good for the old back?"

But Willits took his shovel again and dug into the sand. Then Billy, with Lola right next to him, began digging again as well.

All the time, he thought, *Only one more combination to try.*

He hoped this was the one. All this digging sand was indeed getting so tiring, his muscles aching.

But now—with all that ache and pain—they worked in silence. The only sound was the *whoosh* of the blades of the shovels steadily digging into the hole as it grew wider, deeper.

So far, nothing was revealed but more sand: darker, wet, mixed with soil perhaps. No crabs here—but that didn't stop Billy from thinking they were, somehow, being watched.

Which is when Lola pushed her shovel in—and then stopped.

Billy hadn't heard anything.

"Okay. *Felt* something just now. Hard? So—I stopped. Think . . . *think*"—she looked up at Billy—"there's something here?"

"Best we take care, you know? Excavating whatever the hell it is."

The police chief nodded. "Nice and slow, just so we can see . . ."

And now, all three of them started using their shovels more carefully to remove sand from the top of whatever it sat on, then from the sides. Willits paused now and then to aim his phone's light at whatever lay on the bottom of the hole.

Eventually a large dark metallic chest was revealed. And with the sand cleared from the sides, he could see a combination lock—one where you twirl cylinders to get the correct numbers in place—was embedded on the side of the chest.

They stopped.

Billy had to ask. "What now? We try to open it?"

Bristow stood up. "No. Pretty clear this is it, right? Has to be where Steiner hid the money, the gold, anything else of value? I think we can leave it to others to dig it out, open the chest, which looks pretty secure. And then *they* can see what's inside."

Willits was still looking down.

"*Secure*'s the right word. That's an Eva-Dry solid steel chest. This whole area could get flooded, and whatever the hell is in there would stay perfectly dry. Whoever picked it out knew what they wanted."

Billy stood there for a second. "So—we're done?"

He also realized, for the first time, why—if Steiner showed whoever came at him, in his boat, the image of the coordinates—*they didn't find it.*

They missed the other clue, the real key. The name: *LUIS.*

The real location, Billy realized, unfortunately he now knew.

Meaning if anyone—the very next night—wanted to make him talk somehow? Maybe using a little torture? He imagined all those guys knew about such things.

Wouldn't take Billy long to tell them where to find this.

And yet, Lola was leaving it here.

Billy thought, *That part, not my problem. They said one more night, and maybe this will all be over.*

But that would all take place back in New York. A place he loved. Where he had worked for so many years on morning TV. Where he even once had his own damn restaurant.

Now—somehow—to be the place where this crazy week of mobsters and missing money . . . would end.

The end? God . . . he really hoped so.

He said to Lola, "Now what?"

"We bury this. Nice and neat. Then head back. And you, well, you have some of your new friends to contact . . . let them know that you just may know something about Steiner's hidden treasure. All to be revealed—"

"At the Park Avenue Club?"

"Yup. Tomorrow night."

Billy looked up at the stars glistening, the night beautiful. Thinking: next time he saw the stars, he'd be on the great patio of the club.

To meet people.

Who definitely were not . . . friends.

37

SOME IMPORTANT CALLS

Billy put the phone down, the burner phone Marco Pierce had given him, the man who had him kidnapped and brought to what he guessed was the Hamptons.

The voice on the other end—maybe Marco himself?—had simply said, "Yes?" on answering. Billy quickly said that he had learned some things, but he would not meet anywhere out here.

Too exposed, too dangerous . . .

Said he had something to tell. About what had actually happened to the "missing man." Then—to really bait the hook—he said he had learned something that he thought Marco Pierce would be very interested in hearing. And he needed to tell him *in person.*

But it would need to be someplace safe, lots of people around. Sure. Nice and safe. Like the Worldwide television event at the Park Avenue Club.

The very next night.

The voice on the other line paused as if pondering how best to—maybe?—strangle Billy.

But then Billy added that he knew other people were watching him. It would be much safer there, on the club's outdoor patio, at 9:00 p.m., just as all the speeches began downstairs. And somehow—amazingly—the voice, which Billy was now sure had to be the boss himself, agreed.

One down. Now to call one Lisa Cowles, who was—Billy now knew—not really Lisa Cowles at all.

He entered the number and waited while it rang. Only on this call, it rang half a dozen times, and then a recorded voice answered.

"Please say who is calling."

Billy figured this was some kind of call screening device.

To which he answered, "Billy Blessing."

Then the pickup.

"Billy. Been waiting to find out what you've learned."

He had to wonder whether this Cowles person—her real name now known to be Celia Kole—had been following him around as well, or any of her friends? Maybe she had sent the people who broke into his house? Or had people lurking in dark and mysterious cars, watching him?

"Yes," he continued the ruse, "it's about your father. I have learned some important things."

"And they are?"

Billy did a slight clearing of his throat.

"But, er, I also found something more interesting, that you need to *know*. In person. But, hey—I don't want to say anymore here. Think—"

He played the same card with her that he had just employed with the boss in his mansion on the Atlantic.

"People are watching me, following me. I'm getting, well, a little jumpy. Yeah, scared."

No word of reassurance from the woman.

"So we should meet—"

She cut him off and started to dictate where the meeting should occur. "Okay. I know a small park, about thirty miles from—"

"*No*," Billy said. "I want to meet in a place with a *lot* of people. Safer for me. Maybe—safer for you."

A pause then. This woman, whatever her role in this, was thinking that over.

Then: "*Where* exactly is that, Billy?"

"Tomorrow's the big TV event at the Park Avenue Club. Invite only but . . . I am sure, someone like you? You can figure a way in?"

She didn't disagree with that suggestion.

"All the speeches begin at nine p.m. I can meet you out on the club's big outdoor patio. Tell you everything."

No immediate agreement to that.

Billy prompted, "You, um, got that? Know the place?"

Still nothing.

Maybe, he thought, *she doesn't like this.* Suspicion aroused? But then, like all pauses, this long one ended . . .

With a quiet, "Okay. Hope you have something good for me. I will, of course, bring a check."

"Yeah. Great. And, um, see you there."

She ended the call.

And then Billy was left with one unsettling thought . . .

▷

Namely, according to ADA Williams, there had been *three* parties—three Associates—who had planned the big heist besides Steiner.

So two of them—or at least people connected to them—were now, in some way, in motion.

What about the third?

But Billy also now knew that this person was most likely someone else with a made-up name. "Tony Hill," who was really Sammy Rose.

Billy had the feeling that some of the odd and intimidating encounters he'd had over the past few days had to be the actions of this player number three—Rose.

But he didn't have to lure Sammy Rose to the event. "Tony Hill" was supposed to be a big investor, and knowing that Billy would be there . . . it would be time for him to play his card.

If it all worked out . . .

All was to be revealed tomorrow when he headed, all dressed up, into Manhattan for the gala event.

For an encounter with some people who—he was sure—would kill for the information he now had.

After all, people had been murdered.

For people like them, what's one more corpse among new friends?

And with that thought, he got up—it was getting late—but went to the bottle of Monkey Shoulder. Poured a few fingers. Then a splash more.

Grabbed a couple of cubes from the freezer.

And sat in his chair.

Sipping, thinking, worrying—but above all, wondering . . .

What the hell am I doing?

38

NEW YORK, NEW YORK

Billy wanted to get into the city before sunset, just at the beginning of the opening cocktail reception at the Park Avenue Club.

The azure sky of the day was slowly fading, giving way to that beautiful deep blue-violet, but the hours were simply not passing fast enough. Then as the hour to leave grew closer, time suddenly seemed to pass too fast, bringing him to this tense point—driving into New York for whatever the hell may happen.

The LIE traffic flowed heavy in an endless stream in the opposite direction to which he was driving. Away from the city, back to the burbs.

And as he sat there, the sun to the right of the highway sank ever lower in the west, a lush orange. Within minutes, it would soon disappear behind the buildings of Queens, the apartments, the warehouses, before vanishing completely behind the wall-like skyline of Manhattan.

Now—*that* was a sight that never got old.

He also felt uncomfortable sitting in a suit. God—with a tie even!

It had been a long time since Billy wore a tie on a regular basis, during his *Wake Up, America!* days. But for this club, like all the other upscale clubs—the University Club, the Manhattan Club—it was absolutely required for all major events.

A damn tie.

Even when he loosened it a bit, it still felt like a noose around his neck.

Bad choice of words . . .

At midday a Fed-Ex package had arrived. Inside was the so-called "wire," which in this case was the size of a credit card, meant to be slipped into a jacket or shirt pocket. The micro battery was charged. And it had some kind of Wi-Fi connection that Billy certainly could not comprehend . . . to broadcast whatever conversations Billy was to have.

While ADA Williams listened. Maybe just to mess with him, Billy would go to the bathroom.

He licked his lips then.

Because he kept coming back to the question of . . . *his protection.*

Williams, Lola . . . both had *promised* he'd be well protected. Eyes on him even when he didn't know, they had said.

But he knew the general layout of the great stone patio of the club.

If memory served, no big lights out there. Place was dark . . . moody even (or he guessed, in different circumstances, perhaps romantic?).

Would he really be seen and heard?

He took a breath.

He really needed to calm himself—or his demeanor and wobbly legs would reveal that something fishy was up.

He saw a sign for the Cross Island Parkway, then the Grand Central to the Van Wyck. Yes. With light traffic, the actual city, Midtown ... . not far now.

Yay, he thought. Which did not reflect how he felt—at all.

As the inevitable came closer and closer.

▷

Billy walked into the Park Avenue Club's grand ballroom.

The place was packed. An army of white-jacketed servers were circulating with trays of champagne flutes and a variety of hors d'oeuvres.

For a moment, no one spotted him; no one recognized him.

But then . . .

"*Billy*—you're finally *here*! Was getting worried. I know how bad the traffic on the LIE can get—"

Billy looked at Gretchen. "Not too bad tonight. Um, this quite the party."

Gretchen nodded. "Oh, yeah. Jim—"

He noted that she referred to the current head of Worldwide—Jim Collins—by his first name. Did that mean something?

Knowing Gretchen, *possibly* . . .

"—wanted to go *all out*. I mean, there are the big announcements, including all about Worldwide's plans for you. That will be a big surprise!"

Billy smiled. "Can hardly wait—" he said, while actually he was preoccupied scanning the crowd for any people who didn't seem to be there for the champagne and the big announcements.

And in the crowd, he recognized a few familiar faces from his past.

The host of a one-time competitor to his old show, *Wake Up, America!*, the former NBA star, Lew Jeffries, who—smart and fast—turned out he could carry off an interview with just about anyone, from the tragic to the comic.

And nearby, the female anchor of the show, Rebecca King . . . someone Billy had known for a long time. They hadn't spotted him yet.

But he thought, *I've been out of the game for so long, a chat with them might be good.* Yeah, with people he would have once called *peers* . . .

Gretchen continued, "And once the paperwork is nice and tidy, let me tell you, Billy. They are ready to roll with all of it, *fast*. The streaming shows, even the restaurants, also guest visits to a bunch of shows in the big buildup to the launch."

"Sounds . . . yeah, exciting." Billy guessed he meant that, but it was so hard to really concentrate on what Gretchen was saying when something else was in play.

Something far more "exciting," if that was the correct word.

Then Lew Jeffries turned, spotted him, gave a big wave, grinned, and came over.

"*Billy Blessing!* Good to see you, *man!*"

And then an intricate handshake, which Billy was pretty sure he didn't navigate too well.

Gretchen looked around and said, "Gonna get a refill . . . be right back. *Do not* disappear."

"Oh, I won't."

Then back to Jeffries, a good foot and a half taller than him. "I hear the buzz is Worldwide has some amazing things planned for you? And we get to hear all about it tonight?"

Billy laughed. "So I've heard."

"But, hey—you were actually doing *okay*, at the end of the island? Just cooking in a small place? I mean, didn't you miss it all?"

"Getting up at three thirty a.m.? Did not miss *that*. And yeah— kinda like it out there just fine."

"You know, I kept thinking I should drive out with Maria. Must have a nice hotel or two nearby? Eat at your place."

"Well, as of next week, I am still there, so you have, as they say, a *window*."

"Good, good, Billy. And hey, glad you are coming back to the arena. I mean, let's face it . . . you're a national treasure."

Hope not a buried one, Billy thought.

Jeffries turned. "Oops, I see my network's head honcho. I better go schmooze. More talk later?"

"Absolutely," Billy said.

Then for just a few moments, he was alone again, standing there, everyone dressed to the nines . . . even a few *tens* in there. He realized he better get his own wardrobe upgraded.

If he was indeed coming back to the . . . *arena*.

But as he stood there, passing on a tray of mini eggroll things on offer, he kept scanning the room. More people were coming over for a chat.

This community of television people was real. That warmth, amaz-ingly—actually genuine.

But fortunately or unfortunately, there was no sign of *any* of the people he'd told to come here, to find their way into this event somehow.

To meet him in just—

He looked at his watch . . .

Forty-five minutes 'til nine o'clock.

And then he observed something else—or rather, didn't observe.

The protection he was told about? ADA Williams? And undercover police? And Lola?

Where the hell were they?

He felt totally alone and—he had to admit—he felt vulnerable.

And that was scary.

But then he spotted a famous UK TV chef who now did probably zero cooking but barked at contestants on a cooking competition show. In truth, actually a good cook—and a friend.

Billy stood there, watching the minutes slip away as he spoke to these people from his past.

And he guessed, what looked like his future.

▷

A steady stream of people kept coming and congratulating Billy, some of whom he knew, many brand-new faces. Fun at first, but a little of that gushing goes a long way, he had learned long ago.

And then Gretchen Di Voss finally circled back.

"*Okay*, Billy—I think the presentation is about to begin. Leading off with a glitzy video thing they put together. New logos for the new streaming network and the new shows. Haven't seen it myself yet, but I imagine *you* will be all over it."

Billy nodded. Another glance down at his watch. The screen came to life with the move. *Five minutes to nine.*

He looked over at the side doors of the ballroom that led out on the right to the Park Avenue Club's rustic tavern, one of the best places in the city to get a serious cocktail, and the other doors, off to the left, to a stone staircase that led up to the top of the building and out to the patio, large enough to be the site of its own sizable party.

Billy turned to Gretchen. "Um—I don't have to say anything, do I?"

"No, of course not. I mean if Jim points to you—and he probably will—maybe a wave? All this, just the kickoff to the *whole deal.*"

"Got it."

Then Billy saw someone he didn't know come to the podium. Some new junior exec, Billy guessed. The affable host for the evening . . .

"Ladies, gentlemen . . . we're about to start the presentation. So, hold on to your champagne flutes as CEO Jim Collins shows you the amazing world of Worldwide *to come!*"

And at that, applause as Jim Collins walked over to the podium, the lights on the ballroom dimming. Gretchen's eyes were locked on the stage.

Billy took a casual step back.

Then another.

Then one more, Gretchen not yet noticing that he wasn't by her side. Wasn't this how Clark Kent would ditch Lois in those movies? *Only, I'm not turning into Superman, unfortunately, and I'm on my way to meet Lex Luthor.*

Finally, he turned and began to weave his way in the darkness, through the sea of people, toward those side doors . . .

39

TIME FOR ONE MORE MURDER?

Billy opened one of the big side doors, the wood thick and heavy, ancient and reluctant to move, and he slipped out.

Here he saw the waitstaff clustered in the hallway area, waiting for the show inside to be over, ready to the hit the floor again with drinks and munchies, a long night ahead.

He turned to them. All of them were chatting, enjoying their respite. A few looked up, perhaps recognizing him.

"Um gonna . . . head up . . . get some air?" he said with a smile. "Getting stuffy in there, if you know what I mean." A few grinned at that.

Then he turned to the wide marble steps, starting up, the stone worn into a depression from a century and a half of people using these stairs, wanting to enjoy the city skyline from the great patio.

At the top of the stairs were more doors. But these were already thrown open wide to the night air. The patio outside looked dark. Not much light here, save for the glittering city that surrounded it.

But when Billy slowed his pace and walked out—New York City in all its skyscraper wonder around him—he saw . . . he was not alone here.

Small clusters of people, two, three . . . *here, there.* Someone even smoking a forbidden cigarette.

People up here were apparently not interested in whatever announcements were happening down in the ballroom below.

And Billy had to think . . . *Maybe the other people up here, in the shadows, are here for other purposes?*

He stopped for a moment, thinking, *I have never felt so damn exposed in my entire life.*

And then he started walking again, spotting a corner of the patio with no one else there.

Good spot to stand as if taking in the sights.

And wait.

To see what happens . . .

Which for a while was absolutely nothing. A few people wandered off the patio, perhaps in search of a refill.

A few more people, all shadowy in the scant light, came out, finding their own private spot along the stone wall that girded the expansive patio.

And so far, nothing else happened.

Had this plan begun to unravel already? The people supposedly lured by whatever Billy knew, deciding to *pass* on the invitation?

Which certainly meant, he grimly understood, that they would have other, probably more dangerous plans for him.

But then—just as Billy pivoted from looking uptown, chunks of the dark Central Park visible, back to the patio—he saw someone walking toward him.

A woman. And she walked cautiously. Not rushing, but there could be no doubt . . . *she was headed straight toward him.*

And when she was just feet away, her face picking up the little light, he recognized her.

Without a thought of what he should do, he forced a smile.

Which he hoped didn't look . . . *forced.*

The woman, only a foot away, simply said, "Hi, Billy."

And he saw that this was the woman who had started him down this dangerous rabbit hole—chockablock with dead people and secrets and apparently so much money at stake—and she wasn't smiling.

Her face was quite serious.

"Hi," Billy said.

"So, alright. I'm here, you're here. You said you could talk, hmm? Time to see what you have learned about my father."

Well, that was one thing he would be telling her right away. That it wasn't her father who had gone missing.

Not at all sure how that would be received. Most people probably didn't like being told they had been discovered lying.

He cleared his throat. He suddenly wished some of those waiters, with their silver trays with their rows of bubby neatly lined up, would magically appear.

He nodded. Ready to begin.

Knowing that—if all went according to plan—this chat was only the start.

But plans are only plans, he knew.

And things often don't go . . . according to any plan.

$$\triangleright$$

"What I learned? Well, funny thing is I have learned a *lot*."

He felt the woman's eyes on him. Those dark eyes locked on him, and it was—quite simply—disconcerting. But he continued: "First, well, I learned that you are *not* Jack Landry's daughter . . ."

She smiled at that, apparently not alarmed by the revelation.

"Then, I learned that Jack Landry is not the man's real name. Actually, his name, it turns out—surprise, surprise—is Paul Steiner. And my guess is you're *still* not his daughter."

He paused to see how this was going down. But the woman simply stood there, the moment chilling.

"And, well, I'll just continue, I guess? Your real name is Celia Kole, and I guess, obviously your *someone's* daughter?"

He grinned at this bit of cheekiness. This was a dangerous game, but at the moment . . . kinda fun.

"Maybe someone named Max Kole?"

But at that, the woman shot up a hand. "*That*—might be a good place to *stop*, Billy Blessing. You seem to have found out a good deal about everything, except about what the *hell* I asked you to look into—"

She actually took a step closer, now inches away, voice lowered though there was no one within earshot.

Billy did a sideways glance: *Where the hell is that damn protection that is supposed to be in place?*

Because there didn't seem to be anyone up here, looking out for him . . . anywhere.

"What I *asked* for—and was going to pay a lot for—was any information that told me what happened to this . . . okay, Paul Steiner. And I'm afraid I must say, right now? I sure the hell hope you do know something about *that*."

Was that a threat? Billy wondered.

Sure *sounded* like a threat, he thought. This steely-eyed woman alone up here . . . or . . .

Maybe not alone? After all, he could see those little clusters of people, all dark in the shadows of the patio.

Just hanging out? Or—?

But at this point, he had no choice but to continue with the plan.

Which he hoped to hell was really a plan.

And not a dangerous fiasco on a nice Manhattan night in October about to turn deadly . . . specifically, for him.

▷

"Okay. And have to say, I'm guessing some of this that I am about to say to you . . . maybe you already know?"

She said nothing back to that.

"Paul Steiner went to sea, as he did most days . . . and he was tracked by some people. Who shot up his boat. Then they shot him up—and *then* made sure no one would find the body."

"But you *did*?"

"Not me. I mean, I was *there* but—but yeah. The body was found."

"And these people, you know who they are?"

Billy shook his head. About to tell her the truth and hoping that she believed it.

"No. To my knowledge, I have not had the pleasure of meeting them. Least I don't think so! But I'm *thinking* they got from Steiner what they thought they wanted, then killed him. And I guess—that's it."

Another pause from the woman, eyes still on him. Billy thought, *This woman . . . she's good at that.*

"I doubt that's . . . *it*, Billy. So, I'm going to ask you a few more questions and—Billy—"

Her saying his name slowly, with emphasis, seemed to carry its own threat.

"—I *really* encourage you to tell me everything that you know. Leave nothing out. Because as you may guess—with bodies buried at sea?—why, absolutely anything can happen in this *game*."

And Billy then realized that—just maybe—she might know about the person killed with Steiner, this Luis.

But as he had discussed with ADA Williams and Lola, back in Northold—which now seemed so terribly far away—at this point, on this night, endgame in play? He should hold nothing back.

"Okay. I found bank statements. Lots of money in, out."

The woman nodded.

"Tracked that to a hospital. Then to someone who—oh, you will *like* this part, unless you already know this—was *really* Steiner's daughter. Though, she saw little of him. But that money paid for her education as a doctor, a cancer specialist . . ."

"How touching."

Celia Kole gave no indication that she might have known this.

"And . . . ?" she said.

At this point, Billy dug out his phone, swiped to Photos. And then—the right picture on display—handed it to the woman.

"This right here? It was on the back of a photo of Steiner and his daughter when she was a baby. And I thought: the name, those numbers . . . must mean something? A clue to the stolen money maybe?"

The woman staired at the photo intensely. And Billy suddenly had a queasy feeling in his stomach. His first lie coming. A big one. Pretending he *didn't* know what they meant.

And if this person *knew* it was a lie, well, that could be really bad.

But she looked up. She smiled. Looked as if she was about to say something.

Billy tried to hide his gulp.

Which is when, from across the other end of the patio . . . three people now made their way, heading directly to them.

Company coming.

The woman turned, Billy wondering who was coming their way.

Was the plan actually *working*? People showing up, bad people, thinking the path to a big payday led to this beautiful outdoor patio on a balmy New York night.

Then the man in the middle kept coming forward, while the two men flanking him stopped. And now Billy finally recognized the trio.

My old pal, Marco Pierce of the Hamptons, he thought. And behind him, the two goons from the night before.

Pierce wasted no time. "*Celia Kole?* Well, I did not expect *you* to be here, hmm? And Billy—must admit, little disappointed that you are *not* alone. And if you don't mind?"

The man put his hand out, indicating to Celia that the phone should be handed over. But she hesitated.

Then Pierce did the slightest tilt of his head, gesturing to the two men a few feet back.

"My people here are armed, by the way. Their weapons silenced, of course. Hate to have to make it seem like—maybe—you have somehow *fainted*? Too much of that cheap champagne? When you actually have a nasty hole in your chest."

A pause, then his hand rose, palm up . . .

"*Give!*"

And then this Celia Kole, not looking happy even in the dim light, handed the phone over to the man. He stared at it for a few minutes, then looked up to Billy.

"What the hell is—? Er, I don't understand this. What is it? What does it mean?"

Billy hoped people somewhere were listening to all this, ready to pounce. So he said, "Well, I can explain what I think it *might* mean. That is, if you like?"

Billy suddenly realized the absurdity of that bit of politeness . . . since he was obviously facing people that would have no problem killing him if he didn't tell them all he knew.

None at all.

And the man gave a nod to the two goons, who came close to Billy, one on each side. Billy felt something hard jab in his ribs. And he could well guess what that was.

"Okay. Easy, huh? Everyone *stay* calm? Right so—"

And that was about as far as Billy got, when *someone else* started walking toward the group.

Yet another new addition to this party.

Billy had hoped it might be ADA Williams, with a well-armed group of associates. Or maybe Lola?

Anyone but the person whom he now saw and recognized as all the tumblers—and the players—*clicked* into place.

The man called 'Tony Hill' at the SoHo meeting just days ago, who, like all these mobsters—funny about that—was really someone else.

Sammy Rose walked slowly toward them.

The people in front of Billy took note that *he* had noticed someone new was coming to the party. They turned as well.

While apparently everyone waited for what was to come next . . .

40

WHO KILLED PAUL STEINER?

Sammy Rose stopped and took in the others. Not saying a word. Just standing there, crisply dressed in a tailored suit, a light and shiny gray. His black hair combed back. Shoes pointy, polished, and looking incredibly expensive.

But alone.

Which, considering the goons that stood next to Billy, both quite clearly armed, he had to wonder: *All things considered, that doesn't seem too wise.*

But Rose stopped just a few feet away. Then, all eyes on the new arrival, he spoke, with a gravelly voice to match his outfit and profession.

No wonder he keeps quiet, Billy thought.

"Good evening, old *friends*. I see you are looking at that photo there? The damn *numbers*?"

Celia said, "What the *hell* are you doing here, Sammy?"

"Same thing as you, I imagine. Trying to find if this moron here has learned where the hell Paul Steiner really stashed all that money, all that bullion, all those fully negotiable international bonds."

But Billy figured—having just been labeled "moron"—this was as good a time as any to ask a question.

"Um. Excuse me. But I assume all of you know each other? Sort of? Cross paths professionally, so to speak? So—that puts me at a disadvantage . . ."

Sammy Rose smiled at that. Not a very warm smile as it morphed into a sneer, Billy saw.

"Allow me," Marco Pierce started. "Yes, we three are all—"

But Rose cut him off: "*That* will be enough."

Pierce nodded. "Oh. You seem worried? That this ex-TV cook—"

"That's 'ex-TV chef,' actually," Billy interjected.

"—could go to someone with your name, what we are all trying to find? Well, no worries—*that* damn well is *not* going to happen."

This doesn't sound good, Billy thought.

And then Celia spoke. "Look, Sammy. Why don't you take a walk? Before one of us—"

"What? Is that a *threat*, Celia? Did you just *threaten* me? Just because I *appear* all alone? A little defenseless compared to you and Marco's gun-toting goons here? No worries. You see—I am most definitely *not* alone. See—over there, that building and its nice rooftop patio? Those two gentleman with drinks, chatting, smoking, enjoying the night?"

He paused, giving everyone a moment to look over.

"Well, *if* you had binoculars, you'd see they have earpieces. Slightest wrong move by any of you—the slightest!—and why, they would quickly get their Cross rifles up, Viper scopes already on, and take all you out." And with that, Sammy Rose pointed at each of them, firing an imaginary gun. "*Bang. Bang. Bang.*"

For the moment, all attention was off Billy.

Which he guessed was a good thing. Attention in this sort of situation was probably not something anyone should want.

But he was curious about one thing, now that it was clear this trio was, in fact, competing for the same prize, bullets and bodies be damned . . .

Wouldn't hurt to ask. And might buy some time.

Time for the so-called people here to protect him to actually appear, who were supposed to be *somewhere around here.*

So far, unseen.

▷

Billy looked at the array of what were obviously top-tier, highly experienced and professional mobsters in front of him.

And if he were a betting man, he would not give himself much chance of getting away from them . . .

At least with all his limbs intact.

So then—how could it hurt to ask the question?

"Excuse me, but I'm curious about something."

Their faces showed they weren't expecting or welcoming any questions.

"You don't ask questions, Blessing. You give us answers to *our* questions. Like, what the hell do you know," Marco said. The goon to Billy's right gave another jab with the muzzle of the unseen gun as punctuation. "Before it is . . . sadly, too late."

"Sure, I can tell when I am outnumbered, hmm? I got it. But—just curious—which one of you killed Steiner? I mean, that—even to me, a mere observer—in hindsight, doesn't seem like it was such an effective move?"

Marco Pierce was quick to respond. "Why the *hell* would I kill the one man who *knew* where he hid all the cash?"

"Right," Billy said, now pivoting to the others.

Celia Kole shook her head. "*Kill him?* You crazy? Get him to talk, hurt him maybe—but kill him? The key to the whole thing?"

Which is when, not surprisingly, both Pierce and Kole—doing the math as it were—pivoted to the new arrival, Sammy Rose.

Suspect number three in the "Who killed Paul Steiner" sweepstakes . . .

Rose finally responded, looking directly to Billy, "You piece of . . ."

"Oh—*you* killed him? Sunk the bodies in the sea?" Billy said, like it was just a causal question.

The other two flanking Rose turned and said in unison: "Bodies?"

Billy nodded. "Oh, yeah. Guess, news to you? See, not just Steiner was in the bag apparently. But someone else, some other unfortunate who also got to sleep with the fishes."

He paused.

"Isn't that how you guys say it?"

But Billy could see that he had hit a *very* hot button with Rose.

"Shut the hell *up*. Steiner gave us what the hell we asked. He showed us the damn photo, those numbers, said they were coordinates. Where the money was."

"Oh," Billy said as if he didn't know that.

"And then—yeah—to make sure that no questions would be asked by absolutely anybody, *he was eliminated*."

"You idiot!" Celia Kole said.

Rose turned to her. "Watch your mouth! You know—*and I know*—that you don't have the muscle that your father had. *Not anymore*."

To which Celia, not blinking or backing down, said, "Maybe not. But trust me. *I have enough*."

"So then . . . you *found* the money, Sammy? That what you're saying?" Marco said to Rose, sounding quite confused and still scurrying to catch up with this flow of new information.

Billy thought, *At least, they are not focused on how to get me to talk before—probably—disposing of me in some equally grisly fashion.*

But Rose shook his head. "No. Damn it. Hang on. I, er, didn't have my people move on it right away. You *understand*? Sure. You know, just in case people came sniffing around? Looking for this 'Jack Landry' character."

Ah, Billy thought, *that's* why Sammy Rose, a.k.a. Tony Hill, had made the push, backed by an influx of cash to Worldwide, to get him away from the North Fork, back to NYC.

ASAP.

So no more questions would be asked about the missing man.

"And the money . . . ?" Celia said quietly.

And now Sammy Rose had to admit the error of his ways. "No. Went there. To the *exact* damn coordinates. My boys dug right the hell *outta* that spot. Middle of the night. And there . . . was . . . *nothing*."

Pierce shook his head. "And you *killed* the only guy who could explain how that happened?"

"Oh," Billy said, to keep this informative chat going. "The second body in the bag?"

Rose increasingly didn't like this line of questioning at all. He gave Billy a quick and meaty jab to his midsection.

For a moment, Billy couldn't breathe and saw spots before his eyes.

"What the hell do I have to do to get *you* to just *shut up*?"

Billy gasped a moment, then sputtered: "That seems like a good way. I'll just be over here, trying to breathe. Don't mind me. Just curious, you know?"

"Yeah. So who was *that*, Sammy? This other guy you killed?" Marco Pierce asked.

"A *nobody*. Helped the old man get to the island, to the money. And this nobody said yes, those were the *right*—*whaddya* call 'em?—*coordinates*? Someone who helped Steiner. That's all. With the digging and all that? When needed? He had to go too, obviously."

Billy knew he could tell them all that the second dead man had a name. And that name was Luis. The same name that was on the back of the photo with the *incorrect* coordinates.

All—*so interesting.*

But then—he discovered—there was no time for that, even if he wanted to, perhaps in the interest of buying yet more time.

Because Celia Kole took a step. And for someone who had done all the hard academic work to pass the New York State bar, she moved quickly, effectively, *athletically* . . .

To suddenly make matters much worse for Billy.

She had produced a knife from somewhere. A long, pointed, and nasty-looking stiletto blade that caught what light could be found on the dim patio.

But first she gave the goon who had a gun pressed to Billy's side a nudge, and she soon—and quickly—had moved that blade to one side of Billy's throat.

And now, having possibly thought about this, she talked very fast.

"Okay. I'm taking Blessing. My guess: he *knows* something more. But we are not going to get at that here. I'll take him. Make him talk."

At that, Kole, being rather clever in how she emphasized a point, made the tip of the blade twist a bit, pressing into the skin, quite near what Billy guessed was his carotid artery. That artery, he had heard . . . supposedly a rather important one.

Again, the thought: Where . . . *the hell* . . . was the promised backup? *The protection?*

Marco Pierce—his goons suddenly outmaneuvered—was not happy. "You think . . . you *think* we are going to let you just take him, Celia? Well, you have—"

"Just listen. I will get him out of here. Make him talk. And *when* I know . . . when I have extracted where the money is? The truth? We split it all three ways. Got that? But I—and I alone—handle this screwed-up thing from here on."

And while that proposal seemingly confused the other mob bosses, judging by their expressions, they didn't flatly reject it.

"And how," Sammy Rose said, "do you plan on getting him the hell out of here? This patio, the building?"

Billy could, with a sideways glance, see Kole smile at that. "Oh, *don't you worry*. You two and your, er, associates here? Just mosey on downstairs. Maybe have another glass of champagne?"

"And you?"

"Well—if you want to watch what I do, *watch*."

At that Kole turned to Billy and said, "Okay, Billy Blessing . . . you are going to step over this stone wall here, hmm? And holding on tight . . . lower yourself down, *nice and easy*. I'll be right behind you. With my knife *very* close."

Billy looked at the wall. Then out to the maze of the city streets at night. "Um, down? Down *to*?"

Again, she made the knife do a little twist and turn on his throat. "*Now*," she said.

Billy thought that, on the other side of the wall, there would be nothing but a steady, steep—and most likely fatal—fall down to the pavement below.

Still—he had no choice.

He started sliding his right leg over, grabbing the top of the stone wall tight, then the other leg, and—holding on, literally, for dear life—he let himself hang.

And when he dared look down, he finally saw what was about to happen . . .

41

ALL PARTIES MUST END

The look down revealed that, as his hands dug hard as he could into the curve of the patio's stone wall . . . *no.*

It was *not* a sheer drop down to the sidewalk below.

Instead, just below, there was a smaller patio, perhaps for private parties, that jutted out with just enough room so that should someone, perhaps, let go from above and fall? They wouldn't fall far at all . . .

"Okay," Celia Kole said. "Now *let go!*"

Billy thought the task being presented was theoretically doable. Still a bad landing, twisted ankle, maybe a good chance of something broken.

But then the alternative—recalling the knife and the equally homicidal mobsters above him—made that risk nothing to even consider.

He released his fingers and fell down, landing on the hard stone floor. But despite sudden pain, he kept on his feet as Celia—rather adeptly, former school gymnast perhaps?—landed beside him.

But when he looked up, he saw that this small patio here was not empty.

Two men in suits stood there, as if waiting.

"Okay, get moving, Blessing. There's a back stairway to this private area. But you have to hurry."

Billy hesitated just a moment, debating whether he had any options here.

Which is when Kole said, "My guys here are *not* like the gorillas up there. They can quickly get you under control and navigate you downstairs—whether you want to or not. But maybe best you move under your own steam?"

The men didn't move at all as Celia spoke. And they certainly did look a tad more polished and professional than the two goons that Marco Pierce traveled with.

Still, Billy didn't want to test their abilities. Especially when—once again—that knife appeared, only now pressed to his side. Billy wasn't sure what organs it would hit should it be quickly plunged in.

But he was *pretty* sure they could be some mighty vital ones.

"*Move,*" she said again. The knifepoint again doing its twisty dance.

But they had taken only a few steps when suddenly, they were joined by others.

And—*whaddyaknow*—Billy at last saw some familiar faces . . .

▷

First, Lola Bristow, looking rather smashing for the gala party, stepped out of the side stairwell entrance onto this small patio. The gun she was holding did nothing to diminish the glamour.

Billy thought, *She certainly is something different when out of her khaki uniform.*

Then just as quickly, ADA Martin Williams appeared, also with a gun out.

But that was not all.

Though he should probably be home watching reruns of *Law & Order* or some such—Detective Deacon Solomon. And though officially retired, he too held a gun out.

And it suddenly seemed Billy was saved. The trio of mobsters and their plans were about to come to an end on this rather pleasant New York night.

But not so . . .

▷

Celia Kole responded quickly.

"Ah. Well. No plan ever goes perfectly *smooth*."

Williams acted as the ringmaster for this circus playing out.

"You can tell your men, Celia, to lose their weapons. You too. Then we will escort you all down. Have a lot of support people . . . in the building, on the street. It is, as they say, game over."

To which Kole said: "Such a cliché. And I'm afraid *that* is not a ccurate. You see, Mr. DA, I have an extremely sharp blade pointed right at the upper torso of Billy here. One jab in, and well . . . *no more Billy Blessing*."

Billy listened to this revelatory news. He could see its impact too on Lola, who moments ago had the confident look of someone in charge of the situation. Now her face dropped.

Billy had seen enough movies to know how this would go. Despite those guns pointed in this direction, Kole had the edge.

At least Billy hoped—alive—he was indeed that "edge," and not just expendable.

Williams tried to frame the argument differently: "You won't get far. Even if you get past us—"

"*I will.*"

"There are all the other people, waiting, ready—"

"Whom you will order to stand down. Or again, old Billy here—"

Not that *old*, Billy thought.

"—will breathe his last. A shame. Used to like him on TV too . . . I mean, when I had time to watch mindless TV."

Mindless? Billy thought. God—the insults were coming fast and furious tonight, it seemed.

Billy saw Williams pause. Hesitating as he debated his options.

And Billy knew that, unless the option of a stabbed, dying Billy was perfectly acceptable, Williams would simply have to do exactly as Kole asked.

So . . .

"Alright. *Okay.*" He gave a nod to Lola, then Deacon.

Deacon offered some commentary: "Son of a *bitch* . . ."

They all lowered their weapons. Except, of course, for Celia Kole.

"Now, on your radio. Tell all your assembled troops to completely and totally ignore us."

Again—a pause. But then followed by Williams turning to what must be a microphone on his coat lapel.

"All units, all units. Williams here. Stand down until further notice. Do not interfere"—he looked right at Kole—"with *anyone* attempting to leave the building."

And that would appear to be that, Billy guessed.

But then a thought.

Funny the things that occur to one, when in such situations.

Which, in truth, Billy had never been in before . . .

▷

Celia hissed at him, close to his ear. A rather unpleasant sound.

"*Walk.*"

And Billy did, toward the door to another staircase, which would lead out to a street where he assumed a car would be waiting to speed him and the not-so-nice lady with a knife at his side . . . away.

To a place where he would be questioned in what—he assumed— would be a highly unpleasant manner.

As to his "protection," albeit well-armed? Now all were frozen with the possibility of seeing the person they were here to protect, suddenly— a mere quick jab away from death.

Tough spot, Billy thought.

Yet—not totally without options. Or at least . . . one.

Because while his time in prison wasn't terribly long, he did acquire a few useful skills since the community there just *loved* sharing tips and techniques of all kinds.

And in this particular moment . . .

He had a move that he learned there that might prove useful.

It was, he guessed, his only shot.

So he moved.

▷

Billy turned his head slightly and said to Celia, just as a distraction: "I assume you know where you are taking me? Just wanted to check."

Her lips were still close to his ear. "Just *walk*, nice and steady. Got that?"

Which is all Billy wanted. To get her to say a few words. Just the smallest of distractions as he brought both arms *back* quickly.

His right arm smacked into Celia's hand that was holding the knife, pushing it momentarily away.

Then his other arm jabbed into Celia's midsection, hard. A backward blow designed to knock the wind out of the apparently murderous woman.

Then he spun around. She did have her two accomplices with her after all, and they were now quick to react.

But Billy took steps backward—rather difficult since he saw that this staircase was narrow, the stone steps broad.

Her partners in literal crime were hurrying.

And now, well, that move done pretty smoothly, Billy had cleared the decks for the cavalry to arrive.

Williams and his men hurried into the stairwell, quickly disarming Celia's two assistants.

He watched Lola hurry past him and get her own revolver up, aimed at Celia Kole's head. Celia still held the stiletto knife, but now, well, like the old saying . . .

You don't bring a knife to a gunfight.

And like that, it was over . . .

▷

Lola, now pushing Celia Kole—gun barrel at her head—back to the patio area, where Billy assumed more police awaited, grinned and said, "Very nice work, Billy."

He followed her, suddenly reduced to a bit player in the scene, even as outside he could see the swirling colors of so *many* police cars arriving, sirens blasting.

And on the patio, someone had already cuffed the other key players: the former "Tony Hill," Sammy Rose, and Marco Pierce of the Hamptons with his goons, now surrounded by well-dressed DA agents and the police.

But in moments, uniformed NYPD policemen, their personal radios squawking, entered the patio as well.

The patio was suddenly buzzy and full.

And with the local authorities taking over, Lola walked over to Billy.

"Okay, Billy Blessing. Guess that's it for tonight?"

"Guess . . . so," Billy said. But then a rather important question: "Does this mean that, with all these lovely people under arrest, well, I'm done with it all? Back to North Fork? Back to NoFo Eats? Cooking and the quiet life?"

Lola looked around. "I'd say it *does*." Then back to Billy: "Why— you gonna miss this?"

To which Billy said: "Oh, I really doubt that . . . And—well, don't know about you, but I could use a drink."

Lola smiled at that as Billy started walking past all those handcuffed mobsters to the doors that would lead to the ballroom downstairs where everyone must be wondering . . .

What the hell just happened up there?

EPILOGUE
BLESSING'S BISTRO TOO

42

JANUARY IN HARLEM

Billy looked down at the multiple drafting sheets showing the plans for all the construction going on.

Above him, a trio of electricians wrangled wires across the room, barking at each other various warnings and instructions that meant nothing to Billy.

He heard a saw whining in the back area, home to what would eventually be the kitchen.

He stood on the new wood floor, looking so beautiful when it was installed the previous week, the wide wood planks so classic. But now it was largely covered with tarps and swatches of thick gray paper to protect it from any debris falling from above.

And as Billy looked, he thought, *Yup. It's all coming along.*

Almost hard to believe.

But then he heard a voice from the front of the place as someone walked in while saying a loud "Knock-knock?"

Billy spun around to see Lola Bristow, a big smile on her face, taking off her puffer jacket as she stepped in.

And Billy smiled back with a simple: "Lola."

▷

"Wow," she said. "This place is coming together, Billy. *Blessing's Bistro Too* will be something."

"*That* it will be. Has to serve, not only as a functional restaurant, but also home to various events for the streaming show, the competitions, guest chefs visiting. *Lots* of ideas in play."

He paused. Then: "You have a good visit?"

Billy knew that Lola was in town to see her mother in Bed-Stuy.

"Oh, yeah. Amazing, her age? Still getting around. Tried again to convince her to move out by me, but she won't hear of it. She says she likes where she is . . . and that the neighborhood is getting trendy . . ."

"Aren't they all? Good for her."

He saw Lola looking all around, taking in the men on ladders working with the exposed ceiling—all due to be closed-up within a week.

She turned to him. "You know, I thought with that money from—what did he call his bogus company?"

"Hilltop?"

"Yeah, that money all gone? Then, well your dream of a new place would go poof?"

"I *know*. Me too. Turns out that Worldwide got so much interest in all the concepts. And in that world, with interest comes *cash*."

"I'll say. Can't wait to come here for dinner."

He laughed. "You will have a bit of a wait for that."

But Billy also took pleasure in that thought: Lola, coming back. For dinner of course.

Sure . . .

"How go things with our friend ADA Williams?"

"Oh, well, you know the courts, all the slimy lawyers crawling out of the swamp to defend their guilty-as-hell clients."

"I bet."

"But well—good, I think. They got the aforementioned Tony Hill."

"Meaning Sammy Rose?"

"On at least three counts of murder one. But once they start squeezing his various associates, who knows how many more?"

"Yeah. Good. Killing Steiner and Luis like that . . . well, I hope he gets the proverbial book thrown at him."

"Yeah. Steiner's daughter has been checking in. Wants justice as well."

"And Celia Kole—?"

"Yeah. The nice woman who got you involved in the whole mess? Looks like she is facing a bunch of charges, maybe more to come."

"Such as?"

"Well, turns out using a knife to forcibly kidnap someone, threatening their life with a deadly weapon? Should earn her—and anyone helping her—a good amount of time in Rikers, for starters."

"Oh, she'll enjoy *that* place. And what about Marco Pierce from the Hamptons? No knife. No murders. What do they have on *him*?"

"Oh, well, you see . . . his kidnapping you too? Turns out that is no small thing. And again, he has people, like the goons who brought you to him. Well, Williams thinks they will start to—as the expression goes—*sing*."

"The whole pack of them . . ."

"*Pack* is right. Lot of bad people going to go away for a very long time."

"Guess I will need to testify."

"No question. But—things move slowly. You will probably already have your first *New York Magazine* review out for this place before *any* of that happens."

Billy nodded. "That—won't be too long. Hey, want to see the kitchen? Had all the major appliances delivered this week. None of them hooked up yet but—"

"Sure. Lead the way . . ."

▷

And then Billy stood as Lola walked down one aisle of the kitchen, specifically designed to be roomy. Big problem restaurants often have is a cramped kitchen.

This one—built to Billy's and the network's specifications—could accommodate the chef and a small army of sous-chefs no problem—along with a camera crew and production staff.

He saw her walk to the range. A gleaming and giant Wolf professional with eight burners.

"Whoa. Quite the impressive stove and oven."

She popped open one of the oven doors. "And inside the oven, different sections?"

"Yup. All capable of different temperatures. Absolutely the best. Never cooked on anything *near* this good. Little . . . intimidating."

Lola turned slowly and noted the other items. The top-of-the-line True refrigerator, a full six feet wide. Then, the blast freezer setup, the gleaming dish station and pickup area.

All of it, Billy thought, looking *ready to go.*

But then Lola turned to him.

"Guess, once this opens, we won't be seeing anymore of you out on the North Fork, hmm? Goodbye to all that?"

Billy looked at her, seeing more than a bit of disappointment in her eyes . . .

▷

"Well—not exactly. Wasn't hard to convince the Worldwide execs that having satellite locations, smaller, but tied to the mother ship here in Harlem, was a good idea."

Lola cocked her head. "You mean . . . you *will* be going out there, still cooking?"

"Oh, yeah. I mean, can't say how much. But definitely. Kinda grew to love the whole area, you know?" A pause as he questioned what he was about to say next. But then: "Would be hard to just walk away. Turns out I don't have to. So—I won't."

And the police chief's sad look *vanished.* Eyes wide, a smile even.

"Good. Can use a really amazing restaurant there . . ."

"Hey, NoFo Eats is *pretty* good."

She took a breath.

Then Billy had an idea to spring on her.

"Look, my place here isn't ready. But . . . you ever eat at the Red Rooster?"

"Um, no."

"Marcus Samuelsson's place. Well, if you have *not* eaten there, then as long as you are in the neighborhood, why not?" A breath. "My treat."

He waited while he guessed she weighed options, including the long drive out to the end of Long Island. Only for her to say: "Okay. Absolutely."

"Good. You will love it. And I can tell you the other plans World-wide has for me. Going to be both crazy and fun."

And then, maybe an impulse on her part, she took his hand. "Sounds great. Crazy? Fun? What's not to like?"

He grinned at that. "Exactly. Okay, let's go then . . . not too far from here."

And he led the way out of the chef's kitchen waiting to be orga-nized and set in motion, out to the front of the house, then to the twin doors that led to the street.

It was January and freezing outside only the way New York can freeze, so he grabbed his heavy coat, rabbit-fur gloves in the pocket.

But then—one last look at Blessing's Bistro Too, coming to won-derful life.

With this thought: *Come spring . . . this place will be absolutely humming.*

In the meantime, I wonder what else is waiting out there for a former ex-TV, now amazingly back on TV chef, to get into?

Second helpings, anyone?